A MURDER OF CROWS

SEVENTEEN TALES OF MONSTERS AND THE MACABRE

by
DEANNA KNIPPLING

Wonderland Press

A Murder of Crows

Copyright © 2014 by DeAnna Knippling

Cover images copyright Mur34 | Canstockphoto.com, AlexMax | Canstockphoto.com

Cover and Interior Design © 2014 DeAnna Knippling

Published by Wonderland Press, Colorado Springs, Colorado, USA.

More information on Wonderland Press titles at *www.WonderlandPress.com*

Table of Contents:

In Case You Were Wondering 1
1. Be Good 6
2. Vengeance Quilt 16
3. Abominable 34
4. Winter Fruit 48
5. Family Gods 65
6. A Ghost Unseen 79
7. Haunted Room 86
8. Inside Out 95
9. Treif 103
10. Inappropriate Gifts 129
11. Clutter 139
12. Lord of Pigs 153
13. The Edge of the World 179
14. The Strongest Thing About Me is Hate 197
15. The Rock that Takes off Your Skin 216
16. Things You Don't Want but Have to Take 236
The End 249

In Case You Were Wondering

It was we crows who took your daughter, in case you were wondering. She didn't run away. We had—*I* had—been watching her for some time, listening to her tell stories in the grass behind the house. She would sit near the chicken coop and watch the white chickens pick at the dirt, pulling up fat worms and clipping grasshoppers out of the air as they jumped toward the fields.

Some of them were good stories. Some of them were bad. But that's what decided it, even more than any issue of mercy or salvation or anything else. Crows are, for one thing, possessive of stories. And also by then I had pecked almost all the elders into coming to listen to her at least once, except Facunde, who was then mad and responded to nobody's pecking, not that I had had the courage to exactly take my beak to her. "She is like a daughter to me," I had pled with the others. "She *listens*." They laughed at me, they rattled their beaks, they came and heard her and were convinced, or at least bullied into pretending they were convinced.

We took her yesterday, on the same cold winter day that you traded your son to the fairies, the wind blowing in cold gray threads, ruffling our feathers. It had snowed a few days before that, a storm that had killed your husband, or so it was said. The wind had snatched the snow out onto the prairie, hiding it in crevices. It had been a dry year, and even though it was still too cold to melt the snow, the thirsty dirt still found places to tuck it away in case of a thaw.

I stamped my feet on a sleeping branch while the others argued. Some argued that we should wait for spring. So many things are different, in the spring. But old Loyolo insisted: no, if we were to take the child, we would have to take her then and there: there had been at least one death already, and no one had heard the babe's cry for hours.

We covered the elm trees, thousands of us, so many that the branches creaked and swayed under our weight. I don't know if you noticed us, before it was too late. You were, it is to be admitted, busy.

The girl played on the swings, rocking herself back and forth in long, mournful creaks. She wore a too-small padded jacket and a dress decorated in small flowers. She was so clean that she still smelled of soap. Her feet were bare under their shoes, the skin of her legs scabbed and dry, almost scaly. Her wrists were pricked with gooseflesh, and her hair whipped in thin, colorless threads across her face as the wind caught it. The house had the smell of fresh death, under the peeling paint and the dusty windows, and seemed to murmur with forgotten languages, none of which were languages of love or tenderness. Afternoon was sinking into evening. The girl's breath smelled like hunger.

"Now!" called old Loyolo, at some signal that not even I could have told you. And thousands of birds swept out of the trees toward her. From the middle of it, I can tell you, it seemed a kind of nightmare. Wings in my face, claws in my feathers. The sun was temporarily snuffed out, it was a myriad of bright slices reflected off black wings. We were no flock of starlings, hatched in formations more intricate than any weaving, just a flock of crows. Some of us were old and fat, and none of us were graceful.

We did not eat her. We did not even peck her to death, although of course there was blood. We each of us clutched her with our claws, in her hair, on her dress—and with a *clack clack caw*, we took her into the air.

She did not scream. Her eyes were wide, and all the way around they were white, but she only pressed her lips together and swallowed over and over again, even as old Loyolo practically tore her hair from the roots.

And then, as you chanted and strained over a small crib, as you hoped and prayed that your daughter would not interrupt you, we took her away so that she was no longer your problem. Although I would not be surprised if you begged me to return her, so that she could take your place, on the other side of the window, now that you realize what you have done.

—

We took her to a place hidden in a dumping ground for refrigerators and plows and empty beer cans and tangled wire. You had been there once a few years ago and shot .22s at us, hitting no one but making bright *pinging* sounds and leaving brass casings behind. We made her nest inside an overturned truck cab. We lined it with twigs and feathers and blankets and scraps of cloth and leather and tried not to shit in it. We brought her insects and mice and the last of the dried apples that hung from the branches on your apple tree. We stole for her, stole socks and jeans and too-large shirts and bright scarves with tinsel in them and rings made of pink plastic because, well, chicks will steal anything shiny.

At first she only huddled and shivered and cried. Then, as the afternoon lengthened, she began to pick her way through the garbage, looking for treasures. She found a naked human doll and wrapped it in cloth and bits of string. She tied a serrated knife to a stick. She watched the moon rise.

She did not speak.

We asked old Loyolo what we should do about that. None of us had had chicks who had been silent, and human children, well, they were a mystery.

Night fell. The snow began to come down so thick (and we had eaten so well on a dead coyote that day), that my part of the greater flock decided to spend the rest of the day with her in her nest. We pecked on her door and she opened it, and we swept in, oh, a hundred or so of us, and found places to roost before too much snow could follow us in.

She sat in the nest we had made her under the upside-down seat of the truck, wrapped herself in her blankets with a pink wool one on top, and spread it out for us to sit on. We gathered on her shoulders and all over her legs and waited, but she did not speak.

Old Loyolo coughed noisily and said, "It is time for stories."

We all looked at her expectantly, even though it's not our way to make a storyteller say anything unwilling, and with good reason.

She said nothing.

And so, after a long moment that felt like a feather caught in the throat, old Loyolo said, "If you will not tell stories, than we will tell stories. *Human* stories," he added. "So that she can remember how to be human."

It was a nice thing to say. A kind thought, for a crow. But mostly we were warm and full, and wanted to hear stories, whether they helped the girl or not.

Old Loyolo groaned to himself, jumped off the girl's knee, and hopped onto the rear-view mirror, which formed a kind of podium. "Me first, then," he croaked. "Once upon a time there was a girl who loved her father more than anything else…"

1. Be Good

"Tornado," Pa said, the wind whipping his hair around his face. It needed cut. We already knew the tornado was coming—it was why we'd come outside—but some truths are so big that they have to be said out loud. "Hope it misses the Home."

"Headed straight for it," Ma said beside me. I squinted, trying to keep the dust out of my eyes.

When kids ain't good, they go to the Home. My Aunt Janet tried to threaten me once when I was throwing rocks at her son Tim that I was going to get sent to the Home if I wasn't good. Tim said I started it which was a lie, but I guess we're all a little blind, and Aunt Janet was blind about her son, who had just picked up a kitten and threw it against the wall of the barn so hard that it threw up in my hands and purred and died.

I wasn't the only one trying to get him. The mother cat was attacking him, too.

"You knock that off, Laurie Lee Jackson!" she'd said. "You piece of shit crazy thing! You're going to kill my son! I'll have you sent up to the Home for this!"

And then Pa was there, and he grabbed Aunt Janet and shook

her and said, "You stop threatening my girl and get your son inside. I saw what he did."

Tim just laughed.

It's good to have a father who will stand up for you, but I shouldn't of been throwing rocks at him anyway. I shouted, "I see your crazy eyes and I will tell everybody about you and how you like to kill stuff and you ain't never going to kill my baby brother!"

For that's what he had threatened to do, if I didn't shut up about the kitten. But Ma and Pa didn't raise no fool. So I threw rocks at him instead, because we both knew I'd get in more trouble for it than him killing that kitten, if his ma had her way, and I wanted him to know I didn't give a shit.

So Tim was the one who belonged at the Home. It was Tim who should have been inside those painted cinderblock walls when the tornado came.

Some people say you got to get along and you got to *be good*. Pa says you got to watch out for those people. Those are the ones who want you to shut up when someone hurts you.

Be good means *be quiet* to them.

We stood outside our house, white on the sides and green on top, and Ma turned around in a circle every few minutes, jigging up Leonard on her hip, and watched the tornado dance back and forth. Everything looked brown. The clouds were black but it was almost as bright as a clear day. You couldn't hear the tornado itself, not to pick it out, because of the wind all over and the clatter of sticks on the house. My hair got in my mouth and I resolved to cut it all off.

I wished we had a basement for the cows, the milk cows at least.

We couldn't see the Home, exactly, just the trees where it was. Dirt in my eyes made it hard to see so I squinted them even tighter closed, like the camel I saw once at the zoo in the one time we went to the city.

If they'd have let me, I would have watched the storm from the roof or from the big cottonwood tree in the garden, or from the tin barn up on the hill to get a better view, but they wouldn't.

Ma said, "Those poor kids."

The wind stopped howling for a second and we could hear the tornado grinding like teeth that never stopped, and I knew it could look over at us any second and see us watching us and come after us as easy as it was going after the Home. All it would take was one glance and it could come after us.

It went over the front edge of the trees and didn't look any different for a second, and then the bottom of it got fatter. I imagined all those kids hiding in the basement.

It should have been Tim down there. The tornado should have sucked him up and turned him into tornado butter. But instead it was killing birds and cows and dogs and real people and kittens, instead of him. Couldn't hear any screaming, but I knew there must be some. If that tornado had been that close to me, I would have been screaming. But maybe down in the Home's basement they didn't know.

The dust at the bottom of the tornado turned from brown like everything else to green, from the leaves of the trees surrounding the Home. Or maybe that was just my imagination.

The telephone was ringing in the house but Pa didn't tell me to answer it so I didn't. Probably someone from the church, but we'd stopped going after they wouldn't do anything about Tim, not even make him go to Confession. What good's somebody who's always saying *be good* and when it comes time to punish someone for being bad, they don't say nothing? When the priest says *be good* he means someone who doesn't *be good* the way he likes and not *be good* in general, I guess, which means he's probably saying *be good* about my folks and me a lot lately.

The tornado ate trees as fast as a lawnmower, and behind it was only green-haze dirt.

Then it hiccupped, an empty spot that travelled all the way from the bottom of the funnel to the top, shaking the whole middle of the tornado.

I seen lots of tornadoes. I seen them starting in the clouds, just barely poking out, until they touched the ground. I seen them rise back up into the clouds like a big drip of water that pulls back into the faucet.

But I ain't never seen one just stop.

One second it was there; the next, it wasn't.

Pa ran to his pickup truck and I ran with him, with Ma yelling both our names, but we were down the gravel road in the truck in a heartbeat. I looked back over my shoulder and there she was, standing with Leonard, who hadn't made a sound the whole time, and then I looked forward and even the clouds at the top of the funnel had stopped spinning and stuff was falling out of the sky.

We drove to the Home so fast I put my seatbelt on and still had to hang on with both hands and keep my feet up against the dashboard to keep from getting jerked around.

Pa said, "You're probably going to see some dead people, Laurie Lee."

"I know. But we got to save them before the tornado comes back."

"I should been down there," he said. "I should have been down there."

I didn't say nothing; I knew he was just trying to make the truck drive faster.

We always feed them and hide the kids from the Home when they run away.

There was a boy named Martin who we kept for six weeks so his ribs could heal; he was my friend. They knew we had him and we had no right to him, but Pa let them in and they searched the house and they couldn't find him in the places Ma hid him, so that was all right. Martin said he was kidnapped from his house because he was in love with another boy and God said that wasn't right. When he sucked in his stomach there was a hole under his ribs, a cave where you could put your hand in. I asked him what happened to the other boy but of course he didn't know. We played cards and he cheated but he joked about it every time so I always caught him.

"If you want to learn how to catch someone cheating, you got to play with a cheater," he said. "That's what my dad taught me. He was always cheating. Said it was so I would know it when I saw it."

I asked him if his parents had him kidnapped, but he didn't know. I say it was his folks who did it. Anybody else, the cops would have been all over them. But when your parents do it, it's okay, so *be good* and shut the hell up about it, all right?

Martin's my friend and Tim's a shit. Shows you what I think about *be good*.

I don't know what happens to most kids when they leave my folks, but I knew about Martin. His folks sent a letter to our church, and the priest tacked it up on the cork board. I copied it down secretly and gave it to him.

Please come home, it said, so my folks let him call his folks long distance, and they came and got him.

Ma had taken Polaroids of him when he first came, and Martin's ma had cried and cried over him and said *no more*.

But his dad just nodded and got this tricky look on his face. Martin taught me how to see it, just like his dad had taught him. He was a cheater. Martin looked at me as he was leaving, and I knew he wasn't blind about who kidnapped him no more. I know Ma made him memorize our phone number before they came to get him.

"Anything happen, you call us," she said.

Only I knew that he wouldn't be able to call, the next place his dad sent him. He might be back at the Home now, for all we knew.

My Pa has never cheated at cards. Now that I know how to look, I look, and he don't cheat. I kind of wish I didn't know how to look, but then again I'm glad. I'm glad because Pa ain't a cheat, but I'm sad about myself.

Soon enough we were off our driveway and on the road to the Home. The road was all tore up. When we got to the highway it had chunks missing and signs ripped up and trees over the road, but we drove over and around everything. It started to hail and went from tiny pieces of white to large cracks on the roof and I was scared the windshield was going to bust in on us.

Pa slowed down when we got to the edge of the trees, although with as much mess as the tornado had made, I don't know that you could call them trees anymore. The trees were piled up in drifts, and the hail blew around in them and left white piles, and we couldn't drive any further.

Pa turned the truck around but we didn't leave. I twisted around in my seat until I couldn't stand it anymore and about the same second Pa turned off the truck because he couldn't stand it anymore either. We got out and he said "Wait" and pulled a bright blue tarp out of the truck box and had me hold it over my head while he went running, over and under and around the ripped-up elm trees.

I grabbed the first aid box out of the truck box that we have for while we're cutting trees for firewood in case the chainsaw slips or something, and I went after him as fast as I could. I couldn't barely see the road, but when I got off it I knew because I slipped in mud as the hail turned to buckets and buckets of rain.

Other trucks were coming. I couldn't hear nothing with the rain on the tarp, but I saw headlights coming down the road.

I wanted to see what had happened before someone decided to chase me off, so I tried to run faster and almost brained myself on a stupid tree. But finally I made it, a lot before anyone else but Pa did.

The Home was gone. Top and bottom, left and right. The roof was gone, the cinderblock walls were gone, the outbuildings were gone, the shed where kids in trouble had to stay was gone, the teacher's trailer house was gone. All that was left was the basement, which was full of tree trunks and quiet and dark.

My Pa was standing on the edge of the basement looking down, and I stood next to him. The water was already pooling up over the linoleum tiles of the basement, and it was brown and black and shimmering green from all the dirt and ripped-up leaves.

I looked for dead kids or blood but I didn't see any. So that first-aid kid was just about useless.

After a while, some people from church came up to us. Aunt Janet's husband Uncle Peter was there, and he dropped to his knees and said, "God has taken them home."

Pa took a step back from the edge of the basement with one foot, which kind of spun him around so he was facing Uncle Peter. Pa punched him right across the nose.

Uncle Peter's nose kind of slid sideways and he fell backwards over his boots where he was kneeling. He gasped, then blew blood out of his mouth.

"Those murdering sons of bitches," Pa said. "Those goddamned murdering sons of bitches made all those kids stay upstairs."

"God called them home," Uncle Peter honked. His nose was all clogged up. "If they're all dead, where are the bodies?"

"The next county over, you ass," Pa said.

"They deserved it," Uncle Peter said, and Pa kicked him in the ribs with his boot, one time, another time, then walked away with Uncle Peter sobbing and saying Pa would go to hell.

Pa knew he was going to be in trouble. He wasn't surprised when the Sherriff came to our house. But he wasn't scared of Uncle Peter either, and he wasn't going to *be good* when Uncle Peter started talking like that. You have to show them you're not afraid, you ain't going to *be good*.

They found the Home halfway to Nebraska, mostly. It was all gone to pieces.

The kids, they found all over the place.

I wished and wished that somehow Tim would be dead, but he wasn't.

Later that week I was just messing around, stomping through the animal paths, making up stories about going on an adventure in the jungles of Africa.

As I was walking, pretending to listen to parrots and monkeys, pretending I was stalking a tiger through the sights of my gun, I saw Martin, all tangled up in the branches of an elm tree.

As soon as I saw him, I thought to myself, Laurie Lee, you are a fool for not smelling the stink of this earlier. You are a plain fool.

His body had swelled up, swarming with flies like he was a beehive, and the crows were having a heyday picking at the maggots that had grown up in him.

Pa was in jail at the time, so I had to get Ma. She took one look at him and marched me back to the house. A deputy came a little while later to get him down, just wrapped him up in a tarp that was already stained brown and black and covered with leaves and sticks, and put him in the back of his truck.

Ma made us go to church that week, and the priest talked about wicked people would get what they deserved. And I knew he wasn't talking about the teachers at the Home. He wasn't even talking about those kids. He was talking about Pa being in jail.

I walked out of that church and waited in the truck. When Ma got, she whupped me and said it was for my own good. She ain't never whupped me so hard as she did in the church parking lot, with other people coming out to their cars and telling their kids not to look.

Tim was there, sneering at me as Aunt Janet hurried him towards their Buick.

I ain't let Ma touch me since.

She told Pa he can't take in kids anymore, ever. She goes to church every Sunday and takes Leonard with her. She won't play cards with me and Pa no more, either. Says it's a sin.

But I been watching her. And I know the real reason why.

The girl's head hung lower and lower, until the crows sitting in the hollow of her legs had to hop away from her belly, lest they be crushed. Finally she put her arms around her knees and wept.

That morning, you had told her to go outside and play, you were tired of her and you had enough to do taking care of the baby. She went outside and fed the chickens and gave them fresh water, tipping over their pans so the dirty ice fell out, then filling them with water from large buckets. She went into the barn and stared at the trampled straw. The cattle were gone, even the milk-cows. They had disappeared during the night—later, when I talked to the rats, I heard some very dark things about what had happened to them, and of course I saw what you had done in the cellar, later on.

You did not notice when she came back into the house with the basket of wrinkle-ended eggs; you did not notice when she watched you from a corner of the door to the babe's room. You can tell yourself that I am lying, but you saw the eggs in their carton in the refrigerator, you ate two of them for lunch.

The girl saw you casting spells over the boy, and did not stop you. Instead she went back outside, sat on a swing, and wept until we took her.

When she had finished crying, surrounded by blankets and birds, she reached one arm out of the blankets and touched the doll she had found, a fat baby doll with a scrap of cloth wound around its belly and tied with dirty yellow yarn.

The wind yowled outside, looking to catch us with the door open.

I climbed up into the thick, serpentine wires of the torn-out seat above her head and stood on them, trying to find a better perch. I was not the only one who shit in her nest, but it was mine that landed on her hand as she petted her baby. She looked at the back of her hand, then up at me.

"Oops," I cawed. Her eyebrows twisted, one up, one down, as if to say, *How rude.* I hopped uncomfortably from wire to wire. She wiped the back of her hand on the blanket, which seemed to absorb the whiteness entirely within the pink wool.

Old Loyolo, who had been standing on the mirror, ruffled his feathers so they puffed out and then bobbed his head. Despite the thinness of his feathers, which looked rather pecked about his chest and head, he looked the picture of the superior crow, killer of snakes and rats, defender of nests. "You tell the next one, Machado. The least you could do."

He swooped into her lap, where she made room for him on her knee. That *baggulo*. He hadn't killed a snake in years, and nobody living remembers him doing it anyway, except Ibarrazzo. It's just a story, like a knight killing a dragon. Ah, at least he tells it well.

I didn't have a thought as to which story I would tell as I climbed down from the wires and dropped to the floor, scaring up a featherstorm of chicks. I flapped with all dignity to the perch on the mirror—the storyteller's seat, now—and suddenly remembered a story that the human priest had told me. Oh, yes, I have talked to him, too.

I said…

2. The Vengeance Quilt

In his own head, he wasn't Father Vincent Paul; he was Sebastian Jennings, a murderer. He hadn't meant to become a violent man. He grimaced at himself in the mirror: now *there* was a face that would inspire his parishioners to love God. He checked his teeth, smoothed down his hair, and smiled. Even worse.

It was an August Saturday evening in the year of our Lord 1960, so he said Mass in his green vestments. He used to take more pride in his robes than any woman over designer dresses; now it was one more sign of his falseness under the glory of God.

He stepped out of the changing room. His older sister, Peggy, was waiting outside the door. "Sebastian? There's a problem downstairs." She wore an apron and twisted a wet towel in her hands. One side of her stylish dress was black from coffee or dishwater.

"What is it?"

"Claire and Eileen are fighting over the quilt for the harvest festival."

"You should have interrupted me." He rushed down the basement stairs.

Claire, a small woman with mousey hair, shouted, "That quilt doesn't belong to you!"

Eileen, a much larger woman dressed in a tent, shouted back, "I paid for it!"

Claire Christiansen was married to Frank Christiansen, one of Don Hart's hired hands. Eileen Hart was his wife. The two women stood in the kitchen with the service window shut, as if that would make them less audible to the people drinking coffee or the kids gaping from their catechism class doors. Sebastian held up one hand to keep Peggy from trying to smooth things over; he wanted to hear what the fight was about.

"You said the money was a donation!" Claire shrieked.

Frank Christiansen came toward the kitchen door, but Sebastian held him back, on hand on his chest.

"I hired you to make me a quilt!"

"You are the most selfish—I'm not going to say! I'll give you back the money after we auction it off."

"It's my quilt!"

"Then just take it, you cow!"

"I'll have your husband fired!"

"I just told you that you could have that damned quilt!"

Eileen noticed the others outside the kitchen door. Her blue eyes creased up at the corners. "You heard that, Father!"

"That's enough, ladies," he said. "You're scaring the children."

Claire turned around. She had a coffee cup and a towel in her hands; she put them down and walked toward him, her heels clicking precisely on the linoleum.

She glared at him with eyes so dark as to seem black. "There's a commandment about those who bear false witness." She went in the ladies' room, slammed the door, locked it, then turned on the faucet, high-blast.

Eileen leaned back on a counter with a grin on her face.

Sebastian said, "I understood the quilt was a donation as well."

Eileen said, "It's my quilt. I paid for it."

"Just for the materials?" Sebastian said. "Or for the time she spent on it as well?"

Eileen frowned. "That ain't worth nothing. She owes me for lots of things. Milk."

"I'd like to see an agreement for payment for her work, typed up and signed by both of you. And it would be very disappointing if I heard that Frank was fired over a disagreement between a couple of ladies."

Eileen turned up her nose and lumbered out of the kitchen. She climbed the stairs slowly, dragging on the rail. "He could get fired for lots of reasons," she shot over her shoulder, just as she turned the corner and went out of sight.

"Where's Don?" Sebastian asked Peggy.

"Outside, smoking his pipe," she said as Frank went back to his table, shaking his head. "I tried to get him to come in, but you know men. They don't want to get involved."

The corner of Sebastian's mouth twitched.

Peggy shook her auburn curls. "Sorry, Father Vincent Paul. Ever since you started wearing black, I don't know what to think of you."

"Me, either," he said.

Sunday went fine, and Monday he slept in late. When he woke up, he couldn't remember whether he had enough hosts to last the next month, so he decided to check. He was out of coffee in the house, anyway. He wasn't about to try to prepare for Bible study without coffee. Those ladies were sharp. Claire, especially, reminded him of himself in seminary; she chased down technicalities like a dog after a rabbit.

He unlocked the back door of the basement and flicked on the lights. He made it about three steps before he stopped. Nobody should have to face this before coffee.

The basement was blue with mold, except for a few steps of the green carpet on the stairs, including the lights and ceiling tiles. The smell made him sneeze and his eyes water. He cursed, made a mental note to confess his cursing later, and backed up the stairs. He put out the lights and locked the door behind him.

First he took off his shoes, dropped them in a bucket, and filled it with bleach water, which probably wasn't good for the leather. Then he called Jim Blackthorn, his deacon. His daughter had had tonsillitis and been up to the hospital for the last few days.

Jim picked up the phone. "Hello? James Blackthorn speaking."

"Don't go into the Gray Hill church, Jim. The basement is covered with mold. Just covered. I'll call the extension office in a minute. How's Celeste Marie doing?"

"She's sore, but she'll be all right. I'll tell her you asked about her."

"Good to hear," Sebastian said. "I'd come and visit, but I don't want to make her sick."

The County Extension Office promised to send someone out. Sebastian told them where he kept the spare key, in case he got called out. Then he remembered Claire and Peggy were supposed to clean the church that afternoon. He warned Peggy first. When he called the little Christiansen house, nobody answered, so he crossed his fingers and called the Harts.

A man answered, which was odd; it was August, and he should have been out harvesting wheat. "Hello? Hart Ranch."

"Father Vincent Paul. I'm trying to reach Claire and tell her not to come to the church."

"Father," the man croaked. "Come right away. It's Eileen. She's doing poorly."

"Certainly," he said. "But will you pass on my message to Claire? The church is full of mold, and I don't want anyone getting into it."

"Mold," the man agreed. "There's mold all over the damned place." He hung up.

When someone was doing poorly, you drove them to the hospital; you didn't call the priest. Unless it was too bad not to bother with. Sebastian fetched his last rites bag. Then he raised the carpet in the closet, removed a section of flooring, and pulled out a lock box, unlocking it with a key he wore with a medal of St. Jude. Inside was a simple traveler's Bible. He riffled through the pages with one thumb. The ink, swirls of brown symbols, was still intact. He added the book to the bag.

He drove over the hill and gasped. Hart Ranch shimmered blue in the late-summer sun. The shelter belt dangled with blue streamers. Haystacks rose blue out of blue drifts. Fields of blue wheat scattered blue fog. He stopped at the edge of the mold; part of him knew he'd already come too far, but he had a hard time forcing himself to drive forward anyhow.

He knocked on the door of the big farmhouse. Don Hart, tall and skinny and a good deal older than Eileen, opened the door. "Sorry, Father. Would you mind taking your shoes off?"

Sebastian slipped off his shoes and washed his hands in the sink.

The living room was full of a quilt frame stretched with the most colorful, delicately-pieced quilt he'd ever seen. Claire was stitching the top and bottom of the quilt together with a fine pattern of flowers. She had a foul look on her face.

Don passed by her without looking and went into his bedroom.

Eileen was lying in bed with her mouth open. Only two days had passed since he'd seen her last. Her gray skin had slid off her cheeks and into her neck; the blankets covered a good deal less flesh than they would have on Saturday.

"Has she been to the doctor?" Sebastian asked.

"Won't go," Don said.

Eileen's breath rattled as she struggled to suck air past something in her throat.

"She was supposed to bury me," Don said.

Sebastian pulled up a chair. "Eileen, Can you hear me? It's Father Vincent Paul. You need to go to the hospital."

Another rattle. Eileen's head rolled back and forth. *No.*

"This mold is going to kill you," he said.

No.

Sebastian sighed. "Do you want to make your last confession?"

Yes.

He chased Don out, started the rites, and asked her whether she had anything to confess.

She whispered, "That bitch is killing me."

Sebastian leaned back. "You can't mean that, Eileen."

The fingers on her left hand curled toward him. He leaned toward her.

"Deal with the devil," she hissed.

If anyone would use last rites to accuse someone of murder, it was Eileen; nevertheless, he was shocked. Sebastian placed the host, which was the kind that fell apart and could be swallowed without chewing, on her dry tongue. He touched the chalice of watered wine to her lips.

He finished the rites and made the sign of the cross over her. Then he backed out of the room, closed the door, and said to Don, leaning on the wall, "May I use your phone? I'll be just a minute, and then I'd like to sit with her again."

Don pointed toward the door to the living room. Sebastian sucked in his gut and edged around the large quilt frame to the small table with the phone. He picked it up and dialed his brother Aloysius.

"Aloysius Jennings farm, Mrs. Jennings speaking," Honey said.

"Is Aloysius in?" He glanced at Claire; her ear pointed at him like a third eye. "I want him out at Hart Ranch. Theodore too. I want them to take a look at something."

"Something to do with the reason Peggy isn't supposed to clean church today?"

Sebastian gritted his teeth to keep himself from grinning in front of Claire. That was Honey for you. "Maybe."

"The walls have ears, don't they? I'll ride out and get them. Sit tight."

—

When he finally left Eileen's room, his brothers were waiting for him, sitting uncomfortably on the couch, almost underneath the quilt frame. Aloysius said, "Did you know that's a Joseph's Coat quilt pattern?"

Claire stitched without looking at her fingers. He could have sworn her eyes were black all the way through.

"Eileen's dead," he told her.

Claire nodded and went back to watching her fingers fly over the fabric.

He called the funeral home and told them the funeral would have to be in Fort Thompson because they were having a problem at Gray Hill.

"Sorry about the wait," Sebastian said. Aloysius and Theodore stood up—"Ma'am"—and followed him into the hallway. Theodore handed around filter masks. "Ain't got no goggles," he said.

Outside was a wonderland. Part of him felt like it was the first snow of the season, pure and untouched; part of him knew it had killed one woman already.

Aloysius closed the door behind him. "Isn't it funny that there's no mold in the house?"

"You bring the book?" Theodore asked.

Sebastian tapped his pocket.

"It's not the demons again, is it?" Aloysius asked.

"No," Sebastian snapped. "I swore I wouldn't do that again."

"I didn't say you had," Aloysius said. "Where should we start looking?"

"Where it's wet," Theodore said.

Aloysius pulled a stick off a tree and wacked at a big blue branch, scattering mold.

"Knock it off," Sebastian said.

"Couldn't help myself." Aloysius pointed at a big stand of trees. "If I remember right, the stock tank is over there. Garden on one side and the corral on the other."

They walked through the mold, Aloysius scuffing his feet and kicking up spores. Sebastian just let it be.

There were two lumps lying under the mold in the corral.

They walked toward the water tank, which was covered with mold, like everything else.

"What are we looking for?" Aloysius asked. "What's that?" He pointed at a pattern in the mold on the fence above the tank. Theodore wiped the mold off it with his bare hand and tried to shake it off. He ended up wiping it on his pants.

It was one of the symbols from the book. Sebastian said, "It's a summoning symbol."

"Summoning what?" Aloysius asked.

"Whatever wanted to come," Sebastian said. They went back to the house. *That,* Sebastian thought, *was too easy.*

Aloysius stopped them outside the door, opened it, and yelled, "Mr. Hart!" He waited a few seconds. "I'm sorry to bother you, but there's something you should know."

A door opened, and Don walked toward them. He didn't bother to wipe his face.

Aloysius said, "We'll have to evacuate; the milk cows are dead already. I'm sorry, Mr. Hart, but you may lose the farm."

From the living room, Claire shouted, "No!" She appeared at the door to the entryway.

"It's up to the Extension Office," Aloysius said. "There may be nothing for it but to kill everything on the farm. Come on, put your shoes on. Is there anybody else?"

"Frank," she said. "He went out this morning—" Her tiny knees folded up under the hem of her dress, and she sank onto the floor.

Don said, "What about my wife?"

"We'll take her with us," Aloysius said.

Sebastian had Theodore help wrap Eileen Hart in blankets. There was a time when he would have turned his nose up at carrying a dead woman in his arms but not anymore. The two of them carried Eileen, Theodore under her shoulders and Sebastian at her feet, to the back of Theodore's pickup truck. She stank already, or maybe it was the room.

"You take Don," he told Theodore. "I'll take Mrs. Christiansen. You look for Frank," he told Aloysius. "And burn your clothes and spray your trucks down with bleach or vinegar, for God's sake."

"He's in the north pasture by the creek," Claire murmured. She swayed, and Sebastian grabbed her by the arm. He bit his tongue and walked her toward his Buick.

"Claire," he said, hands at ten and two. "What did you do it for? We found the summoning symbol on the water tank."

"The what?" Her hands were folded in her lap; she sat as straight as a fence post.

Sebastian drew the symbol—incompletely—in the dashboard dust. "That." He brushed it away.

"Oh, that," she said. "That was the water tank last Saturday. Is it a hobo sign?"

"Claire, we priests study many things at seminary, one of which is devil worship. This is one of their signs." He was distorting the truth; another item for his next confession.

"Devil worship," Claire said. "You mean it's real? Eileen had a Bible with all kinds of weird things like that in it. In her bedside table."

Sebastian stopped at the stop sign. "I'm going to take you to my father's farm."

"But that's back the other way."

"So it is. Peggy'll take care of you." He turned the car around.

Claire didn't say anything for the longest time. "What'll me and Frank do?"

"We'll take care of you," he promised.

"We, as in the church, or we, as in the Jennings?" she asked. "I don't want any handouts."

"Probably the latter," he admitted. "My father could use help, now that Aloysius is on his own. And Peggy wouldn't mind the company."

Claire put her pointed chin in her elflike hand on the window ledge. "I wish we'd known that. I would have dragged Frank off like a shot. That woman hated me. Did everything she could to make my life miserable. We didn't know there was anyplace else to go."

He didn't have any answer for that.

Sebastian left Claire with Peggy, who shoved him out of the house with a broom and told him to get his Buick away from the elms. He drove back. A white van from the Extension Office was parked at the Hart Ranch farmhouse. His friend Jasper stood next to it with a paint-fume mask dangling around his neck, smoking an unfiltered cigarette. Sebastian shook his hand. "Jasper."

Jasper Long Horse was a jack of all trades in Buffalo County. He'd grown up on the reservation, gone to school in Sioux Falls, and had come back to work for the county as a repairman, tree-remover, snow-plower, killer of rabid dogs and coyotes, and agent of the County Extension Office. What he'd come back for, Sebastian had never been sure.

"What the hell, Sebastian, I mean Father?" he asked.

Sebastian chewed on a nail, then realized he was contaminating himself more than he already was. "Would you think I was crazy if I said it was black magic?"

Jasper let it go. "The inside of that house is untouched. I don't get it."

"You saw the church?"

"Sprayed it down. With any luck, you should have the place back by next Saturday. But this place, I don't know."

"I left something inside. Mind if I go in?"

Jasper waved him toward the door. "Be my guest."

Sebastian found the book where Claire had told him, the same kind of Bible they'd used in seminary. He stopped in the living room to take another look at the quilt. The blocks seemed like random patches of different colors of scrap, sewn together any which way, but if he looked at the quilt as a whole, he could pick out patterns. Then he took another look at it and swore (another item on his list). The stitching wasn't of flowers; it was protection symbols.

No wonder why Eileen wanted the quilt.

He unclamped the quilt from the frame, put it in a trash bag, and brought it with him.

Jasper peeked inside the bag. "Whatchoo taking that blanket for?"

"It was supposed to be a donation for the church at the Harvest Festival next month," Sebastian said. "I don't want anything to happen to it. Don't worry, I'll have Peggy wash it."

"You should get a lot of money for that," Jasper agreed. He got in the van, and Sebastian followed him off the farm. Jasper stopped, rolled his window down, and waved him over to the side of the road. "Don't tell Don and them, but we're going to have to spray everything. Might have to go into your dad's property, too."

"Do what you have to."

Jasper nodded. "I get the mold and you get the black magic, all right?"

"Deal."

Jasper laughed, rolled up his window, and drove away.

He threw down the quilt in front of Claire, who was sitting on the couch next to Peggy, wearing a dress about five sizes too big. "You lied to me. That flower pattern is a protection symbol."

Claire ran her fingers over the stitching. "It's just a nice design."

Sebastian said, "What I don't understand is how, if the house was protected from the mold by this symbol, Eileen could die of it."

Someone coughed from behind him. Sebastian turned and saw Frank Christiansen holding his cowboy hat in both hands. "It wasn't mold," he said. "It was cancer."

Claire looked up at him over the stitching. "How do you know?"

"I knew," he said. "She's been hiding it for a long time."

Claire pressed her lips together.

"Don't blame Claire," Frank said. "I told her to put the symbols on the quilt. I'm sorry. She was going to get me fired. I had to do something to make myself look too good to get rid of. But it was too strong for me."

Claire stood up, dropping the quilt, and went into the kitchen. "That bitch." Sebastian heard drawers rattle and slam. He followed and saw her with the top of her dressed pulled open, holding a paring knife against her chest. She was covered in blood; she had carved the symbol from the water tank on her chest, upside down.

Sebastian looked away modestly from her naked breasts, then told himself to stop being an idiot. He tried to take the knife away from Claire; she shoved him. She was too small to make him lose his balance, but she stumbled out of arm's reach anyway. She stretched her neck, making a twisted face in order to see better as she cut herself. She touched up one of the lines with the knife and tossed it on the counter.

"Goodbye, Father Vincent Paul," she said.

Frank was standing beside him. "Claire. Wait."

Without turning around, she said, "How else could you have known about that Bible? By her bed? She never told anyone about it. You *saw* it, you cheating son of a bitch." The back door slammed and the screen door creaked shut after it.

By the time they nerved themselves to follow her outside, she'd roared down the road in Frank's truck. Fortunately, it hadn't rained in a while, and they could follow the dust trail. Frank pushed on the dash, trying to make the Buick drive faster.

"Do you know where she got the book, Frank?" he asked.

"Of course I didn't want to. Have you seen how beautiful my wife is? But Eileen told me we'd lose our home if I didn't." Frank had left his hat behind, and the sun was shining straight into his wide, blue eyes.

"The book, Frank. Where did Eileen get the book from?"

"I don't know," he said. "She just had it."

"Does Don know about it?"

"He didn't go rummaging around in her bedside table."

They turned onto the Hart Ranch road and found the pickup truck abandoned beside the road. The door had been twisted off its hinges. He swore again and decided to stop keeping an itemized list of his sins.

On foot, they followed the trail through the grass, stopping just past the mold. The mold crept toward them; Sebastian stepped back, but Frank started to run into it. Sebastian grabbed his arm and swung him around so hard he ended up on the ground. Frank hissed at him, got up, and ran into the blue.

It wasn't quite as blue as it had been earlier. More of a soft gray.

Frank ran down the hill, mold covering him from head to foot as he kicked up spores, until he disappeared into a tree belt.

Sebastian had failed them again—God, family, parishioner, and neighbor—and there wasn't anything else he could do, so why he gunned the engine and sped down the hill toward the farmhouse, he never knew. He parked the Buick, pulled the revolver that Theodore had given him out of the glove box, and loaded it.

He found Frank by the milk barn, almost at the stock tank. The mold covered him as Sebastian approached him; the blood splatters turned blue and disappeared. One of the three mounds in the pen reared up and hissed at him.

Claire.

"Don is dead," he lied. "Heart attack. It's over. There's no more vengeance to be had."

The summoning symbol had worked, all right. She was more like a knee-high snake than anything else, but with several small, warped limbs. Her chin puffed out like a frog's, so close to him that he could have reached out and touched it. Greenish, spotted, tiny gold-colored eyes.

Claire opened her mouth, sorted through the mold with her long tongue, and pulled out one of Frank's legs. She gulped it down whole. Sebastian backed toward the stock pond, pulled out a pocket knife, and started to gouge out the summoning symbol.

Claire spat out bone and rushed at him. He had a split second to decide between shooting Claire or not. Instead he jumped backward as Claire smashed, face-first, into the symbol on the fence. How she'd cleared the stock tank with her spindly limbs, he didn't know.

The fence shattered, breaking the symbol. If Sebastian was expecting a miracle, he wasn't going to get one; the mold certainly didn't disappear or turn into daisies. Claire backed up, shook her head, and tried to charge him again.

He pulled out the revolver. "Sorry, Claire." He shot her on the head, which stunned her for a moment; then he rolled her on her side and shot her in the chest, ripping the summoning symbol there to shreds.

Quick as anything, he dropped the gun, pulled out his penknife again, and carved the protection symbol onto the first whole piece of skin he found. She shuddered and thrashed, knocking him down. He grabbed onto her, and carved, from memory, the symbol for banishing, over and over, until she lay still.

He asked God to forgive them and receive their souls, sinners all.

Aloysius kept Jasper from sending in the crop dusters until he and Theodore had dragged Sebastian, Claire, and Frank out of the mold.

"Holy shit," Jasper said, when he pulled back the tarp and saw Claire underneath. Whatever she'd called inside her was gone, but it hadn't left her gently. Her jaw was shattered, and her skin was stretched out so badly that Aloysius had barely been able to carry her back to the truck for all the flopping around she did. No two bones seemed to be stuck together, and of course she was covered with bloody symbols. And then there was Frank, in pieces.

"Eileen Hart blackmailed him into cheating on Claire." Sebastian coughed up gray phlegm. "Claire decided to take revenge on him since Eileen was already dead. But I didn't tell you that."

"Black magic," Jasper said. "Shit."

"I took care of it."

Jasper gave him a look. It was the first time Sebastian could remember that anybody had looked at him like he was a real, live priest instead of a kid whose diapers they'd changed or who had last been seen guzzling beer out on the reservation.

The mold was obviously dying, turning a flat gray, but nobody wanted to risk it, so Jasper sent in the crop dusters with heavy-duty fungicide. They'd been lucky. Don Hart took his savings and moved to Minnesota, near one of his daughters by his first wife. Liam bought the farm and hired more men to work it; the land grew well enough after a few years had passed.

Peggy finished the rest of the quilt using the protection symbol, and they sold tickets for it at the Harvest Festival. Sebastian put in twenty bucks and won it.

He put it on his own bed and slept very well indeed.

"And," I said, "as far as I know, that priest still has it."

That priest. You might think he doesn't know what you've done. You might think you have him fooled, with his soft face and kind eyes and thick black glasses. You think your weeping and wailing over the death of your husband has deceived him. Perhaps it might have, once, before I started telling him tales about what I saw you doing at night, about the tales the girl told.

When I finished, the girl's lips were pressed together in a small tight circle, as though they were a worm curled up tight. Her back was straight, barely brushing the seat. Twin streams of anger jetted from her nostrils, hot as dragon steam.

If *she* ever believed you, that is over now.

I hopped down from the mirror and strutted through the younglings, who parted before me, until I reached the girl's foot. It was a good story, enough of a story to part chicks. But what did the elders think of it? It was a new story, one that I had not told before. Of course I had stolen it from the priest, but that wouldn't save me, if there was no good in the telling.

The elders said nothing, but Old Loyolo looked down on me with his black eyes, weighing.

After a moment, he pushed Facunde forward. Facunde who had been lovely, Facunde who had been eloquent. Facunde who I had long wished to be my mate, but who had ever eluded me. Her mate, Guerro, had been killed last year, killed by cats, and she had been mourning him ever since, building towers of sticks all over the dumping ground. She had gone mad. Her feathers were dull and gray, and crawling with lice. She was fed by her grown chicks. Always she was building her towers of sticks, even in the snow. The cats would take her soon.

Old Loyolo pushed her until she fell off the girl's knees and landed beside me, on her back in the middle of a huddle of chicks.

They pushed her upright, then over to the storyteller's perch. She cawed unintelligibly, nipping at them, flapping her wings. But they were inexorable.

I followed her, and pinched her along the wing with my beak, and helped lift her onto the perch.

Old Loyolo made a spot for me next to him. But I stayed at Facunde's feet. Her ragged claws clutched the mirror over and over, leaving smears on the glass.

"Speak!" ordered old Loyolo. "A story!"

A story, a story!

"A *human* story," I said. Meaning that muttering the tale of how Guerro had died under her breath, as she had been doing ever since he had been eaten, would not do.

"A story," she croaked. "I will tell you a story. It is not a human story, though. It is a *winter* story that happens to have humans in it. And it has nothing to do with making our girl *talk*," she sneered down at me, "when she doesn't want to. It doesn't mean anything. So don't blame me if you don't like it."

What? What? cried some of the chicks who were at the edges. The ruffling of feathers was almost loud enough to drown out her voice.

"Speak louder," old Loyolo ordered.

Facunde cleared her throat. It sounded as though she were coughing up a dry, sun-killed lizard stuck in her throat. Or, I thought, her heart.

When she had finished, she bent over and clawed something from her beak. A shimmering, sparkling bead, the size of a fat crow's eye. It landed in front of me. As fast as anything, I pecked it up. It was bitter-tasting, and seemed to move, although I was sure that it was not anything that had been recently alive. I held it under my tongue.

Facunde said…

3. Abominable

You meet a woman.

In a bar, sitting at a table, with a long, white cigarette between her pale fingers and smooth, pale nails. Her lips are red, her dress is red. She stares at you like a beautiful monster, hungry. The smoke curls toward you, she brushes her blue-black hair off her face. A cynical Snow White, the fairest of them all.

You're charming.

You turn the chair next to her backwards. You sit and smile. You're Jack. Her name is Laura. You say you'd like to share your life with her, starting with a drink. Hers is a gin and tonic. You're charming, and she enjoys you.

———

Taking her to your apartment is smooth and easy. You brush away your usual lines, your foreplay falls away like heavy winter clothing, you're making love—

It's not making love, she murmurs, moving her satin and fur around you. You hardly know me.

You touch her face and grin crazily, We've had at least what could be considered a formal introduction, yes?

You insist that she meet you every night, she cannot resist.

For months you pamper her, cooking, brushing her hair, flowers, conversations in the dark. She loses some of her cynical chill, you teach her how to tell jokes. She tells you she used to be a country girl with shit on her cowboy boots, never so sophisticated, but she's forgotten how— You tell her the city bores you, you're playing with the idea of moving on—

I wish I could take you back home sometime, she says. Out to the old place, so many things I wonder if they're still—

You'd like that.

She means something to you.

She's the only thing that holds fast, stays perfect and pure. Everything else stinks of tar, mildew, or rust. When the night fills up with assholes yelling to wake up other assholes whose car alarms have gone off, she sleeps, so quiet you can barely hear her breathe. You talk about all the crazy things you did as a kid. She listens, she really listens.

You aren't sure—nobody's ever sure—but you're good to her, just in case.

She's crying.

She clings to you and wipes snot off her face with her sleeve. You calm her and stroke her tangled hair, trying to put her smoothness back together. You beg her, no matter what, we can—

When she can talk she tells you she's pregnant.

Shock, panic flashes, your ears cloud up and echo with thunder. Yet you find yourself smiling like a damn fool as she pushes you away.

I don't want it, she says. I can't stand kids.

It wouldn't have to be just your kid, you say. Our kid. Baby. You're not going to kill it, are you?

Fear, cold fear.

Her, she says. It's a girl. My family always has girls. —No.

We could move back to the place where you grew up, you say. Don't you have family out there? Your parents?

My cousins, she says. My parents are dead, remember?

If it didn't work out your cousins, would they take it? Her?

—Yes. They only had the one, and he died.

This is your chance to gain solidity. Gravity, roots, earthiness. You were about to float away with indifference before you met her. Turning point, settling down, rock-hard foundations. Please? Pretty please?

She doesn't want this, but she says yes.

—

Laura swells up like a stubbed toe, puffy and complaining. You don't have to feign attention through the birthing classes. You buy her simple, sweet gifts. You make sure she dresses well: you don't want her self-image to suffer any more than it has to. You take her out, but she hates it because her back hurts or her bladder is full.

Laura, you tell her. I love you. It's only a matter of time.

—

When the baby is born you name her Flora after your grandmother who lives on the other side of the city. Your grandmother is cross and uncaring when you take Flora to meet her.

You take the baby to Laura's cousins, they coo and cuddle.

Of course we'll take her if—if. But Jack, they say, when are you two lovebirds getting married?

This, she says, is the way I want it.

—

Leaving Flora with the cousins, you see the house.

You're deep-sea divers, you're men on an alien moon in your borrowed insulated coveralls and boots, wandering through the icy house. The sun filters in, trying to melt the dusty frost that sparkles everywhere. Upstairs, one of the windows has shattered. You pull off a glove, the cold presses on one side of your hand and not the other. You turn your hand in the breeze.

You find Laura downstairs turning the pages of a photo album.

Mother, wife, cousin, daughter, she says. I have all this family I didn't remember I had.

You can't make out the faces on the ruined pictures.

Really, the house is in great shape, the cousins have been wonderful keeping it up for the day that Laura would come back, her trust fund paid for it and all, but there was love—if only that damn window upstairs hadn't busted—if only all that time hadn't passed—

Laura cries on the way home to the city, you tell her—you don't know what you tell her.

—

Four weeks, you go. It's something of a drive, but not that bad. Works as a commute, barely.

It's a white house with green shingles on the roof. It's so old you thank God for the running water and electricity. The woodstove heats the center of the house like a heart, and the cupboards and closets and the attic and the basement are like cold fingers and shivering toes.

You've hired someone to check out the wiring, the plumbing, the cracks in the cement downstairs, but it's you, one slow week after another, who cleaned out, fixed up, and furnished the house again. You saved as much as you could, but you couldn't save everything. Some of Laura's past is gone, trashed, wasted, refused, no matter that she's back now.

Laura stands in the house with her arms open, for the first time seeing the changes. You see the world spread out for her, open up her claustrophobic urban future into a white prairie with red sunsets. She trots through the house, she stretches in front of the stove, dressed in a red flannel shirt and blue jeans. You've never seen her wear blue jeans before. She chops wood in the morning, she takes long walks into the shelterbelt in the afternoon. She sings in the kitchen.

She hates you.

Everything she sees and touches is a reminder to her that her past is gone. You've thrown away the rags and scraps that used to be her home. You've taken her away from the city, from the woman she used to be. Never mind that she's happier now.

You're the father of her child.

When she's undressed her belly sags and her cunt flops around like an empty sack. She doesn't make love to you, she fucks you, sloppy and bored like your grandmother's kisses. She's stopped shaving her legs and wearing makeup.

Yet you're happy, you tell her, and all it will take is time for her body to go back to the way it used to be.

At first, Laura nursed Flora, but Flora's teeth came in early. She said her breasts were sore from being bitten, you couldn't blame her. But that wasn't all. Nothing Flora did pleased Laura.

Little monster, she called her.

Wouldn't change her, wouldn't feed her her formula, wouldn't hold her when she cried.

Not my baby, our baby, she says. I did all the work for nine months, now it's your turn. I'm going out to the shelterbelt to clear some more deadwood before the storm. I'm taking the pickup, do you need anything from the store?

The usual, you say, make sure you don't forget the diapers.

It's almost March before you convince yourself it isn't a matter of time, change, adjustment. You're afraid to leave Flora alone with her mother, always know that the little monster means less to her than a sodden teddy bear that you threw away months ago.

Laura's body hasn't recovered, and she says she'll never forgive you. Her callused hands will never be pale and smooth again. The nails are hard-bitten now.

You decide to leave.

You tell Laura.

She smiles.

I'm taking the pickup out to Gundersen's, she says. Think I'll start raising some orphaned lambs this spring. I'll keep them in the garage where you used to keep your car. With heat lamps. What do you think?

I don't think you're fit to raise anything.

I've been ready for you, she says. She pulls out a well-creased, dirty envelope from the pocket of her coat. I'll be back tomorrow afternoon.

Thank God. I'll never see the little monster again, will I?

Then she skips out to the pickup truck and leaves.

———

You read the note.

She doesn't want you to leave her anything you've touched. She doesn't want the baby, doesn't want the car, doesn't want anything you picked out for the house. You made her realize that she needs a home and a family, but you're damned useless and she doesn't want you around. You pushed her into all these decisions, so live with it. She's been sleeping with that sheep-farmer Gundersen. He thinks her body is just fine.

But so did you.

———

You're leaving first thing in the morning, you think. Your grandmother is unpleasant, but you can stay there. Just until. When you take Flora over to the cousins, you tell them as much as you know.

We heard, they say, about Gundersen.

You've been hurt before, you say. You hate to leave, but—you've been rootless for so long that it isn't much of a readjustment.

Will you be back for Flora, they want to know. Please say no.

Yes, oh, yes, you say. Tomorrow morning. I just need to pack. I want to keep her, I've been raising her myself. Laura hates her.

We know, they say.

You go, you just go.

———

You put more wood on the fire, briefly you consider burning the house down. You pull as much of yourself and Flora out of the house as you can, packing it tightly into the car. There's too much left over. You decide it's enough to let the fire go out in the morning and throw the windows open. The pipes will freeze, and the snow will get in, ruin everything.

You fix yourself a sandwich and ignore the storm coming up, thinking only, I hope Laura gets caught out in that—

———

The windows rattle.

You can hear the wind picking up outside and a knocking sound upstairs. It's a window, the one that was broken before, the one that always jiggles loose from the broken yardstick you used to wedge it shut. The snow's coming in, the wind slams the closet door against the wall.

You let your heart wash itself out in the cold, close the window, then jam the yardstick tight.

———

You sit with a beer in front of the television.

You wonder what she'll do with everything you're leaving behind. Burn it, put it in boxes marked "asshole," shit on it, and mail it to your grandmother. Or she won't notice it's even there.

Suddenly there's a gap in the wind, and you realize the house is silent. You turn down the volume on the television, wondering if the storm is dying down or if you've just gone deaf.

Then you hear the moaning.

It isn't the wind, but it's definitely coming from outside.

You look but you don't see anything. Jesus. You hope it isn't some kid lost in the snow.

It's too bright to see out the window.

You turn off the lights. Nothing.

You bundle up, grab a flashlight and (remembering a couple of stories they made you read as a kid) tie a rope to the porch railing before you take a walk around the house. Your cheeks sting as snowflakes knife into your face. And melt, dripping into the neck of your coveralls.

The moaning sound is just a trick of the snow. It moans as it clings to the side of the house, slips, and the wind rips it away. It gathers and huddles in little piles as if for warmth. The wind throws leaves and sticks and bits of ash from the trash barrel and knocks the snow screaming out onto the prairie.

The snow seems to sense you, and starts begging, scrabbling harder and harder at the siding of the house like a puppy or a drowning man.

You go back inside and turn up the tube.

You get rid of the beer.

After an hour you wake. Hadn't realized you were falling asleep.

It's louder.

As if someone were speaking backwards. Muttering.

Then as if someone were taking a small ax to the outside wall. Loud.

It's colder.

You pull back the drapes, and the window is covered entirely with white.

Goddamn snow.

Give me back the city and the municipal plows, you think.

The house bangs and shudders. You hear another groan at the window.

You pull back the curtains, but this time the window is black. You can't see anything. No snow.

It comes at you so hard it seems to bend the plate glass window toward your face.

Bang.

Weird.

Bang.

The snow ripples with the impact as it strikes.

Bang.

It's so cold.

You realize that you've let the stove go out.

You hear a sob from the window, and the snow disappears.

You turn off the lights and peer through the corner of the window at the side of the house. Nothing. You turn the lights back on. Nothing. Christ, you turn the televisio—

Something scrapes against the wall. You can hear it.

You haven't taken off your coveralls or boots, you pull on the rest of your gear and open the front door. You don't shut it behind you. Something's stuck to the side of the house, moving up the gutter, snatching snow out of the air, getting bigger. Heading toward that loose upstairs window.

You go back inside, run upstairs.

You see the mass of snow outside the window. It splits into tendrils and wedges itself into the cracks of the window frame.

The window frame grunts and creaks.

The snow starts beating on the window.

Bang.

Harder. Like a fist.

Bang.

Harder.

The glass shatters.

———

Warm, warm, it only wants to get warm. You run. You run to the heart of the house, but the stove is out. The only warmth left is you.

It takes shelter in you, cell by cell. You aren't warm enough. Nothing is warm enough. God. You flake up and blow away.

So cold.

———

The nearest farmhouse is Gundersen's, just across the shelterbelt and another mile or so. Half a mile out, heading back to the farm, you find Laura.

She runs into you with the truck. You cling to her windshield, you force her into the ditch.

You can't get in. You huddle around the truck cab, begging her to let you in. You don't mean to torment her, but you do. If only you could reach her, touch her—Laura—

Laura—

Just leave me alone!

She screams until she falls asleep, blue at the lips.

Laura—I'm sorry—

Laura—

You go on moaning her name until springtime, looking for warmth. Not your fault, really.

And then you melt and flow away.

When she had finished, Facunde peeked at the chicks underneath her. "My bead," she croaked. "Give me back my bead." Her voice, so long unused, had gone rough and prickly, like pinfeathers. "One of you has it, you filthy things. My bead!"

I did not open my beak.

The girl was looking at me, her eyes two narrow, suspicious slits peeking out from under her blanket and her carpet of crows. Oh, yes. She had seen me take it. I winked at her. The bead, if that's what it was, wriggled under my tongue, trying to crawl down my throat, and I had to clear my throat over and over, to keep it from going down. It was as bitter as a soul turned rotten.

It *might* have been as bitter as your heart.

Facunde heard me clear my throat, and pecked me on the head. "You have it, Machado. Don't try to lie. If you do, it will jump out of your mouth and down the throat of one of these chicks. And who wants that!" She laughed and flapped off the mirror-perch, her frayed wings beating the thick air, and crashed into the girl's lap. Old Loyolo, of course, hopped out of the way. He can't be having crows knock him about; it upsets his dignity, which is a cupped leaf full of rainwater, likely to tip out with the slightest breeze.

Facunde crawled up the girl's arm and settled on her shoulder, with her beak almost in the girl's ear. "You keep it, Machado," she very nearly hissed. "See how you like it. And see how you like the thought of another bird having to carry it under their tongue in your place." Her feathers seemed darker, with more sheen to them.

As for the bead, already I did not like it at all, not the taste, and not the feeling of it in my mouth.

"Who will be the next storyteller?" Old Loyolo said.

The chicks called out their suggestions, naming those who were chicks themselves, foolish downy things who couldn't describe a rotting corpse on a snowy hill in the moonlight with any kind of poetry. The ones they named tucked their heads under their wings and stamped their feet, shuffling away from the girl and, more specifically, the elders sitting on her lap, whose eyes can be so piercing, so dark and threatening.

Strange to think of myself as one of *them* now, an elder.

Facunde whispered in the girl's ear, but the girl shook her head. Facunde chuckled wickedly, a sound that set my feathers shivering with near-forgotten longing. Already her eyes were brighter, her feathers more ordered. As for myself, I felt old and tired (at least, more old and tired than I usually did, and not as old and tired as I do now). Despite the crowding in the truck cab, there was space around me, as the chicks leaned away from me, trying to keep from brushing their feathers against me.

Old Loyolo saw this, and beckoned me forward. I began to hop toward him, even though I felt weak. Better for whatever sickness I carried to be surrounded among the old, than among the chicks. We tease them, but they are all the future we will ever have, and the only ones who will remember our stories.

"I will tell a story," announced one of the chicks, an arrogant male named Zubalo.

Zubalo, Zubalo, cheered the other chicks, as though their approbation meant anything at all. And yet when Old Loyolo looked at him, Zubalo did not cower, did not hide his eyes under his wing.

"You will?" Old Loyolo cawed in annoyance. "Are you sure? Are you ready? Have you come to me in humility, to practice?"

"Who made you master of the stories?" the young chick said. "Who said that you could choose who tells stories, and who does not?"

Old Loyolo jerked his beak in the air, and Zubalo's tail feathers shuddered. "Who am I? Who am I?" The old crow danced on the girl's knee, hopping and shifting his weight from side to side. "The chooser of the stories? No! The storytellers choose the stories! Don't you pay attention? I do not choose the stories!"

Zubalo ducked his head up and down, lower and lower each time. "What does it matter? You choose the storytellers, then! That is the same thing!"

"No," Old Loyolo said. Now he stood completely still, his wings spread a little and his feathers turned a little so that they looked like a row of sharp knives. "I do not choose the storytellers. They choose themselves. What I do is to keep those who are not storytellers from telling things that are not stories!"

"Anyone who tells a story is a storyteller." Zubalo's crowing was thin and weedy, a call that barely carried throughout the girl's tiny room.

"Then tell yours," Old Loyolo said, with the voice of death. "And take the consequences, if you are wrong."

"The consequences?"

But Loyolo only glared at him. And so Zubalo hopped over to the mirror and flapped awkwardly up to the perch. He struck the window and tumbled backward, only barely catching his claws on the perch. They screeched against the glass.

But then he caught his balance and hopped around to face his audience, his first full audience.

It reminded me of my first story. And so before I tell you Zubalo's story, let me tell you this one…

4. Winter Fruit

Miklos had always wanted an old-fashioned Catholic funeral, with incense and a tomb, so he'd converted a few years ago, when the doctor started to warn him about his heart. He didn't change his diet.

The tomb was cold, but not actually unpleasant.

I locked the door of the tomb behind him and placed the key on a black ribbon inside my dress, singing an old song under my breath. Outside the tomb, it was cold but sunny, and a light breeze played with the black silk scarf covering my hair.

I had to choke back an appalling giggle. Miklos would tell horrible jokes at funerals—the one about switching heads—the one about the man who wanted to be buried with his money, so his wife wrote him a check—

Andros stood next to me with his hand on my shoulder, squeezing hard. The family looked like dancers at a costume ball wearing masks of tragedy, which would soon be cast aside for the hideous grimaces of comedy at the dinner.

If only they had known how hungry I was.

The family stood near the man-made lake across the street and watched the wintry sun set behind the mountains. As soon as the arc of the sun left the sky, the aunts drew their scarves away from their faces and sang. It was not a Catholic song. It was not a Greek song. There were no words, no wailing, only harmonies.

Afterwards, we walked the half-mile to the restaurant. Andros had prepared the food himself: chewy, spicy kollyva, toasted paximadia, and piles of pomegranates, their crowns sacred to Miklos's old religion and least worth an old-fashioned superstition from his new one.

And meat.

Andros had roasted an entire lamb in the parking lot behind the restaurant. He'd marinated it with yogurt and salt over three days while we prepared for the funeral. One of his cooks had stayed with the lamb during the last rites, basting it with garlic, lemon, oregano, and olive oil. Andros and I had viewed the lamb before the service had started.

He had left the head on, the spit driven grotesquely through the hole in the bottom of its jaw, making it seem as though the creature had suffered horribly, dying in the flames.

I swallowed back my desire to fling myself on the roast lamb. "Is it ready?" I asked Andros, casually.

Andros arched an eyebrow at me, making the hairs along my arms stand on end. "Certainly," he said. "Hungry?"

I bit my lip. "I haven't eaten since last night," I said, lying.

Andros pulled a switchblade out of his pocket and cut off a thin sliver of charred meat. "For you, the first cut."

I held it under my nose for a second and popped it into my mouth. It tasted of bitter ashes.

Miklos was a mad clench of muscle and gristle, not an inch taller than I. His hair was wiry and black; his jaw couldn't stay clean for over an hour. He was made like stone, so incredibly dense that on our honeymoon, he stood on the ocean floor near Naxos while fish and tiny octopi darted through his fingers as if he were a fallen statue. Perhaps he was.

The Harbor, white and Greek blue, shimmered in the twilight like a ghost. Miklos and Andros had claimed it was haunted by a third brother, a lost triplet who had died in the ocean of their mother's womb. Andros opened the door. Inside, the tables had been heaped with the feast and the wine stood ready to pour. Although I had been the first to walk through the door, Andros seated the aunts first. But who could blame him? I was only a beautiful young widow. Hardly family.

As he held the chair for me, he whispered in my ear, "Be with me."

I sat, and he pushed the chair to the table. His arms weren't as strong as Miklos's, but they were strong enough.

"What, lovers?" I whispered.

"I will satisfy you in ways Miklos could not."

"Ah. Food."

"You never gain an ounce."

I pinched Andros in the waist, and he jumped. One of the aunts glared at us.

"You are the perfect woman to me."

"Let me mourn in peace, Andros."

"I know your secret."

"Which secret?"

"You killed Miklos."

I hissed through my teeth. "I did no such thing."

"You were hungry, weren't you?"

"Not that hungry."

"You gave him the heart attack. You frightened him."

"It was your over-rich food that killed him," I snapped out loud. "Andros, respect the dead for at least one meal."

And then I started to eat.

If Miklos was a statue, Andros was an avalanche. Andros would seduce women by changing their children's diapers, then insist the brats be left to cry while they made love. He would sell lobster with sea-urchin sauce for less than the food cost, because his customers must *taste* it. His staff quit within weeks or lasted for years: students, sadists, perfectionists. He regularly took waitresses for lovers, then fired them when he tired of them. He never admitted to fathering a particular child—but never denied it, either.

Andros's hair was a soft brown, falling in soft waves that he tied back when he was in the kitchen. His hands were softer than Miklos's—but covered with scars. Miklos could stand still for hours on end. Andros was light on his feet; he loved to dance. Miklos could only manage a stately waltz.

The feast lasted well into the evening, and Andros was generous with the Amethystos. I ate heartily until I saw one of the aunts frowning at me; then I pushed my plate away and groaned at my fullness, tugging the waistband of my skirt.

Being so close to the mounds of food remaining on the table made me foul-tempered, so I stepped outside for air. Andros followed me. He put his arms around me, and I pushed him off.

"I want to make love to you," he moaned.

I snorted. "Here?" The garbage was redolent.

"Here. Anywhere."

"Go find one of the cousins. They won't mind a little incest."

"Please, Adrienne—" He ran a hand across my chest.

I slapped him. "Andros! Your brother is dead!"

"You killed him!" He reached for me again.

I tried to walk past him into the restaurant; he grabbed for me again. But I have known Andros for years, and I was ready. I rushed him against the trash bin with a loud, empty clang, slammed his head against the rim, and stormed off. Andros is persistent but easily shifted. And I am strong.

As I yanked open the door, the family doctor, Dr. Alex, stepped out. "Are you all right?"

"Fine," I said. "I'd be more worried about Andros if I were you. He might not survive the night, if he doesn't keep his hands off me."

Dr. Alex put an eyebrow up at me. "Several drugs, when combined with alcohol, cause erectile dysfunction. Perhaps it's time for a prescription."

I laughed. My stomach growled.

Dr. Alex said, "You can't possibly be—"

I shoved past him. "It's just gas," I said.

"Ah," he said, looking at Andros.

I fumed and helped myself to some wine and a plate of cookies, regardless of the aunts and their observations. Dr. Alex glanced at me, a bland look on his face—he had the most remarkably bulging forehead—from across the room.

I hadn't killed Miklos! Dr. Alex knew it for the truth, no matter what poison Andros whispered. Miklos was older than I, with a heart even older than the years on his birth certificate could show. I wanted to shout the truth into the room.

Instead I picked up a pomegranate and shredded the rind and pith with my fingers. I left the vermillion, jeweled pips piled on a plate. I promised myself I could leave as soon as I had finished them, eating the vermillion jewels one by one to pass the time. And then I would take my memories of Miklos and go home, away from his squabbling, glowering relatives.

I was just about to eat the first pip when Andros returned. He tried to steal a handful of pips from my plate, but I grabbed his hand by the wrist and forced it away, unceremoniously knocking the spectacles off a nearby cousin.

Before his blood-kin could protest, Andros shouted, "A toast!" He picked up his wine, but his glass was empty, so he picked up my glass instead. I stood up, taking my plate of pomegranate pips with me, so quickly I nearly knocked over my chair.

"A toast! To Adrienne!"

"Andros," I hissed. "Shut up!"

"To Adrienne and her hunger!" he roared, his voice echoing through the room as all conversation stopped.

No one echoed his toast. He drank regardless.

"May it never fail," he concluded.

I flung the pips at him—the plate fell and shattered—I refused to eat anything he'd touched—and left, weeping tears of outrage and humiliation. I swore to myself never to walk through the door of Andros's restaurant again.

You may judge for yourself whether I succeeded.

Halfway home and almost blinded by the moon in my eyes, a hand gripped my arm, and I wrenched myself free, ready to launch myself down Andros's throat.

"Adrienne—" I should have known it was Dr. Alex, following me again.

"Leave me alone!" I shouted.

"Let me examine you," he said.

I laughed. "You told Andros, didn't you? After all these years, he knows. You think I killed Miklos, don't you?"

Dr. Alex shrugged, turning his enormous forehead into a beachside of creases.

"I didn't kill him!"

"Don't tell me you never thought about it. He was almost as bad as Andros. In his own way."

I shook my head. "No. Never. I would never hurt either of them."

"All right," he said. "Now, will you come back to my office tonight?"

I sighed. "Go back to the restaurant, Dr. Alex. People will talk. I can't afford it."

"Promise me."

"All right. Monday."

"We open at eight."

"All right! Now, go!"

He smiled, the moonlight turning him into a ghost even before his scent left my nostrils. Then my stomach growled, and I turned and ran all the way home.

Oh God, what am I going to do? I thought. Miklos, Miklos, why did you leave me?

The phone was ringing off the hook, but nobody had left any messages on the answering machine—Andros. I locked, bolted, and chained the doors, put a pile of sliced, roasted lamb from the refrigerator on a platter, and went downstairs, eating as I went. The smell from the basement raised the hairs inside my nose, as always—disinfectant, bleach, and rancid fat.

Miklos had left me with six clients; our assistant Yuri had taken care of all but the two who needed more than rouge. I flipped on the lights.

The two clients were alone, sadly, their families leaving them to my care rather than spending the night. I would guard their bodies from the spirits, I promised them.

The dead are always heavier than they look. To move one part of the body is to try to move an entire life, they are so heavy.

I pulled open the gentleman's drawer and pulled his gurney out, then wheeled it under my lights. The man had died young and handsome—until the automobile accident that had put him through the windshield and onto the asphalt. Yuri had done his best. He'd cleaned the face down to the pores, rebuilt the jawline and teeth, and attached the skin as securely as possible without damaging it further. Luckily, the eyelids were undamaged.

I scrubbed and dressed and left the empty platter in the sink. I'd already set up the man's photograph at my table, along with a molded latex cheek I'd cast from the other side of the man's face. I never try to make the dead look like the living, no matter how much the clients' families beg me; it's never a mercy.

A couple of hours later, I was still fussing with the way the bones of the jaw molded the cheek to match the photograph (they didn't) and decided to take a break. Despite the ache in my back, I felt at peace, my stomach finally settled. I stripped off my gloves, washed up, and went upstairs.

The light on the answering machine was blinking. No messages from Andros, thank God. One from Dr. Alex reminding me of my appointment tomorrow morning. One from Yuri, begging me to unchain the door, because he couldn't get in and finish with the female client before morning.

"Oh, hell," I said, just as someone pounded on the back door. I unchained the door and flung it open before Yuri could leave. "I'm sorry—"

Andros shoved his way through. "You should be."

I slammed the door, but it was too late. "Get out! I won't sleep with you, no matter what lies you yell from the top of the mountain, you bastard!"

Andros walked into the kitchen and flung open the refrigerator. "Where is it?"

"Where is what, you fool?"

"Don't play with me. It's downstairs, isn't it?" His voice crackled, as if he'd screamed himself hoarse, which would have taken some work, for him. Andros ran out of the kitchen, leaving the refrigerator door open.

My peace of mind had melted like grease in a frying pan, spitting and hissing in the heat. My stomach growled again. I slammed the refrigerator door and stalked after Andros.

Andros was looking inside the refrigerators downstairs, looking inside the other client's bag.

"Get out of there!" I shouted.

"Where is it?" he gasped, trying to shout but unable to raise his voice above an ugly whisper.

"What? What? What is so important that you violate the peace of the dead?"

"Miklos's heart!"

I was too confused to shout. "Why would his heart be here? We just buried him."

Andros's eyes seemed to turn to lightning, and he rushed me, both hands out to shove me or strangle me or both. I hit my head against the concrete wall. For some reason, my nose hurt like all the rages of hell for a moment before I passed out.

When I awoke, I was locked in the refrigerator downstairs. I knew this because the air was cold and humid (to keep skin from cracking in the dry air), I was surrounded by the smell of old blood and metal, and the door at my feet was locked. I kicked, saddened by the dents I must be leaving in the refrigerator door but unable to keep myself from lashing out.

After a few dozen kicks, I twisted myself around (I am just small enough; Miklos could never have done it), and fumbled around in the dark until I found the catch. I forced it with my fingers, pinching the rollers until the spring forced back, and pushed the door.

It opened only a fraction of an inch. The room outside the refrigerator was hardly warmer than the inside. But I could tell, from the padlock rattling as I beat the door, I was well and truly locked inside my drawer.

I howled. "Andros!" My voice echoed back to me.

I could have begged Andros for my freedom, but he would have heard the threat in my voice regardless. I meant to kill him, as I had never meant to kill Miklos. One way or another, the body would never be found. I howled again, and my stomach howled with me.

But Andros didn't answer me; no one did. Eventually I fell asleep.

I awoke to the smell of heaven, of succulent meat. Pork, burnt and smothered in a piquant sauce. Lamb from the ceremonial feast. Sautéed mushrooms, onions. The deep-earth smell of pickled cabbage with wine and garlic. Olives, bitter oranges, oregano. I could list the scents for you, one by one, until you covered your ears and laughed at me to stop, mocked me for my over-delicate nose. Cumin, turmeric, coconut. Mussels. Fresh cream. Cheese so passionate about its own molds it stung the nose to be within a dozen feet of it. Coffee, as fresh as a new-killed rabbit.

Another might call it a kind of seduction or a peace offering, a feast meant to tantalize or lull me. But I knew Andros, and Andros knew me.

I growled, "What do you want?"

Andros chuckled. "So you're awake." The lock of my cage rattled, and the door opened.

I listened. Andros backed away from the door quickly, almost running, then stopped. Someone else was in the room with him; I heard the breathing, which was so slow and even you would have thought the other was asleep. Yet how could anyone have slept through that jackhammering of smells?

I slid the drawer free and dropped into the room like an animal, crouched until my hands were touching the tile floor, my nostrils open wide.

The room was filled with food. The gurneys were piled with it, the shelves, the tables, the chairs, every inch of space was crowded with a feast.

Andros stood next to the door, halfway out already. "Hello, Adrienne. This is all for you—help yourself." He slammed the door behind him, and I heard the sound of a padlock quickly closing home.

I stalked to the door and tried it. Of course it was locked. I rammed the door with my shoulder. The door was too solid simply to break through, but I might have heard the hinges creak a little.

I rammed the door again and felt a little give.

And then the smell defeated me.

"Andros!" I howled, then started to eat.

—

Of all things, it was the kataifi, an almond dessert, that I reached for first. Ah, they were so good. And closest. Then I started on the dishes that would fade first. Olive oil ice cream with lemon-basil sauce so sour I could feel it burn my lips. An omelet with spinach, tomato, and feta. Sesame-seed biscuits with butter. Then red-snapper soup with zucchini, tomatoes, and potatoes. The lemon and olive oil in the soup was like silk on my tongue. How had he made all the food? In such a short amount of time?

With that, although I eyed the octopi, I was sated enough to attack the door again. "Let me out!" I screamed. My shoes were missing, so I beat at the hinges with my shoulders until they were raw, then cleared the food off a side table and used that until I had smashed it to bits. I had almost twisted the bolt off when I heard a moan from within a mound of food on a gurney.

I froze.

The moan came again, thick with mucus, like something drug up from the depths of the sea. "Aghch—"

A platter of crabs slid onto the floor and lay still.

Oh, God. What had Andros done? What had he tried to make me do? Had me meant me, God forbid, to *eat* someone?

I walked back into the room, my heart thudding with fear for the first time, so hard I thought it would choke me.

On tiptoe, I approached the gurney. The cement floor was cold on my bare feet, colder than death. I do not fear the dead—but I feared whomever or whatever was on the table, breathing harshly. A dozen skewers of shrimp slid to the floor. I held my breath and reached out one hand to push aside the platter of garlic and wine-steamed mussels—

"Dr. Alex!"

Food didn't trouble me until I became a woman. I have always been strong for my size, but it wasn't until I developed these hips that I started to feel a terrible hunger.

Perhaps, when I was a girl, I might have lost control and eaten someone, in the depths of my need. But at thirty-five, there was no chance I would do so, no matter how hungry I was. I would—and I swear to you that I truly would—eat my own leg first.

That damned Andros!

Andros had not used subtle arts to make Dr. Alex unconscious—Dr. Alex's head was tender on the back, bloody and obviously swollen through his thinning hair.

His eyes were open but wandering. I waved my hand in front of his face, and he twitched but could not follow it. I squatted next to him and murmured in his ear, "You must be quiet, Dr. Alex. We don't know what Andros will do. He believes in his heart that I killed his brother. Perhaps he believes you helped me hide Miklos's death."

"Don't eat me," Dr. Alex whimpered.

I snorted. "I swear, Dr. Alex, I will pick those crabs off the floor before I eat you."

His eyes flicked toward mine, almost seeing me. He smiled a little. I reached over, picked one of the crabs up, bit through the shell—and swallowed. His eyes went wide and I laughed, spraying chunks of shell on the floor.

I was calm then, or calm enough to hold myself back from either breaking down the door or consuming the feast. The food had all been made with fondness, if not love.

How could I tell that? Ah, how could I not?

I thought Andros would burn down the house with myself and Dr. Alex in it. I thought he would shoot me if I tried to take Dr. Alex to safety. But he did not. He wished to kill the woman he loved—but first, the horrifying, loving feast.

Dr. Alex must have come to the house to check on me when I did not appear for my appointment and been hit on the head for his trouble.

"But what about the heart?" I murmured to myself.

"A bull's heart," Dr. Alex mumbled. "I used a bull's heart. And it was barely large enough."

I grabbed the gurney to keep myself from sliding to the floor, knocking loose a pattering rain of oysters in their shells, alabaster calamari rings laid on pasta ribbons dyed black with their own ink, and a plate of lobster, bright red shells like the armor of the god of war. Dr. Alex wobbled, but I steadied him as I steadied myself.

I saw it then, as plain as I can see the sky.

"Where did you put it?" I asked.

"In a jar," Dr. Alex said. "In storage."

And it was I who had given Dr. Alex permission to perform the autopsy, his little look-see to determine the cause of death: heart attack.

"When?" I asked.

"Why did he have to—I sent him all the—why did he have to ask so many questions?" Dr. Alex panted and turned his head from side to side.

"What about Yuri?" I asked.

"What about him?" Dr. Alex asked. He sounded suspicious, and I guessed I might have only one more question before he was fully conscious.

I leaned closer, so my hair, which had come loose, trailed across his face and filled his nose with my scent as though I were his lover. Of all the things I wanted to know—proof of his guilt—who else was involved—blackmail—revenge—I wanted to know what he saw when he looked at me, when he stood next to me and implied that I had scared Miklos to death with my appetites.

I purred seductively, "What about my heart? Don't you want that, too?"

"I will take it soon, my lamb," Dr. Alex said. "It will fit into the same jar easily."

It was easy enough; the room was well-stocked with knives and saws and served with an abundance of drains.

Because I had told him I wouldn't hurt him, I hit him in the head with a bone hammer first, knocking him out like a steer. His expression was stunned even before I hit him. The idea of his raw flesh disgusted me, so I called for Andros to let me out, so I could cook it. But I received no answer. I called again. Nothing.

Either the police would come, or they wouldn't. Either Andros would open the door, or he wouldn't. I did not think, one way or another, that I would have time to prepare Dr. Alex properly, as meat. As offal.

Miklos! With that cry and a scalpel, I cut Dr. Alex's throat. The hammer had not killed him: the living blood pumped free. I leaped back. Even though I had taken care to stand behind him, the blood sprayed widely at first. After a time, I rolled Dr. Alex onto the floor, kneeling on his back until the blood had stopped running, long after he had died. Then I washed him and hung him from a ceiling joist, after I had pushed away the acoustic tiles.

I decided not to damage the door any further—the story I would have to tell would be complicated enough without having to explain having torn the bolt out of the door.

I was only just finishing up the last swirl of juices and grease from the bottom of a platter of fried oysters, a splash of water I'd poured in to save myself the indignity of having to lick it clean, when Andros unlocked the door. I tossed the platter at his head; he gulped back whatever he had intended to say and disappeared as the platter rebounded from the door frame.

I laughed.

"It's all right, Andros," I said. "It was only a joke."

He peeked around the corner like a little boy. I growled; he vanished again. I almost burst from laughing.

When he reappeared, his eyes wandered the room.

But for a pile of dishes stacked neatly by the sink—I had been only just about to wash the last platter before I had thrown it at him—the room appeared as it normally did.

"I suppose the clients' families are worried," I said. "Or is it still only Monday yet?" No clocks in the preparation room; Miklos had insisted. And a lock on the massive door; it could only be opened from the outside. A mystery. I wished I'd asked him while he'd been alive, asked, and not allowed myself to be turned aside.

"Just now Tuesday," Andros said. He glanced at the refrigerator and away, but not so quickly that I didn't notice. I wiped my hands—wet with suds only—and opened the door to the autoclave.

The silvery dental amalgam was cool to the touch, barely. I took the mass in my palm and crushed it with my thumb until it tangled together. I tossed the mass to Andros. "A memento," I said. "Or use it for blackmail. Your choice."

Andros caught the amalgam in his fist, held it over his heart, kissed it, and put the metal in his pocket. Then he shuddered.

I told myself it did not matter whether Andros believed me or not.

We interrupted each other.

"Did—" I asked.

"Did you kill—" Andros asked.

"I killed Dr. Alex," I said. I tried to smile ironically, but I think I merely appeared bitter. "Isn't that what you wanted? Miklos is avenged."

Andros dropped his head on his chest, his face trapped in as ugly a grimace as I've ever seen. "You didn't kill Miklos then," he said.

I suppose I should have rushed across the room to comfort him, or at least pretended to cry, so he could comfort me, but I am not that kind of woman. That was not what had made

Miklos steal me away at sixteen, his brutal, sad eyes more thrilling than even his caress.

Also, I admit I was angry.

"It is time for you to go," I said. "I forgive you. But you must go."

He nodded, unable to speak. I closed my eyes, smelled ozone and felt the thunder as the hot air shocked through me, counted three, and opened them again.

He was gone.

Upstairs, in the kitchen, a cake box and an envelope had been placed on the breakfast table, a place of pleasant memories.

I cut a slice of the cake and opened a bottle of Irish stout to drink with it.

The cake flesh was supple chocolate, its fine crumb supple enough to spring back under a caress without crumbling. Between its two layers was pomegranate jam, sweet yet astringent, just barely blessed with thyme.

The entire cake was draped in ganache, rich as butter and bitter as death. In fact, I think he mixed in ashes—but not many, not many at all.

Across the top of the cake he had scattered pomegranate pips, blood-jewels, love-jewels. The symbol of both marriage and death.

I ate it all.

I did not open the envelope, although I treasure it still, because I already know what is inside.

Later, I found that Andros had deeded the Harbor to me, for moneys and services rendered. It thrives under my hand and the aunts' cooking, but I cannot make it sing, not the way Andros made it sing, and not the way the women sang beside the lake the night Miklos was sent home.

Rather, I am happiest here, with the clients, sharing their peace. In the summer I will visit mother. And, of course, the aunts make sure I always have enough to eat.

I told you that story because it reminds me of your situation, and the monster outside your door. It has eaten those I love; it will eat the thing you try to defend yourself with; it will eat you.

And yet *you* are the hollow one, aren't you?

But to return to my chick, and his first story.

Zubalo shivered on his perch. He saw the eyes looking at him, the eyes of his brothers and sisters, the eyes of his friends and flock-mates, the eyes of his elders. Believe me, when one is standing on a real storyteller's perch, whether it be a mere branch or the top of the roof, the eyes that one has always known change into the eyes of demons, the eyes of greedy cats.

I chuckled, then had to cough up the bead, as Zubalo shivered on his perch.

If he hopped down before he spoke—then all would have been well. The chicks would chatter their beaks with laughter and batter him with their wings. And all would be forgotten.

But no, he would not, and I knew he would not.

Zubalo cleared his throat and said…

5. Family Gods

"Aunt George," I said. "I tried to kill my wife and baby girl yesterday."

She reached across to the glove box and pulled out two cigars. Her eyes didn't leave the road as she unwrapped one and handed me the other.

"Here. He likes the smoke."

"Who?"

She bit the end off her cigar and spat it on the floor. "I'll tell you later."

"What about Serenity?" My daughter, in the back seat.

"So open a window. There are worse things that could happen to her than a little cigar smoke."

I lit Aunt George's cigar, then mine. My lungs released after months of holding back half a breath. I leaned the seat back. Cornfields flashed by outside the window, countless fence posts, rolling hills decorated with black cows. I rolled down the window. The air smelled like coffee and manure.

"Tell me about it," she said.

"I'm not the kind of guy who kills people," I told her. "That's not how you raised me.

"The first I heard about Tammy leaving me for John Fox, who is this thick-necked man who works at the stockyards, was when I got home from Afghanistan to see Mom put into the ground. Tammy was writing me all kinds of dirty, sexy letters telling me how bad she wanted me to be home while the whole time she was screwing around with a guy who smells like rotten meat. He must have been a hell of a fuck.

"I walked into the house just after midnight and threw my bag on the floor. Tammy was waiting up for me. She said, 'I don't want you to get the wrong idea, Michael. You can stay here tonight, but that's it.' And then she told me.

"I didn't wait until morning. I didn't even kiss my baby girl. I walked out of the room, out of the house, down the driveway, and down the street. The cab had already left, so I walked to the nearest gas station, bought a gallon of gas in a red plastic container, went back to the house, and poured gas all around the place. Then I lit it on fire with a series of flimsy matchbook matches that kept going out.

"The gas finally went up. I walked around the building to make sure it all caught, and then I saw my daughter through the window.

"Just then the fire went out, almost like I'd never lit it. Just disappeared. The only thing left was the smell of smoke. It wasn't until then that I felt upset about what I'd done, and then I was so angry that I kicked the side of the house so hard I think I broke a toe."

"I know all that." Aunt George sucked air past her cigar. "I put the fire out for you." I stared at her. She adjusted her steel-rimmed glasses and brushed a white-blonde hair away from her face.

"You put it out?"

Aunt George lifted two fingers off the steering wheel, as if to wave at a passing car. She flicked the tips of her fingers against her thumb, and a blue curl danced on her blunt, stained fingernails. She flicked them again, and the flame went out. "But then you went inside, and I couldn't see. What happened then? How did you end up with Serenity?"

"I don't understand," I said. We turned off the Interstate.

"What I need to know is, are the cops looking for you? Are you AWOL?"

"No. I, uh. After I calmed down, I went back inside to talk to Tammy. Serenity was awake and screaming her head off. When she saw me, she cut off like somebody had pushed her pause button. Tammy made me promise to take Serenity with me to the funeral, just to get the kid out of her hair. I slept on the floor next to her crib. After a while, I picked her up and laid her next to me to sleep."

"So Tammy's all right then?"

I nodded.

"Good." She turned off Main Street and into the church's gravel parking lot. "The short, short version is that we have a family curse. Sort of. A family god." She pulled into an empty parking space and put out her cigar. "A murder god."

I'll skip a description of the post-funeral funeral we had. My mother had long since been buried, but the people at church went through the motions again, for my sake. I shook a lot of hands and lost track of my daughter as she was passed around. Old women would tell me how much she looked like her grandmother and insist on "giving me a break" from her even though I ached to keep her close. I felt like I had to protect her from something awful, just out of sight, and I hated those women for taking her away from me. If I'd thought I could get away with it, I would have hit them until they'd let her go.

I stood next to Aunt George at the graveside. She stood shoulder to shoulder with me, her cream-colored hair tied with a leather thong and draped over one shoulder. She'd raised me after I'd proved to be too much for my mom and dad to handle, but she was always gentle with me.

"You've been having the dreams, haven't you?" she muttered. I gaped at her, which must have been answer enough.

"I've been dreading this day since your mother brought you to me," she said. "I've always known. But your mother thought if she hid you long enough, he'd let you go. Of course he wouldn't, but she was always a fool. Do you know how she died, Mike?"

"A fire," I said.

"You don't know the half of it. It wasn't just a fire; we Kaufmans don't burn easy.

"I woke up one morning in West Branch, and I could smell Vivi break; it was something you couldn't sleep through, like a gas leak. I sat up in bed and threw off the covers. Within a minute I was driving to Coralville, speeding like a demon down the side roads.

"But I was too late. When I pulled up, Vivi was standing on the sidewalk with her hair down and her feet bare, wearing nothing but a bathrobe open at the front, screaming at your stepfather. She had a cleaver in her hand, and he had blood running down his face and undershirt. The police pulled up to the curb, and Vivi was off like a shot, disappearing through the bushes around the side of the house, over a chain-link fence, and gone.

"The cops, who were too scared not to talk to me, didn't have anything to go on but what your stepfather could tell them. She'd tried to kill him with the cleaver, stopped, pulled a pair of t-bone steaks out of the fridge and seared them until they were black on the outside and bloody in the center, eaten them both, and run screaming out of the house. I followed the scent. The trail led to an abandoned house on the outside of town.

"I pulled up beside the house, smelling booze and sex all over the place. I had to light a cigar before I could get out; I found myself itching to cause some mayhem myself, following a scent like that. I heard a crack, and a man wearing only his shirt came running out of the house.

"A second later, the windows broke, and fire poured out and downward onto the ground, it was so heavy with death. The fire poured and poured until it reached the sidewalk and only stopped when it reached my feet."

I said, "Why didn't you put the fire out? Like you did with me?"

"She wouldn't let me."

I screwed up my face like I was going to cry, but I was thinking about that fire, and how it would feel to put blood all over my wife's face, lock her to her bed, and set the whole house on fire. Aunt George punched my shoulder hard enough to leave a bruise.

"Pay attention," she hissed. "The docs said she had a stroke, and that there was a gas leak, but I know better. When we were kids, she was just as bad as me. Worse. She killed a horse one time. Tore its throat out. Uncle Scott took her aside, and after that she wasn't the same. Always pretending to be the upstanding type, too cold to let butter melt in her mouth. She wouldn't kill a fly.

"She couldn't take care of you. You reminded her too much of what she gave up, and it would set her off.

"You don't know how proud I am of her, Mike. She could have taken a lot of people with her, and she didn't. But then again if she wouldn't have been so stupid in the first place, if she'd paid her dues and lit the fires, done the small killings, she'd be alive today to hold your baby girl."

She chewed on the cigar, then stoked it until it glowed through the ash.

"You have to decide whether you want to be a monster—or be like your mother—or be like me."

She waved the cigar over the coffin, which seemed to soak up the smoke. It was probably just the wind.

After the "funeral," I took Serenity back to her mother. I had another nine months before I was done in Afghanistan. And

I wanted my daughter when I came back. So I had to play nice.

What got me was, I was still paying Tammy's rent. She was sleeping with a cattle-lot worker, in my own bed no less, and letting me pay her rent.

Serenity screamed with rage when I handed her over to her mother, and I knew I'd eventually win, as long as I kept my head on straight.

And then I got back in the car with Aunt George and went home.

Aunt George's apartment was in the old Opera House; even the paint had turned from white to sepia. I opened the screen door and almost had a heart attack from the second-hand smoke. And the way nothing had changed. The Felix-the-Cat clock; the prints of semi-naked, fat women; the barstools at the kitchen counter.

Aunt George started a pot of coffee. I stood there dumbstruck until she pointed me at a stool. "So you decided not to kill her. I can see it on your face."

I shook my head. "I want my daughter too much."

"You're going to have to live with it," Aunt George said. "The feeling of wanting to kill, and not being able to kill. You're the only person alive, save your mother, your daughter, and your great-uncle Scott, that I haven't wanted kill at some point or other. The whole human race, the only reason they're alive is that I need them to make a world for you and the rest of the people I love. And to keep me out of jail. Not much of a reason, but good enough, I guess."

"You ever kill anyone?"

She nodded. "That's a story for another time. Stories, I should say. But tell me about when you started having the dreams."

I was in Afghanistan looking for some Taliban in the Safid Mountains. It was the most beautiful country I've ever seen, nothing like Iowa.

Not that Iowa's not beautiful, but in Afghanistan, the mountains erupt out of the ground like a reverse waterfall, with cliff edges like knives. It was the kind of place where your neighbors can't see you, and you can't see them, and everything's sharp under the sun. Black and white. Life and death.

It was in a cave. We were following a tip from a man who had been turned out of the Taliban for beating another man to death over a dog, of all things. The man had been frothing at the mouth by the time we'd found him, so angry that he was willing to betray his group.

I went inside first.

The cave was covered in dark tiles carved or molded with tiny, sharp-edged marks, with a fire pit in the center. The place was abandoned; we were too late to catch anybody. But I could tell from the state of the garbage in the corner that they'd been there not long ago.

On one wall was a group of tiles, each no bigger than the tip of my thumb, that together showed a winged, footed snake surrounded by smoke and fire. I looked at it for two seconds and passed out. My squad had to drag me out.

I used to be the kind of guy that other guys go to for advice, because I could see things from all sides. I used to be the kind of guy that stopped other guys from shooting when they shouldn't.

I haven't been the same ever since.

"I'm going to kill John Fox," I said. I wasn't sure why I said it. I was in the same mood as when I tried to set my house on fire, feeling nothing, only knowing what had to be done.

"No," Aunt George said.

"I am. Really I am."

Aunt George gritted her teeth. "You'll do it alone, then, so I can take your daughter when Tammy flies off the handle and won't keep her anymore, and you're on death row. Damn it,

Michael. Just because a man steals your worthless wife, that's no reason to kill him. It isn't."

"I want to send Tammy a message."

"She doesn't give a damn, Mike. Scaring her won't do you or your daughter any good."

We argued, but that was the end of it. To tell the truth, I wasn't disappointed. What was John Fox? A man too scared to serve his country. A man who walked in cow shit all his days. A man who fucked a woman whose only talents were writing dirty letters and giving birth to Serenity.

That night, I had one of the dreams. About the family god. I liked thinking of him like that; it sounded right.

I was in the cave again, only the fire was lit and smoke filled the room. I breathed in the smoke like it was clean morning air. The god stepped out of the shadows on the other side of the room. I'd always been afraid of it, but not because I feel like it's going to attack me. The god's big, bigger than a man. You could call it a dragon or a dinosaur, but that's not right. It's a serpent, as thick around as my chest, with hips and legs supporting it off the ground. The god stands before me and holds its wings over its head, feathered wings big enough to suck the air out of me when it beats them. Then the god shakes his wings and drops to the ground, waddling sinuously toward me. I've never seen anything so awkward, yet so fast.

The fear is a sick feeling, and then I'm angry. I pull my lips back and bare my teeth; the god grins up at me and puts his forelegs on my shoulders. I fall backwards.

This is usually where I wake up. But this time, the god pushes his snout into my chest like I'm made out of cotton candy. He pulls my heart out and crushes it between his teeth. Blood, dripping with fire, squirts from between his teeth. The sick feeling goes away entirely, and all that's left is hate. I hate the god. I hate myself. I push the god away and run out of the cave.

Suddenly, I'm on a highway, bathed in moonlight. There's a truck in front of me, driving fast.

John Fox is in that truck.

I catch up to him easily and land in the back of the truck. He swerves. I run my nails across the glass in the back window, then tap it. It splits and tumbles out of the frame, pebbles of glass.

John Fox screams and runs the truck off the road. The truck rolls in the ditch, and I fall out, but not before the truck crushes one of my wings and part of my chest.

I drag myself off the road, toward the truck. It hurts, but I know I'll be fine as soon as I make the kill.

John Fox eels out of the truck's back window. The doors must be jammed. He's got a shotgun, which he raises toward me.

A shape darts out of the sky and slams into Fox, knocking him down. At first I think it's the god, but its skin is yellow-silver under the moonlight, like Aunt George's hair.

She stands between me and John Fox. I drag myself closer to them, and she hisses at me to back off, whipping the tip of her tail against the ground in annoyance.

I try again, getting to my feet. She bats at me. I hiss back at her. Then I hear the grass rustle in the field and go still. A deer leaps across the road, and I jump after it without thinking, catching it. The blood smears over my face, my forelegs, my belly, then flashes as it catches fire and turns to smoke. I lean back and shriek in exaltation as the fire spreads into the fields.

The next morning I woke up and heard the cops outside the apartment. I wasn't surprised when they asked to see me, but I was surprised when a neighbor came out of her apartment and volunteered the fact that she'd seen both my Aunt and I at the kitchen table not half an hour before John Fox died in a fiery wreck, two hundred miles away. She'd been snooping in the window, hoping to get a look at me, having heard so much about me from my Aunt.

John Fox was dead, then.

I waited until the neighbor and the cops were gone. "Did you kill him?"

Aunt George had a black eye. "I dragged him out of the fire. But not fast enough. He punched me in the face, and I passed out for a few seconds."

"Why did you stop me, if you were just going to let him die?"

"You're my family," she growled. "Give me a little credit for trying to keep you from turning into a monster."

"I *am* a monster," I said.

"Not that kind." She lit two cigarettes and passed me one.

I smoked it.

When Zubalo had finished telling his story, his beak opened and closed over and over again, and he moaned like a dying chicken. His feathers were puffed out and his claws tapped on the mirror, as though fear were inside the glass, knocking to get out. A thin thread of shit dripped out of him.

His friends, who at first had gathered under the mirror, edged away from him, their claws dragging in the dirt on the overturned roof of the truck cab.

Crows don't speak of it, even amongst ourselves, but it is so: if a storyteller displeases his audience, then the other crows turn on him. If only one or two of us dislikes a story, well, then there is no danger. But if a flock of crows moves together, and more and more crows join it, then a storyteller might be pecked to death, little more than a pile of bones remaining.

It hadn't been a bad story. But the fear had gripped him, in the middle of the telling. If a good storyteller can brazen through a bad story, a bad storyteller, well, can drop a good story into the dirt.

"Stop!" Old Loyolo shrieked.

But the chicks would not stop. They crept up on Zubalo, more and more chicks joining their ranks. Their throats thrummed with malevolence, and even some of the elders were feeling the pull.

The first chick reached Zubalo's feet and pecked him in the chest. It drew no blood, not then. But it was as though the wind had been unloosed from the clouds. A mass of chicks rushed at Zubalo, pecking and clawing and cawing madly.

Facunde whispered into the girl's ear. Her eyes widened, her mouth opened, and her chest shuddered, as she took in a long, twitching breath.

"Stop!"

The chicks froze. The girl's shout was the sound of a gun, it was the sound of a hunter.

"I liked it," the girl said. "It was good enough. He's just a *baby*. Stop pecking him."

A few chicks, unable to restrain themselves, got in one last peck before they hopped away. Old Loyolo's eyes followed them, and counted them all.

When Zubalo was finally revealed, his head was tucked under a wing. His feathers were scattered, and even a few patches of skin showed through.

There was blood on the mirror now.

Sometimes, it doesn't matter if the story was good or not. It only matters that sometimes when the elders are listening, it all turns flat. As thin as a picture. As false as a reluctant lie.

As bitter as a writhing pebble in the throat.

Now that the girl had spoken, it felt as though a kind of barrier had been broken, as if a thin film of ice on a cold stream had been shattered with a sharp gray stone. We waited with bated breath, but she only settled back into her nest of blankets, with thin pale hands pulling the pink wool blanket further over her head, tucking the sides together under her chin. Facunde settled back on her shoulder, worrying at the stained, stinking blanket with claw and beak until the girl's ear was visible again.

Outside, the storm had thrown the night across us even earlier than usual. The world outside the window of the truck appeared thick and white, but its lightness was a lie: the world was dark but for a single light that rose high over the dumping ground. We were buried in the snow's shadows, the inside of the cab a lightless, hollow gray.

After everyone had settled again (and after Zubalo had hidden, almost buried, under the wings of his friends, who had abandoned him before but were back now, which Zubalo put up with; it can be *very* cold without one's fair-weather friends), Old Loyolo said, "I have another story for you. That is, if you would rather not go to sleep for a while. It is dark out, and it will be a hungry night. Better to sleep through as much of it as you can."

But the girl shook her head.

Old Loyolo cleared his throat. "Very well, then. Facunde, tell another story."

"Me?" She ruffled up her feathers, and the girl squinted her eye shut to keep out Facunde's disgruntled, thrusting wing feathers. "I just told a story!"

"Not so," Old Loyolo said. "Zubalo told the last story."

"What about Gorria? Or Ibarrazzo?"

"They tell pleasant stories. Stories for summertime, stories for fat bellies in autumn. You and Machado, you have always been the ones to collect human stories that go well on a winter night." He sighed. "Elke, my Elke used to be the one who had to tell all the stories in the winter."

"Where is Elke?"

"Elke is dead, Facunde. Elke died in the autumn while you were piling sticks in your grief. The one who taught you all of your stories—"

"Not all of them!"

"Died while you were buried under your grief. She was killed by hunters, Facunde, and you did not come to tell stories at her boneside." Because Loyolo was looking at Facunde, he was also looking at the girl, who retreated further into her blankets, the pink wool falling over her eyes, as though she, too, felt guilty.

But it was not guilt she felt. She was grieving, too, you see. For her father, for her brother. For her dead.

And for you—but not for you, for an eidolon called *Mother*.

Facunde rattled her beak in annoyance and, without leaving the girl's shoulder, said, "Fine! Another story, when I am poor of stories! When I owe all my best stories to someone I didn't even pay my respects to! Because the storms forgive me, if I grieve my mate! And if I carried a burden that none of you could ever understand!"

She throated this to the roof of our bower; she screamed it at the winter wind.

But then she looked at me. Well, I was the exception, with her bead in my mouth, wasn't I?

6. A Ghost Unseen

Hey, man, thanks for coming, and, um, hang on a sec before you hand me that. I'm sorry to be such a pain, but I have this plan. The thing is, I'm a horror writer who can't see ghosts, and I want to do this experiment.

What I tell everyone, from my agent to my lawyer to those kids who did this article on the writing rooms of successful horror authors last year, is that my house is haunted. Which is actually true. This four-year-old kid supposedly drowned in the pool in the back yard in the 1960s, right after the house was built. The pool's filled with gravel now. I bought the house because it was supposed to be haunted. I mean, I asked the realtor to sell me a haunted house, and she did.

And then I got here, and I couldn't see it. But of course I still bought it.

It's the front room that got me. Blood red. The nuts who'd owned the place before me did it. I bought this place just so I could write in this room. I can sit at my old roll-top desk over there, punching the keys on my laptop—they sound just like typewriter keys except for the semicolon, which makes this little scream. The whole place smells of old books and leather.

Spilled wine. A little dirt from the coffee table where I put my boots all the time.

And blood. This room. It's so inspiring.

Except lately.

I found out I got the big C, man.

All week I've been numb. I couldn't type a fuckin' word. I couldn't think. I couldn't eat. I sat out in the back yard on my rusty old patio chair next to the filled-in pool and chain-smoked until my tongue felt numb and covered with ash. I read books and put on headphones and lay in the sun, because who's scared of skin cancer now, bitches? Fuck it.

I know there's, like, a million or more fans out there who wouldn't mind giving me a little sympathy. But that's not what I want. Sympathy? Shit. I don't write sympathetic books. I write about how the dead don't die. They come back from the grave and haunt you and rip up your life.

Why? The fuck if I know. They just do.

Actually, that's not true. They haunt you because otherwise you'll kill yourself from depression and boredom and feeling like you're never going to escape your day job. When you're like that, you can't tell whether you're alive or dead. If someone told you the world was gonna end, you'd be like, "Hey, okay, bro, you only live once."

I used to be like that. I felt like nothing I did had any meaning, nothing anybody did had any meaning. I was standing behind a veil, and on the other side was life, and it was too fucking stupid out there to give a shit about.

I just wanted to take all the shit that normal people believe in and break it. And I thought, either I become a serial killer or a writer, and if the writing thing doesn't work out, then I can always take up the hatchet, you know?

Because having the shit scared out of you will, unlike anything else ever could, make you appreciate being alive.

So, in my own way, I write about hope. Just, you know, with a lot of fuckin' blood and guts to oomph it up a little.

But even someone like me runs out of hope sometimes. Which is where you come in.

If I pursue this thing aggressively, which is what my doctor wants, I have six to nine months to put everything in order, lose my hair, vomit all the time, and turn into a mummy. And I don't want to do that. And I feel like I wrote everything I needed to write, you know?

But don't worry! I'm not turning serial killer on. See? No ax behind my back or anything. You're safe.

I talked to my doctor about some test results this morning—stuff's getting a lot worse, really fast—and I knew I had to do something fast, before I went too far downhill, but I couldn't figure out what. So anyway I was hanging around the window seat in the library, staring out the window like a dork, when the neighbor across the street waved at me. He was poking around with his roses again. Roses must be a huge pain in the ass, because he's out there all the time. He uses a wide variety of garden tools, and they all look like they'd make great fucking murder weapons. I like watching him work. It's kinda soothing.

I went outside, because what else did I have to do? "Yeah?" I said.

He leaned his hands on his knees and cracked his back. It sounded painful. "Just thought you should know, cops drove by earlier this morning, before you got up. Six cars full of them."

"What did they want?" I asked, feeling like my gut's full of lead. I'm always afraid someone's going to come to my house and accuse me of killing somebody right after I finish a book. Because in my head I feel like I really did. But that wasn't it.

"Just checking out the ghosts," the old guy said. "Sergeant MacMuertie brought some new guys to see 'em, because they never will just take his word for it. His way of making sure you don't get hassled."

I sighed. "Look, I know I'm a horror writer and all, but I can't see ghosts. Just tell it to me straight. That kid didn't drown, did he?"

"Nope," the old guy said cheerfully. "Right in the front room. I saw part of it. They never did catch whoever did it—and all I could see was a couple of shadows, didn't think twice about it until later. But blood got all over the place. That's why it's painted red in there. So the ghost blood doesn't show so up bad when the ghosts are acting up. I'm surprised you don't smell it. Some days I can smell it right through the window."

He stuck his hand spade into the ground with a sound like an axe chopping through someone's neck. The green blood of the grass filled the air. Then he leaned back on the spade. Roots ripped like flesh, and a piece of grass that'd grown too close to the roses popped out.

Dirt sprayed.

I looked back at my window, but I couldn't see any ghosts. Fuckin' nothing.

Okay, I lied about one thing. Misled you, anyway. I did see a ghost once. Only once, when I was kid. Down in the basement of my parent's house. I didn't know what it was at first. It didn't look like a ghost; it looked like another kid. But of course it wasn't.

I was in the basement, playing with a couple of old knock-off Barbies and a steak knife, when suddenly this kid about my age slid out of the spare bedroom. She was crawling on her stomach because her legs had been chopped off just below her waist, leaving stubs that looked kind of like ham. She was dragging herself along by her forearms; her hands were balled up in fists. She'd slap one fist down on the tile floor, drag herself forward a couple of inches, and then bam, slam another arm down. It seemed to take forever.

As she passed me I smelled something that was a lot like bad cat breath. She was leaving a trail of glowing green slime behind her. She didn't see me. She went into the laundry room, and I followed her, holding that steak knife in both hands in case she changed her mind and attacked me.

The slime soaked through my socks. It was as cold as walking on wet snow.

In the laundry room, the ghost dragged herself over to the drain, inch by inch, then shoved her face down the hole and slid in. Her body folded in on itself, then stretched out. Her arms sank into her sides and disappeared. Her dress—she was wearing this white nightgown thingy—sank into her skin and disappeared. The stumps of her legs stretched out and blended together into a snake's tail.

Then she was gone.

I was eight, and I never went into the basement alone again.

They say Mother Theresa spent the last fifty years of her life begging God to talk to her again. He talked to her a lot as a kid. I mean, a lot. Then one day, nothing, no matter how hard she begged. But she never stopped serving God, even though she didn't believe in him anymore. That's faith. That's the kind of faith I want. Just…not in that direction.

After I got back from the neighbor's house, it hit me. The whole plan. Here it is. I ordered a pizza.

I picked you guys because you have the pepperoni that curls up into the little grease cups. Oh, it's horrible. But, I mean, it's not like it can hurt me now. Here's a hundred. Keep the change.

What I want you to do—just as a favor—is look through the bay window. Just a favor.

Do you see them? The ghosts?

Fuck. Well, I had my hopes. Thanks for looking. And thanks for the pizza.

No, I can't take it—it's too heavy. You keep it. I just—I just wanted to smell it, one last time.

Yeah, um, there is a woman behind me on the floor. She's dead. It was quick and clean and she barely felt it, I promise. She used that steak knife, I mean, she sharpened the holy shit out of it first, but it's the same one she used when she was eight.

Hey, man.

If you want a souvenir before the cops get here, all you have to do is step in and take it.

"There!" Facunde cried, clacking her beak at Old Loyolo in a manner that was as ridiculous as any hatchling's. "Are you happy?"

Old Loyolo shook his head at her. "Too short. I'll only call on you more often, if you keep telling stories that are too short."

"I'm done telling stories."

"You're not done telling stories until I say you're done. If you keep being this rude, then I'll make you choose the storytellers when I'm gone."

"Good!" Facunde shouted. She beat her wings in the air. "I'll choose someone else every time, and I'll never have to tell stories again."

"You're a silly chick," Loyolo said.

"You're a…" Facunde hopped around on the girl's shoulder, raised her tailfeathers, showed her vent, and shit down the girl's shoulder.

Old Loyolo laughed. He laughed such a laugh as destroys silence for days, a laugh that would be talked about until spring came and we were too busy gorging ourselves for talking. He laughed a laugh that echoed in the ear. A laugh that mocked death.

I was glad of it.

The rest of the chicks were chuckling nervously, the way chicks do, not because they understood the humor of it, but because one of the elders was laughing and so they had better laugh too.

The girl's hand snaked out and stroked the back of the crow that was nearest her on her lap, who happened to be Ibarrazzo. Ibarrazzo preened under the girl's hand, rubbing her old head against the girl's warm skin, rolling it around on a neck as flexible as a snake's.

"Zubalo!" Old Loyolo shouted, startling them all into silence.

Zubalo, the poor chick, was shoved into the middle of the truck's roof, with all the other chicks pulled back from him.

"You next!" Old Loyolo said.

Even I was surprised, and I thought that he would refuse to speak. You can, you know, if you're willing to put up with Loyolo haranguing you the rest of the night. But the young crow jumped into the air and flew to the mirror as though he had been expecting to be called, had felt it coming like the pressure of a storm. Perhaps he had.

7. The Haunted Room

Andrew had had plans for the front parlor since he was six. The lace curtains were old and yellowing even then, and the heavy brass rod had smashed his toe when he'd pulled the curtains down to shove them in the fireplace.

It had only taken a minute. Aunt Pamela was bringing sandwiches for their tea so they could sit in the high-backed armchairs and pretend to be fancy for a few minutes while they discussed school. She didn't know much about kids. Having raised two sons, Andrew couldn't imagine any outcome of having a sticky little boy in the front parlor where it didn't end in tears, broken china, and smeared sofas. But she'd tried.

The curtains had gone up like flashpaper. He had stood between the fire and the metal fire screen, watching the flames run up the curtain rod and onto his arms when she'd found him. She'd screamed and dropped the silver tray with a clang and an explosion of crustless white bread that sprayed ham salad on the striped yellow-and-pink cabbage-rose wallpaper. She beat at the flames curling around him, then flung the fire screen aside and rolled him on the floor. *Andrew, Andrew!*

Somehow the curtains had been replaced and the pale carpet and girlish wallpaper cleaned without stain.

Even when Andrew had become an adult, she'd refused to change the room. The wallpaper seemed as fresh (yet stale) as ever, the carpet pile as tidy and bright as it had been when he was six.

Now she was dead, and he could do whatever he liked with the place. He wanted to open it up. Add more windows. Strip out the carpet and see if the floor underneath was as beautiful as it was in the rest of the house, just waiting to be finished. He wanted emerald green and hardwood and chrome in this room.

But Aunt Pamela wasn't going to let him.

First thing, he'd taken the curtains down. Then he had a double of Scotch, having rolled the curtains up in a loose ball and left them on the dining room table stacked with moving boxes and broken things that hadn't survived the trip.

When his wife had left him, after their second son was safely off to college, Aunt Pamela had sat him down in the front parlor with seriously stale coffee and told him that he had to let his wife go, the same way his father had, the same way *she* had. It was a kind of family curse.

She hadn't so much refused to change the room as let his suggestions slide off her, unheard.

After he'd rinsed his glass in the sink and left it upended in the dish drainer, he'd gone back to the table to put the curtains in the trash, but they were gone.

The front parlor was unchanged. He unhooked the curtain rod, pulled the decorative fleur-de-lis off the end, and slid the curtains free again. He put the rod back up.

"Andrew! What are you doing?"

He froze guiltily. Turned.

Aunt Pamela was in the chair next to the fire, reading a book. He listened to his own breath as she glared at him.

"Leave those alone."

He laid the curtains across the back of the nearest chair (pink with feet in the shape of dark-stained claws clutching at balls) and walked toward her. She glared at the curtainless window still. "Andrew! Stop that!"

She was talking to a little boy, not to him. He reached the side of her chair and touched her arm. His hand moved through it, touched the arm of the chair, gently. The starched doily was stiff under his hand.

"Aunt Pamela?"

"Out," she ordered him, or rather the little boy he had been. Then she sighed. "I suppose it *is* time for a snack. I'll be right back. Don't touch those curtains," she warned him. She set the book aside, stood up, putting her hands to the small of her tiny back, and stretched.

He tried to follow her out of the room, but she vanished at the parlor door. He gathered the curtains, took them outside, and stuffed them in the trash. Poured himself another double and stood at the doorway of the front parlor. The curtains were gone.

He had no warning, no chill breeze or involuntary shiver. Aunt Pamela just appeared in front of him, her elbows jutting out a little from carrying the tray. She shrieked and dropped the tray, kicking it as it reached the hem of her dress. The little white triangles of ham salad sandwiches flew across the room just as he remembered them.

She threw herself at the fireplace, waving her hands at the air, then leaning back and putting her forearms to cover her face. *Andrew, Andrew!*

She sobbed and crawled backward, turning her face to her shoulder, coughing, then collapsed. It seemed like she stopped breathing. After a while, her body jerked up into the air, bent almost in half, then floated jerkily past him, vanishing again at the door.

No. It hadn't happened that way.

He blinked and the curtains were back, and Aunt Pamela sat in her chair next to the fire, reading.

He wanted to take the curtains down. Was that so hard? So bad? She'd left him the house. It was his to do with whatever he liked, not something he had to guard for the rest of his life, unchanging. He didn't have to keep faith with the damned curtains. He didn't have to put up with this ghostly, unreasonable tantrum.

His whole life he'd spent doing things her way. It had to stop. Yes, he owed her a lot. She'd brought him up. Hadn't wanted to, but she'd done it when it was clear that his dad would be worse at it even than she was. And now she was dead.

He'd let her have her way when she was alive, to honor the fact that her life would have been different, if he'd never been dumped in her lap. Maybe it wouldn't have been much different. But he'd honored her wishes.

Until now.

Maybe he would have had a different life, if it hadn't been for her, and she needed to respect that, too.

Andrew didn't question his own sanity; his aunt's lack of compromise over this one thing, this room, was too familiar.

His glass was empty again. He refilled it and set it on the dining room table. The rest of the house had evolved over time, becoming more modern, less girlish, bearing pictures of him and his family on the walls, their fashions changing over time, Aunt Pamela staying more or less the same, only getting slightly smaller as she got older. The tiny waist, the flowered dresses, the hair that was always just barely escaping from her severe buns.

The fact was, he'd lived and she hadn't. Her hands stayed folded in her lap, in photo after photo. She looked sad and lonely, no matter where he'd taken her.

His foot sank hesitantly into the carpet. The ghost of his aunt crossed the room in front of him to the chair by the fireplace. She lowered herself into the chair as though her back hurt, then reached over for the book.

Andrew took another step closer to the curtains, and another, watching her but careful not to bump into the coffee table in front of the yellow sofa with the tiny pillows. He just wanted a place he could call his own, without having to constantly think about someone else. A place where he wasn't defined by someone else, or by the lack of someone else.

Then he was around the couch, next to the curtains. He lifted the rod off, loosened the fleur-de-lis, and slid them off again.

"Andrew! What are you doing?"

He replaced the curtain rod, then tiptoed toward the fireplace. It hadn't been lit since she died. She wasn't watching him; again, she was watching where he would have stood, as a child, next to the pink chair.

He passed her and pulled back the fire screen. She still wasn't watching him, and he noticed the book she was reading. It wasn't a book but a photo album with a childish yellow horse on the cover; he'd made it for her when he was eight. After the fire.

"Oh, Andrew," she sighed. "I'm too old for you to haunt me anymore. Just leave them alone, will you? It's been forty years already. I'm tired." She looked back to her book just as he tossed the curtains into the fireplace and lit them with one of the long matches in a tin she kept nearby.

They went up like flashpaper, and then he had her attention.

"Andrew, Andrew!"

The fire jumped onto him, even though he could have sworn he was standing far enough away. He looked at his arms, disbelieving, as the fire swarmed up them.

Aunt Pamela flung the album aside—that wasn't right, either; she was supposed to be carrying sandwiches—and tried to beat out the flames on him, but her hands only passed through the air.

The fire jumped onto the old furniture as he frantically waved his hands.

Pamela woke in the hospital, alone. The curtains. Always the curtains with Andrew.

They told her the house was gone, and she wondered if his ghost would leave her be, now. She almost didn't want him to go. She longed to be the content old woman who looked out of the ghostly photograph album; nobody else could see them those pictures, taking their ghostly vacations by the shore. It spoke well of the afterlife, that it had already been happier than the life she'd lived, even if Andrew's ghost-wife had left him.

But nearly forty years was too long not to admit you were dead.

When he had finished, Zubalo hopped off the storyteller's perch and onto the roof of the truck—our floor—which had by then become a thick paste of feathers and shit, enough so that even I was disgusted. And then he waited, slowly picking up and lowering one foot, a mingling of arrogance and terror that made me chuckle in the back of my throat. I remembered my first real story—and then the bead writhed in my mouth, and I had to crush my laughter against the roof of my beak, to keep the bead from escaping down my throat.

I think that Zubalo was waiting for us to approve of his story. My head felt heavy from holding the bead, a heaviness not unlike the craving for sleep. I shook my head to try to keep myself awake.

Among crows, it might seem as though the elders need to approve of a story before a storyteller is determined to be worthy of life or death, but that is not the case. Elders add something to an audience, that is all. Approval from the elders? Well, I suppose we have forgotten more stories than most chicks have ever heard, and might be trusted to know a good one from a bad one more often than not. But it isn't the elders who decide.

At any rate, Zubalo did not need the elders' approval of the story; he had approved of it himself, which is part of the secret of being a storyteller that nobody tells you. A story is a lie, and nobody believes a liar who doesn't, at some level, believe what is said.

Zubalo, after discerning that he was not about to be pecked again, began to hop toward his coterie.

"Mother," the girl said.

Every crow's head turned to face her. Our eyes watched her face slowly emerge from the blanket, a paler shape among the gray shadows.

"Mother killed Papa, and I think she killed my brother." Her voice was so strained that it broke, and she coughed, a deep and worrisome burr of a noise. Her eyes rolled upward, and her eyes became white moons in the reflected light of the snow.

"I left my brother. I left him to die."

I shook my beak. The snow seemed to crawl along the outside of the window like smoke with eyes, to seep through the glass and coil about our feet in cold streams. I wished to tell her—I wished to tell her a thousand things. But the bead seemed to shimmer on my tongue, the way sunlight shimmers across a field of snow, the morning after a blizzard, and I could not speak.

"It is your turn," Old Loyolo told her.

The snow began to hiss in my ears, almost deafening me to his voice.

The girl's voice was far away, too. "I will tell you how Mother—"

"It cannot be a *true* story," the old crow said, softly. "Not today."

Through a fog of white flakes, I saw her eyes unroll themselves and her face lower, so that she was looking at him, at the meat-and-bone-and-feathers of him, at the pure stink of him, at the loose feathers and the wrinkled skin, the twisted claw on his foot that always made him hop in a circle during hop-races with the new chicks, making them roll on their backs and laugh while he won the race.

"Why not?"

"Because if you do it will be a bad story, without an end, and then we will have to peck you to death."

She nodded slowly, as though unrolling her eyes had made her dizzy. I squinted. Around the edge of my eyes was nothing but whiteness. "But what if it's secretly true?"

"That," Loyolo said, "isn't my problem."

She nodded again, this time more firmly. "Then let me tell you one that I haven't told any crows yet, a story about mice—"

8. Inside Out

Mice are the small enemies who will eat you up from the inside out. But I don't mind that. It's the pellets that I mind. They leave them everywhere! If only they would nibble discreetly and shit back in their dens, or within the walls, I might leave them alone.

They were in the pantry, they were in the wash. They were behind the cat-litter box, cat piss or no. They were in my dish cupboards. They ate old love letters and lace. They ate my marriage license.

The only room they didn't touch was my daughter's bedroom.

So when I went to the witch, and she served me tea with the tea bag still in the cup, which I knew meant that she didn't like me, and she told me it would cost me my daughter to get rid of the mice, I said yes.

Then I said, you won't kill her, will you?

And the witch said no, no, she just needed an apprentice. Nobody wants to be a witch of their own free will, you see, it doesn't pay enough and the men will never trust you enough to marry you. So you have to work two jobs and spend your Friday nights listening to other people's problems.

I squirmed in my hard chair, and she winked at me.

When I got home, my daughter, who was too beautiful to be a witch and looked nothing like me and was probably switched at birth by the hospital except hospitals don't do that anymore, said what happened to all the mice?

I said I made a deal with the witch to get rid of them.

Like the pied piper? she asked.

Yes I said, except instead of the whole town losing their kids, it's just you.

She cried and she raged and she threw a fit, but she knew that I didn't like her, and she didn't like me, and her father was dead, so there was no reason to stay. When I drove her to the witch's house in the morning, her bags were already packed.

Darling daughter I said—

Oh, stuff it she snapped, and off she went.

I threw the rest of her things out of the car, and off I went, too. But soon the mice were back and I went to the witch's house to demand my daughter back so I could sell her to the witch again, and get rid of the mice.

The witch said those are the wrong mice. They are not very nice mice at all.

Oho, I said, you're the one who sent the mice in the first place, so you could get my daughter. Well you're just going to have to take care of these ones too. I left and went home but the mice were still there. They drank the cleaning supplies, they ate up the toilet paper. They ate up the wood in the window frames and the windows fell out. They chewed the wires to all the lights and I spent the night in the dark and the cold, covered in mice pellets, and the next morning you know where I went.

I just don't know, the witch said. I've tried everything I can think of, but those mice still won't leave. They're the wrong mice, the wrong mice. I don't know their provenance.

I said that's fine but I'm staying here until they're out and now you have to fix everything that's ruined in my house because I gave you my only daughter in exchange for no mice and if you'd done what you said none of this would have happened.

Then my daughter appeared. You're staying here?

I am.

You can't stay here. You have to leave!

I'm staying here until the mice are gone, to remind you witches to work harder. You a pair of slatterns, that's what you are.

She was still as beautiful as anything. I wondered if she was the witch's true daughter and my true daughter had been thrown out with the trash.

How are we going to get the mice out of her house? my daughter asked.

The witch shrugged. Instead, she said, we should ask how they got there in the first place.

My daughter bit her lip and I laughed. You brought them! I said. You brought them! You brought the mice to eat me up from the inside out!

I was tired of waiting for the witch's mice, my daughter said. So I called some of my own. I called them up out of your heart. I called up jealousy mice, and resentment mice, and petty mice, and angry mice, and revenge mice; mice of spite and mice of nagging; a thousand and one stingy mice; a thousand and two frowning mice; a thousand and three never-quite-right mice. They have always been eating you up from the inside out, and the only way to get rid of such a curse is to…

Is to purify your heart, the witch said.

Bullshit, said I. You said you'd get rid of those mice and you're the ones who are going to do it. I'll not lift a finger, I'll not drop a bead of sweat, I'll not pray a single prayer to get rid of those mice. I am the mouse in your house now, and I'll eat you up from the inside out. And I lifted the cover of their stew pot and ate all of it, bite by bite.

The bead in my mouth burned with a bright white light, such that the inside of the truck cab was illuminated into almost pure whiteness; even the black feathers of the flock turned white from the brightness of the light reflecting from them. No one but myself seemed to notice. They watched the girl and nodded at each other, bobbing up and down. A good story, perhaps not the best one that we'd ever heard told from her, but a good story, and they had liked it.

My beak was wide open, and I had not remembered opening it. The bead burned on my tongue, burned and crackled and threw sparks.

I tried to shout, but no sound emerged. A large lump moved in my throat, blocking all sound, and then all breath.

I raised my wings, and a few heads turned my way, but I knew that it was too late.

"Machado!" Facunde shrieked, over the chatter following the girl's story.

My wings went limp, my legs lost their balance, and I fell over, my face lying in the muck on the truck roof. I closed my eyes, yet it seemed as though I could still see through them: Old Loyolo turning slowly. Facunde shouting—screaming—something in the girl's ear. The uproar of a dozen birds being flung away from the girl as she threw off the blanket and reached for me.

Her hand wrapped around my chest, crushing it. My beak—I could have sworn it was open already—was forced apart, and the girl's fingers pinched something from my throat.

She flung it from her, a white and burning thing, glowing for a moment, then turning black as night and scuttling into the shadows of the wires overhead, where no one would dare reach for it.

Ibarrazzo cried, "The Crouga! The Crouga! Mother of all crows, we must flee!"

I do not know what happened then—I was gasping for air, gripped in the girl's hand more tightly than was good for me. The world spun, because the girl spun me, and because I spun within myself. The world seemed to explode, the glass to shatter, the snow to burst into the truck cab at us. That is all I know.

We found shelter under a deep ledge made of that which had been thrown away, mainly within the hollow of a large white box suitable for freezing food. With all of us packed inside, it was also suitable for keeping most of the cold out, although the door had been removed and the wind thrust in after us, trying to tear our feathers off. It was still better than the open weather of the pit.

We huddled around her. That is, the others huddled around her. I lay in the girl's hand and breathed, one breath after another, which was a difficult piece of work. The girl blew in my face, trying to make sure the air I breathed was warm, and although it did little to ease my hurts, I was still grateful for it.

"Machado, Machado…"

Facunde sat again on the girl's shoulder, peering down at me. Every time she said my name, I could see her tongue moving, I could see the back of her throat. The single light of the dumping ground shone down almost directly upon us, and even though it was shadowed, I could see that the inside of her mouth was scarred and bleeding.

She had held the bead for so long, and I, after only a few moments, was reduced to a gasping corpse on the girl's palm. It was not my proudest of nights.

"What…" I said.

Facunde shook her head. "I do not know. I found it while I was looking for grief-sticks and picked it up. I have been guarding it ever since, trying to find a place to bury it where the chicks would not find it."

Ibarrazzo clung to the girl's other shoulder. "I know," she said. "I know what it is." She of the stories of matings, of chance meetings between lovers-to-be and flirting in the trees. *She* knew this horror.

"The Crouga," I gasped. "That's what you called it. The boogeyman."

The girl leaned forward to hear better, and tilted me on her palm. That is when I noticed that our numbers were fewer, and that some were missing feathers, and others were bleeding.

"Where are the others?" I asked.

"Dead," Ibarrazzo said, with such confidence that my heart seized inside me, and I coughed. "They have been absorbed into the Crouga."

"What is it?" I moaned. "What have I done?"

Ibarrazzo lifted one claw, an almost human gesture. "I warn you, this is not a proper story. I do not tell this kind of story, normally I refuse. The world is dark enough without dwelling on it. Oh, you can tell what you like—" she snapped her beak in Facunde's direction— "but as for myself, I will tell stories that bring more light into the world, and less heartbreak. But I know the darkness, yes. I know it better than either of *you*."

"Please," I begged her. When I had wept over Facunde mating with another, it was Ibarrazzo who had comforted me, who had told me lies about love until my heart could resume beating on its own again. "Please, Ibarrazzo. You know I believe you. Please tell me what I have done."

She cocked her head with pity, looking at me with her good eye, the clear one. "Ach," she sighed. Then she turned her head, so that she was looking at me with her other eye, the one that had turned to moonlight and milk.

It was startling; Ibarrazzo never looked at anyone with her bad eye, only the good one. Under the harsh light, the bad eye seemed to move from within, as if it were full of smoke or small worms. She said, "The Crouga, it is the boogeyman. He started out as a crow who was unjustly pecked— or justly pecked, some say—and whose spirit lingered in the form of a small, shining seed. Any crow who picked it up would summon his spirit, see? And it would grow and grow…and eat, and eat. And it would have to be fought back, or else it would eat until every living crow had been consumed and it starved itself back down to a tiny seed. Facunde carried it, but because her heart was so cold," Ibarrazzo shrugged, her wingtips flipping with contempt, "there was nothing for the Crouga to eat. It was only when this sentimental idiot picked it up that it awoke."

Facunde turned her head away.

"How do we fight it?" I asked.

"With stories," Ibarrazzo said. "Why do you think we tell so many stories? Only to pass the time?"

I blinked at her, and thought of her as a foolish old bird for the first time in a while.

She saw the look in my eyes, the gape of my beak, and said, "I know a story that was once used to fight the Crouga. A story about eating the darkness…"

Foolish or not, she was a good storyteller. I settled in.

9. Treif

Nitzaniya stood outside the corral at dawn, feeling the huge behemah butt each other through the vibrations of the ground and smoking one of Caleb's cigarettes. She stuck the toe of one boot into the wire; the fence rattled, and some of the behemah spotted her and trotted closer, hoping for a treat.

She shook her head and stepped back. Zombies grew the best tobacco, and the behemah's hands, if thick and calloused from running on all fours, were quick to snatch. Caleb said they were trained not to knock down the fence, but she didn't want to push her luck any further than she already had.

One of the behemah, a big bull whose shoulder came up to her ear, lowed and pushed his way to the front. He moaned at her and shook the fence with his shovel-fingered hands.

"Well, you poor mamzers, how about a story?" Nitzaniya asked. Her voice was still raw from what the Goodlanders had tried to do to her, but she was a storyteller, damn it, and if you didn't tell your stories when the opportunity knocked, you deserved to live in a hell without them.

The shaggy red bull lowed again, and some of the females joined the call, rubbing up against the temporary fence, leaving handfuls of thick red hair behind. Despite the cold and the storms coming off the lake, it was starting to turn to spring, and they were losing their fur. It only made their shocked faces and thick eyebrows look funnier, without their beards.

She liked coming here, liked the smell of them. Liked the taste.

Daniel watched the old storyteller, Nitzaniya, from his window, which looked over the walls of the stockade. As she waited out her three days in the quarantine hut, she drank the last of her liquor and smoked the last of her cigarettes. She was even shouting stories through the wall, depending on who was there to listen:

The story of the zombie who had followed a man of the Burial Society through a rainstorm—washing off his ipish until he had to abandon his cart and the remains of a dead woman, unburied—and the way the zombie had wept over the corpse then eaten it, wrappings and all (told to a group of old women); the story of the two ravens who plucked out the eyes of a zombie by taking turns cawing at it (told to a line of kids with their ears pressed against the wood); the story of the man who had lost his ipish and was surrounded by seven women zombies, and survived only by pleasuring them, each in turn (told late at night to a group of drunken men who knew better). Daniel knew none of the stories were true, but they were good stories nonetheless.

Finally, the storyteller entered the city of Goodland, picking her way through the rusting cars and tilted asphalt, while sharpshooters aimed rifles at her from high, broken windows and gaggles of people surrounded her, begging for news. She waved them off and shouted that she'd start her work first thing in the morning, but right now she wanted a bath.

Daniel's son, Ely, who had thick, dark hair and a laughing eye, knocked on the door of his father's library. "Nitzaniya's here, father," he said.

"I see that."

"I'm off to help Elaine with the bathwater. See you in the morning."

"In the morning," Daniel said. "Did you tell your mother?"

Ely nodded. He was eighteen and anxious to be out in the world, traveling from place to place, killing zombies and having adventures. Ely had to make his first circuit soon, picking up young men and women to be trained for the Burial Society, but he'd waited when he'd heard that Nitzaniya was coming back.

Ely thought the world of her. The first time he had met Nitzaniya, she was telling the story of the two boys who had been trapped by a zombie at the top of a tree, one of them offering to throw himself to one side in order to give the other time to save himself, but the other finding a way to trick the zombie into thinking that a boy woven of branches was a real boy, thus saving them both. Ely must have been six, and he had announced that there was no finer profession that that of storyteller.

Daniel had been horrified, but Nitzaniya hadn't skipped a beat. She'd leaned over on the bench into the gaggle of little boys, pointed at Ely, and told him that she had seen his future. He was destined to become part of the famed Burial Society, just like his father, killing zombies and burying the dead. The other boys had worshipped Ely for days after that.

It was safer hunting zombies than being a storyteller, after all.

And so Ely became his apprentice, years too soon, and knew more about death and rot and murder than anyone else in Goodland but Daniel. He knew the secret of the ipish by the time he was ten, and hadn't breathed a word of it.

It was a bittersweet thing, to know one's only son had chosen to follow in one's well-respected but somewhat outcast footsteps.

The storyteller had a house in Goodland, although she wasn't often home; she had been raised there as a girl, and the city council hadn't had the heart to take it away from her or burn it, even though it was a haven for rats and other vermin.

The house had no basement, which was probably why it had survived for so as long as it had, without someone to keep it up for her.

Daniel knocked on the front door and heard the storyteller call, "Come in." He entered and picked his way through the house until he found her, in the ancient, claw-footed bathtub, one wall of the bathroom fallen in and covered with wool blankets, the mildew black upon the tiles. The water was steaming hot and frothed with bubbles. Nitzaniya held a yellowed and precious paperback romance novel in one hand, her middle finger marking her place as two lovers embraced on the front cover. Even though the light was only just dimming, candles had been lit on overturned buckets behind her; there were enough buckets stacked around her to fill two bathtubs or more. Daniel supposed she'd taken another bath already, one to get the grime and ipish off, and the other to ease the feel of the road.

"How are you?" he asked.

"Well enough."

"Have you seen Ely?"

"He helped Elaine carry water for me. Strong as a behe—strong as an ox. Sorry I ran late. There was a behemah stampede in Mount Horeb. Hell, Daniel. You better watch out for the Madison zombies. They want a route to the lakes so they can ship behemah to Chicago and onward, and you're right in the way."

"I know," he said. Nitzaniya's body was thin and flat and as hard as he remembered it. Her breasts were flat bags that reached almost to her belly, which sagged the way an old woman's will. She was only fifty, the same age as he was—he could remember a time when that would have meant they were middle aged, rather than old. "We're too old for this. You should retire."

"Retire. That's a word that lost meaning thirty years ago."

"Twenty-seven. At least come by the house."

"We both know that's not a good idea." She stretched out her legs, raising her toes into the air and spreading them wide. "Now, did you come to make trouble, or are you just here to lust after my body?"

Daniel laughed under his breath. "No, no. Neither."

Nitzaniya snorted.

"Did you bring it?" he asked.

She took a loud breath, raised the book, and pretended to read a page. Then she lowered the book and looked at him. "You know I did."

"Why?" he asked.

"I want to be able to give him a future, Daniel. Goodland won't be here forever."

"He—"

"I'm an old woman, Daniel. I don't have anything else to live for."

"You should write your stories down instead. Let that be your legacy."

"Oh, he can read now?"

"Or train an apprentice."

She looked at him; she didn't say, *I don't want to get anyone else killed*, although it was on both of their minds.

"Just get rid of it," Daniel said. "Please. For Ely's sake. Or keep it for yourself. Don't get people started on it. Not here."

"Don't you want to know who it's for?"

He shook his head. He wasn't the law around here, not unless it was killing someone who had turned; then he was the law above all others.

"Get a move on, then," Nitzaniya said. "My water's getting cold, and if you're not here to lay me, I want to soak in peace." She sank back into the still-steaming water, pulled up her knees, and let her feet sink under the surface.

There was one more thing he had to know. "You aren't—eating it yourself, are you?"

Her eyes caught the glint of candlelight off the mirror. Her long, white eyebrows met in the middle of her forehead, and she said, "Get out."

A breath of cold air rose up behind him, almost as though it were at her command, and he backed out of the room. Either she was eating it or she wasn't, but she wasn't about to tolerate him a second longer. She'd be up and out of that tub with a knife in hand in a second if he stuck around, he knew.

He met Elaine on his way out. "Hello, Mr. Lieberman," she said. "I'm afraid that the storyteller is in the bath right now."

"I found that out in a hurry," he said. "I guess I'll get my news tomorrow, like everyone else. Let me or Leah know if she needs anything."

"Leah made her supper." Elaine showed him the basket filled with his wife's home cooking, and his mouth watered. They were all that way, terribly impressed to be able to wait on the storyteller hand and foot—although he wouldn't have expected it of Leah.

What stories would she tell if she were rich and had no need to go wandering? Would she still wander? She would; he'd offered to marry her, long ago, and she'd refused him. Still, all she had to do was say the word, and he'd support her for the rest of their lives. Unlike storytelling, handling the dead always paid well, even in the years before the plague. But those who did it, although wealthy, were always held aside from the rest of the world, unclean.

Daniel walked the street, listening to the sound of his boots on the broken asphalt and cement. It was wet out and getting colder. It would probably rain all night, wind coming in from the lake, laden with moisture. He rubbed a hand over his stubbled jaw. Funny. All that rain, and he still felt like time was just drying him out.

A few streets later, while he wandered through the sunset more or less at random, he smelled it. He'd broken into a trot before he'd known why, then realized he'd smelled a zombie.

It turned his stomach, as always; he hoped it wasn't a child. His nose led him deeper into town, into the middle of streets of houses, away from the lake. It started to sprinkle, the wind picking up at his back faster than he could run. Later, he would wonder if he could have really smelled what he smelled, with the wind blowing the way it had. He heard screaming and loosened his revolver in his belt and shrugged his shoulders, gripping the machete sheathed between his shoulder blades to check it.

Clapboard houses with porches out front lined the streets; it was the kind of place that would have been real neighborly, back in the day. It was one of the first neighborhoods to recover from the plagues, with people trying to help each other out, even if it mean blowing their heads off if they started to turn. Ely lived nearby.

He knew every damned one of those houses like the back of his hand.

He followed his nose, his guts, and the screaming until he was almost, but not quite, in front of his son's house. The zombie was two houses down, in front of a place that used to be lilac but had gone patchy and faded between sunlight and whitewash. A nice young couple lived there with their elderly father, who was a bit of a bastard, if Daniel remembered right.

The old man—Mac-something, MacIntosh—was standing in front of the house. For whatever reason, here, in the middle of Goodland, years after the last turning inside the palisades, MacIntosh was turning.

Daniel pulled out his revolver. A bunch of idiots surrounded MacIntosh. The light was fading fast, and a lamplighter was standing in the crowd, holding his pole at his side, making no move to light the streetlights in his rush to watch the excitement.

It was just excitement to Daniel; to the people on the street, it was death.

"Get back!" he yelled. He ran toward them as fast as he could. "Get back! Go on, get out of here! Heeya! Get! Get!"

People got out of his way, but they didn't leave the street. They never did.

"MacIntosh!" Daniel yelled.

The old man looked up. The left half of his face wasn't working anymore, and his left arm and leg were dangling. His skin was a dull gray, and a rope of spit hung out of his mouth. He moaned.

"You poor bastard," Daniel said.

The old man held a paper-wrapped parcel in his right hand still. The paper had been ripped off, and a hunk of meat, apparently bacon, was sticking out of one end of it. Behind him lay a woman's body, a long, bloody rip down one side, probably caused by a dull knife or a pointed pair of scissors. She was kicking, turning herself around in a slow, dirty circle on the ground, bleeding out. The daughter-in-law. He saw another body lying in the doorway, boots facing out and down, and assumed it was MacIntosh's son.

Daniel reached behind his waist and pulled the machete out of its sheath. He kept it terribly sharp, but it always seemed dull at times like these.

"Stay away from the house," he yelled. At least he'd reached the old man as he was turning, while his body was still converting from human to zombie. Their nerves tended not to work so well during the transition, leaving them slow and easy to kill. Easier.

With his left, he shot out the man's right knee, toppling him down to the ground. A few steps later, he was close enough to kick the man's arm out from under him as he tried to raise himself up again, then step on his back. Daniel hacked with the machete at an angle to get around the ridge of bone protecting the spinal cord. The blade got stuck for a moment, so he drew it out and cut again, this time slicing through the front of the old man's neck. MacIntosh's head tilted onto its forehead, then toppled sideways to face the crowd.

With a few more twists and slashes, Daniel cut the arms and legs off and pushed them out where they couldn't touch each other. Then he checked the woman. She, too, was turning, so he did the same for her, murmuring words of comfort.

People, thinking they were safe, crowded in closer, and he yelled at them. They backed off a tad, and he took the opportunity to climb onto the porch and check the son.

The man was dead, stone dead. Except it wasn't MacIntosh's son. It was Ely.

Daniel was too stunned to feel anything except wonder why his son was in the doorway of MacIntosh's house. Daniel dragged the body down the stairs, then told the lamplighter to send word back that he needed his cart. Daniel had another one of Ely's neighbors light the lamps.

He had someone fetch and light him a torch, then squatted over the mess on the ground.

With the tip of his machete, he poked the paper-wrapped package still clutched in MacIntosh's twitching hand and tried to find a label or other sign of where it had come from.

The stuff smelled. It smelled bad, like rotten meat. But it also smelled good, like aged cheese. He'd had lutefisk once as a kid, and it was the same kind of smell—not as fishy, but still there.

It was behemah meat. It was treif, the worst thing you could possibly eat.

And Nitzaniya had smuggled it in.

"What's that?" a woman's voice said behind him. He looked over his shoulder; it was another one of Ely's neighbors, a woman of about seventeen or so, the wife of a farmer who kept her in town so she'd be safer. She was just barely starting to show.

"Evidence," he said, without thinking.

"Is that what turned him?" she asked, and he cursed himself for a fool. She yelled, "Mr. Lieberman thinks he found what turned Old Man MacIntosh!"

The crowd started to pull in tight, but he waved them back, then pushed the paper over the end of the package as best he could with the machete. He scratched a circle around the bodies and the package with the tip of his machete and said, "No closer. None of you come any closer than this, unless you want to get infected."

It was full dark by the time the cart arrived, pulled by Sheriff Dustry and three deputies. Daniel washed his hands with moonshine from the kit, then lifted two rolls of white gauze from the side boxes.

Dustry said, "I see three there, not two."

"One of them died too soon to start turning," Daniel said. "My son."

Ely's throat had been cut from ear to ear.

Daniel had been trying to put it together while he waited; it was hard to collect his thoughts with the crowd watching over the bodies inside the ring. The limbs rolled and twitched, the torsos flexed and shuddered; the heads mouthed words endlessly, still trying to communicate. Laughing and crying soundlessly, unintelligibly. He just wanted silence, time to think, and the freedom to pace beyond the direct line of sight of the bodies.

Nitzaniya had brought the treif. She had sworn time and again that it wouldn't change anyone—it wasn't infected. It was the dried, cured meat of the behemah that had been rubbed with herbs and rendered brain-grease and smoked over a fire of apple wood and burning bones. Zombies at it all the time, like jerky, except on their main holiday, to celebrate escaping destructions by humans, when they butchered the oldest of the behemah and ate them fresh.

Daniel could remember when the behemah had been human. Like all the Burial Society, he'd been outside the walls, smeared in ipish, to render the dead. Zombies had come up to him time and again to smell him, or rather the ipish, and passed him by.

At first they'd been leading human prisoners, and he'd had to watch the zombies lead them away, lest he be attacked and killed, possibly drawing an attack down on Goodland. Over the years, the prisoners had changed. More hair, fewer clothes. Bigger. Fewer pleas for help, until they lost the ability to talk at all. The dumb, panting, open-mouthed look of them. The smell.

Behemah smelled delicious, like food—the older they were, the better. His mouth watered whenever they passed. Zombies preferred them to human flesh. That was the reason that humans lived at all, he supposed; they were second-best on the menu. How the zombies had changed them so fast, he'd never know.

He'd never eaten any. There were some things you couldn't do, and remain human.

But if it wasn't the dried behemah that had done it, what had?

Daniel tried to imagine it: Ely had come to the door, and Old Man MacIntosh, turning into a zombie, had slit him from ear to ear.

No. Zombies didn't use knives, and they didn't bother to kill; they just ate. Whatever the plague did to them, it made them hungry until they'd finished turning. They ate more like normal folks did after that—except for *what* they ate—but at first, they couldn't eat enough. More like a pregnant woman than anything else, as though they were eating for two.

Ely had to have been killed by a human, for human reasons.

Dustry had the deputies help him wrap the bodies. Fortunately, Ely didn't have to be chopped up; he hadn't so much as twitched the whole time. He really had been killed, not infected.

Daniel wrapped the heads and limbs of the zombies and left the torsos for the deputies. Sure, the torsos were the goriest parts, but they were the least likely to turn around and claw you, too. Daniel had on thick leather gloves and an ancient set of goggles with cracked rubber seals and a leather strap that had to be replaced every few years because of how he had to clean it. The deputies had on thick aprons made of plastic tarp, which was better than nothing, but not by much.

As each piece was finished, they loaded it into the back of the cart inside a rigid, ancient children's swimming pool. The cart was heavy, because of the corrugated steel they'd used to cover the back, top and bottom, front and back. The pool took care of most of the drips; the steel took care of the limbs that dug their way out of their bindings and tried to escape. Daniel scraped up the area as best he could, then threw the dirt in a tin pail and slid it into the cart next to the pool. He scattered bleach over the ground, then salt.

Dustry gestured to the deputies to haul the cart away, and the two of them walked next to each other, following the cart, watching for trouble.

Dustry shouted, "Go home now," at the last of the crowd. There were only a few folks left, most of them having drifted off when the last piece of Old Man MacIntosh—his head—had been tossed into the back of the cart.

As the two of them followed the creaking cart, Dustry said, "I saw the treif. You know what that means, don't you? We got a smuggler. And that means death."

"I don't like it," Daniel said, which could have meant anything. There was something else bothering him, and he couldn't put a finger on it while Dustry was distracting him.

"It's that woman."

"Nitzaniya?" Daniel asked.

"She's the only who's come in lately. But I have to wonder if Ely was involved."

Daniel exploded. "Ely? How dare you—"

"Hang on now," Dustry said. "I have to wonder. It's my job. I'm sure there's a reason he was over at his neighbors that had nothing to do with the treif. Hell, for all I know, he was sleeping with the daughter-in-law."

Daniel snorted.

"I know that Elaine was fussing over that woman all day. He could have used it for an excuse to head on over."

"Not likely."

They went back and forth over it. Daniel didn't dare defend Nitzaniya. The treif might not have turned MacIntosh, but it was *human flesh*. And she was selling it like jerky. No. Whatever had been between them was over.

He'd lost his son.

She'd have to understand that.

Except she wasn't likely to be too understanding while they were stringing her up, were they?

All the while, he was thinking he was missing something.

It wasn't until he noticed the smoke—which had to have been coming up from Nitzaniya's house—and started running alongside Dustry that it came to him, and then was gone almost as quick: MacIntosh was dead. His daughter-in-law was dead. Where was MacIntosh's *son*?

They were going to string her up, right then and there, but Dustry wouldn't hear of it. "Cut her down!" he yelled as they started to hoist her over the crosspiece of an old light pole.

They hadn't bothered to tie her hands, and she was holding onto the rope with both of them, trying to keep her windpipe from being crushed. Her face was lit up from the burning lamps around her, including the one above her. The way she was swinging back and forth as she rose, the lamp was shaking and spilling burning oil. It landed in her hair, on her clothes, on the ground. She was going to go up like a torch any second.

"Cut her down!" Dustry yelled again, and his deputies surged forward, jerked the rope out of other men's hands, and let her down. Daniel grabbed her and wrapped his arms around her to smother the fires blooming in her clothes; dirt spilled over their heads as someone else put out her smoking hair.

Nitzaniya gasped for breath, eeled out of his grip and dropped to her knees, threw off the noose like she was a greased pig, and started running. The crowd chased after her. Daniel stayed where he was; there was nothing he could do for her now. If she'd gone to the jail with Dustry, he might have been able to talk her or bust her out, but there was nothing to do for her now.

No stories, no talk, there was nothing that was going to stop that crowd, he was sure.

The deputies had gone, but Dustry had stayed behind, probably for the same reason Daniel had. There was nothing he could do, and the town would heal faster if he didn't see who did what when they finally caught the woman. They'd tear her apart.

Dustry walked over to him, his boots crunching on dry grass. "There's just one thing I have to know," he said.

"The son," Daniel said. "Where the hell was the son? I'm going back."

"Mind if I join you?" Dustry said. "I can't do any good around here."

The two men walked back to the cart, pulling it with them back to MacIntosh's house.

Elaine stood in her doorway, watching them. "Ely's dead," she called as they passed.

"Yeah," Daniel panted. "I wrapped him myself. He didn't come back."

"Good."

The two men trudged with the cart. It had to have been after midnight by then.

"It was all *her* fault, wasn't it?" she asked.

"Workin' on findin' out," Dustry said. "Gotta check something."

"What?"

"Never…you…mind," he said. He lowered bend over, lowering his pole toward the ground.

Daniel laid his down, too.

"Hell," Dustry said. "I don't know how you do it. Alone. Hell."

Daniel shrugged. "Part behemah," he said.

Dustry spat. "Don't say stuff like that. You don't know who's listening."

Something shifted in the back of the cart. Daniel checked, but it was just body parts sliding around in the pool. "Okay," he said.

They walked into the house, and Daniel got another whiff of it, the smell of something turned. He cursed; if he hadn't been so upset about Ely, he'd have smelled it a mile away.

"What is it?" Dustry asked.

"It's another turn." Daniel pulled his machete out of its sheath and drew his revolver. At the top of the steps, he raised his hand for Dustry to hold still. Something was making a sound below them, in the basement.

Daniel stepped over the stains of his son's blood and fully into the house. "Don't get all wound up and shoot me now," he said.

"You want me to go first?"

Daniel shook his head.

The house looked almost untouched, like the years has passed it by without letting it age. Lace curtains, bright paint, nice rugs. The furniture was protected under heavy plastic covers, and the rugs had clear plastic runners laid over them, but that wasn't too unusual, even for the years before the plague. Photos everywhere, some of them faded. Heavy curtains that blocked the light. Dustry had him wait a minute while he lit a heavy hurricane lantern using a sparker, then they moved forward.

Under the stairs was a small door standing open. In Daniel's experience, nobody left the door under the stairs open on a regular basis, so he looked inside. Sure enough, there was a hole in the wall behind it. The hole was blocked with a thick slab of wood with a padlock on it. The lock was covered in dried blood, and there were drips of it puddled under the lock.

Daniel ducked under the doorway to get a better look at the lock, then straightened up and hit his head, thumping on the stairs overhead. He cursed. Something moved below.

Daniel pushed Dustry out of the doorway, aimed, and waited.

Footsteps came to the door, which shifted slightly as a weight rested on it. Long seconds passed, and a woman's voice called,

"Ian? Is that you?" The door shifted again. "Ian…I'm so sorry. I'm so sorry."

There was a moan from below, and a gasp. "No!" the woman said, then ran down what sounded like stairs.

Daniel leaned forward again and spotted the shotgun just inside the stairwell. He holstered his revolver and set his machete aside. Both barrels of the shotgun were loaded.

"Ready?" he mouthed at Dustry, who nodded.

Daniel shot both barrels at the door, blowing the lock off the wood. He tossed the gun, picked up his machete, drew his revolver, and toed open the door with one foot.

Dustry held up the lantern behind him.

A hole had been dug down into the ground, a secret basement shored up with railroad ties and rotting plywood. A passageway led through the dirt, around the regular basement, and down further, until the bottom edge of the foundation passed overhead. The stench was unmistakable. As they went down the last set of plank stairs, they saw a light ahead of them.

Under the foundation was a small room dug out of the dirt with plywood walls and mud all over the floor. There was a bed, a bedside stand, a lamp with a scarlet shade, a rug, and a hole in the far corner covered with more plywood, ragged around the edges. Daniel looked under the bed; Dustry peered at the books on a bookshelf and tried to see whether there was anything behind it, finally tipping it over to see the rotted wall behind it.

"Nowhere else to look," Daniel said, pointing at the cover to the shitter.

Dustry pulled back the plywood while Daniel aimed.

Two sets of eyes looked up from them as the smell of zombie shit filled the room. Daniel was used to it from the ipish, but Dustry gagged and spat. Luckily, neither of them had eaten for a good long time.

It was a fully settled zombie woman—gray, sagging skin, gaping mouth and jutting teeth, and not a lick of fat on her—and a young man in the middle of turning, the two of them squatting in the shit hole. Daniel recognized the boy as MacIntosh's son.

"No," the woman said, hanging onto the boy so he couldn't jump out at them. "I'm so sorry, I'm so sorry..."

The boy just moaned and tried to eat them.

Daniel aimed at them. By the time Dustry was done heaving his guts out, both of the zombies were at the bottom of the shithole, black sludge drooling out of their shattered skulls and the smell of gunpowder almost covering up the rest of the stench.

Dustry said something, then grinned. Neither one of them could hear a damned thing.

They came out onto the street, each holding a laundry basket full of chopped up body parts that they'd wrapped in furniture covers to keep them from putting themselves back together.

Daniel thought he had it worked out by then, and promised himself he'd tell Dustry his theory when they could hear each other without screaming themselves hoarse. Nitzaniya had somehow gotten Ely to make a delivery for her—probably because Dustry had had someone watching her. The treif was probably for the woman zombie, MacIntosh's wife, and now the son. Ely had come to the door at a bad time, while the son was turning, and MacIntosh had killed him for what he'd seen.

In the middle of all that, the woman had lost control, attacked MacIntosh and her daughter-in-law, and...a big damned mess was what it was.

He was almost sure Nitzaniya was dead by then. Had got what she deserved.

He blamed her for Ely's death. Hell, hadn't she just said that he was all she had to live for? Maybe she was better off dead, anyhow.

One of Old MacIntosh's arms had untangled itself from its gauze wrapping, so Daniel rewrapped it before adding the rest of the parts to the pile.

"We're going to have to be careful with this," he said. "I really don't need these to spill out."

Dustry sighed and grabbed a pole. Daniel hefted the other, and they were off.

Dustry left him as they passed the jail. "Sorry, Lieberman. But I have to check on things."

By *things*, Daniel understood he meant *find out what the crowd had done to Nitzaniya*. By that time, he was settled about it. She'd got what she deserved, and that was that. She never should have sent Ely out with that package.

His feelings were bubbling up in him, and he wanted to get out of town before they spilled out, so he kept walking, both poles on his shoulders now. He'd stop inside the quarantine area to put on the ipish.

But he hadn't got more than another hundred steps when Dustry caught up to him again.

"Come on, Lieberman. You got to see this."

Daniel put the poles down gently, checked the body parts to make sure they were secure, and followed Dustry into the jail. It was a tidy place, for all that rioters had been through there with spray paint, baseball bats, and shotguns when the plagues had first started.

Dustry led him into the holding area, and there she was: Nitzaniya.

Outside the cell his wife was sitting on a rusted folding chair. Both women looked miserable, but not, strangely, mad at each other.

"What the hell are you doing here, Leah?" he asked. "You know she's the reason our son is dead."

"Shut up," Leah said. "You old fool. Who do you think took orders for her?"

Daniel felt his legs go weak, and he grabbed onto the bars of the cell. "Leah," he gasped.

"I'm ready to die," Nitzaniya said. "Don't worry about it. I panicked, that's all."

"How are you even alive?" He had to know.

"I talked them out of it. I told them I had a good bit of money saved up, and I'd give it all to the widow, if they brought me to the jail and let me be strung up instead of ripped apart."

Daniel shook his head. He couldn't believe it.

"But don't try to be noble and get me out of this," she said. "I'm ready. I'm ready to go. I don't have anything to live for. No reason for it."

"Good," he said.

"Daniel!" Leah said.

He shook his head. He didn't have it in him to forgive Nitzaniya. Leah was a different matter; it had been the storyteller who'd talked her into it, obviously.

Dustry tugged on his sleeve. It would be good to be gone for a few days, that was true.

"I'm going to take the bodies out," Daniel said. "One way or another, Nitzaniya, you better be gone when I get back." He studied his wife the way he always did before he left. She was beautiful, and she was angry at him. He opened his arms stiffly; she stood up stiffly; they embraced each other stiffly. He didn't want to have anything happen to him while he was out and her thinking he didn't love her anymore. He put his lips on her cool neck and kissed it. "I love you," he whispered. "Just you."

"I know it," she said. "But we're old now. It doesn't matter anymore, if it ever did. You should say goodbye."

Daniel sighed. He should, even if only to make his wife happy. He kissed her again and stepped back so he could see Nitzaniya.

"I wish it hadn't come to this," he said.

She gave him a little half-smile. "I wish I'd had time to find that apprentice. Teach him some stories. Something to keep that part of me alive, at least. You're right. I shouldn't have drug Ely into this. And I shouldn't have let these stories die. They're lies, but they're good to hear now and again, eh?"

He nodded. She walked up to the bars, reached her hand through. He took it, held it a second, and let go. Followed Dustry out of the jail. Didn't speak another word; didn't have to.

Dustry said, "You want some help taking that the rest of the way?"

"Nah," Daniel said. "You might get me a couple of sandwiches and something hot to drink, though." He picked up the poles and staggered forward until the cart started moving again. It seemed to have gotten heavier since the last time he'd picked it up, but he wasn't about to put it down; he'd never get it started again. He was just too damned tired. He should probably spend the night in quarantine was what he should do.

Daniel heard yelling from over by the jailhouse; a group of people were standing outside the building, yelling. He tried to look away, but he couldn't. He kept twisting his head around to see what was happening until his neck was sore.

He wasn't afraid for Leah; Nitzaniya would never betray her; she'd kept her secrets well, even from him.

The smell of zombies got stronger, and he set the poles of the cart down. It would just be the kind of thing that would happen tonight, another turning. He spun in place, trying to filter out the smell of the zombies on the cart, but he couldn't figure out what direction the smell was coming from.

The rioters at the jail got louder all of a sudden and moved in a group toward the wood frame that served them as a gallows.

Daniel found himself running toward them. He had no idea what he was going to do: but when he got close enough for them to hear him, he yelled, "Run!"

Screamed it and kept screaming it.

"They're coming! Run!"

In his gut, he knew it was true. Like so many things about zombies, when it came to smelling them, his nose could work miracles, if he let it.

The ground started shaking, and there was screaming everywhere, and shots. The zombies were sweeping from behind him toward the jail, across the town. They'd surely swept over most of the living already.

He didn't have to look. He ran toward the frame, where Nitzaniya was already standing, her hands tied behind her, the noose around her neck. She was looking at the zombies behind him, mouthed, "I told you so."

"You surely did," he said, although he doubted she could hear him.

He pulled the noose off her head and drew his machete, started to cut through the ropes around her wrists.

The zombies rode up around them on behemah as big as small elephants. In other circumstances he would have laughed to see their identical faces with their eyebrows raised and mouths in small, shocked-looking circles.

One of the zombies reigned to a halt in front of the platform, and Daniel noticed that Dustry had been ridden down in the dirt underneath him. The zombie was gray and hairless and gaunt and had blood-red lips drawn back from his white, white teeth. He was wearing a cowboy hat and a silver star on the breast pocket of his threadbare shirt.

The zombie glanced at Nitzaniya, then at Daniel. "Kill him," he said. Another one of the zombies swung down off his mount onto the platform, holding a revolver.

"No!" Nitzaniya yelled.

The zombie looked at her; she looked at him. Daniel finally cut through the ropes, and she winced as he cut just a little too deep without meaning to. She shook off the ropes and walked over to the zombie. "Let him go."

The zombie jerked his head toward his mount, and Nitzaniya climbed up behind him, just like that, no ipish or anything to cover her scent.

The other zombie holstered his weapon and climbed back onto his mount.

"If he hurts anybody or the behemah, kill him," the leader said and rode off with Nitzaniya behind him.

The other zombie watched him for a moment, then rode on. The wave of zombies passed him by, and he heard more behemah coming, herds and herds of them, running through the streets toward the lake.

Daniel climbed off the platform and went into the jail to watch. Leah was at the window already, watching. He squeezed her around her shoulders. "I'll make sure they don't hurt you," he said.

"All you have to do is eat the treif," she said. "It marks you to them. I'm fine."

He clenched his eyes until the tears went away. The behemah toppled the gallows, tore down trees, broke into houses, set fires.

It was a stampede. Fortunately, it was easier for the huge, shaggy red half-men to pass the jail by than knock it over, although it did sound like they were trying from time to time.

"What are we going to do?" he said.

"Don't worry," she said. "Nitzaniya and I were ready for this. As much as anybody could be. Goodland was doomed, and we knew it."

He believed her. And so he burst into tears, watching the behemah knock down his town, and mourned his son.

Nitzaniya stood back and stretched, trying to work the kinks that being hung one and a half times had put into her.

Caleb had come up behind her while she was telling the story and was waiting patiently for her to finish. She cleared her throat, rubbed her neck, and said, "Thank you again."

"It was nothing," he said, and she knew it was more or less true.

"It was good timing, though," she said. "Sometimes, that's enough to make a good story."

He nodded. His gray flesh moved differently than a human's, but it wasn't truly rotting away or anything like that.

"I have a favor to ask you," he said.

"Anything."

"There's a girl…" he sighed. "She was my daughter, in life. Now she's just trouble. I was wondering…"

"If I'd take her on."

He nodded. His hair had long since fallen out, all except the stuff in his ears and nose.

"I'll talk to her," Nitzaniya said. "I need to take on an apprentice sometime. I'm not getting any younger, and I would like to die at some point."

Caleb shrugged and spread his hands. They'd had that discussion already.

She was going to have to change some of those stories around when she told them to the girl. But that was all right. None of them were, strictly speaking, true to begin with.

"How is *that* story supposed to help get rid of the Crouga?" Facunde demanded from the girl's other shoulder. "That makes no sense whatsoever. You're just making this all up."

Ibarrazzo ignored her and looked at Old Loyolo, who sat on the girl's knee, and then at me. Both of us, she looked at with her bad eye.

Why she called it that, and how she had got it, I have never heard. I *had* assumed that it wasn't a story worth telling—a sickness, old age. The same kind of thing that happens to all of us, eventually, if we are lucky, and doesn't need to be dwelled upon. But now I think that she hid the true story of her bad eye under a few shrugs of her wings, as though she had always had one bad eye, and one good one, and that's all there was to it.

And now I will never know the real story.

Old Loyolo cleared his throat and said, "Eating is important. What you take in."

I wish he had not reminded me. It was a hungry time, and it was still a long way off until dawn. I glared at him. The top of his head was almost bald, his feathers were so thin. And his twisted leg was oozing blood.

Ibarrazzo clicked her beak and made a little nod that I think that I was not meant to see. "It is," she said.

Then I thought to myself, *there is something between them that you don't know. Lovers?* But now I know. We couldn't fight the monster with stories, not the way she suggested. She was using the story instead to tell him what needed to be done.

"It has been a long time since you have told that story. You should tell it more often."

She watched him, this time not nodding. "No," she cawed softly. "I shouldn't. Every time I do..." she shrugged, this time without that little flip to the ends of her wings. Her feathers were spread wider, with gaps between them. Hollow wings.

"It's not because you tell the story, my dear," Loyolo said. She lowered her head, and he hopped over to her—there were so few elders on the girl's lap that it wasn't difficult—and rubbed her beak with his own. When he had finished, she buried her head in the girl's shoulder, pushing the pink blanket closer to the girl's neck, and held her head there for a long time.

As though she were hiding her one bad eye.

The snow began to come down more thickly, turning the light over us a swirling gray that reminded me of bugs in the summer and made me feel even more hungry than before. The girl was shivering constantly and the elders began ordering the younger chicks to come up and huddle with them, both to keep warm together and to help cover the girl with a blanket of crows. She had pulled her hand back inside the blanket. As for myself, I was able to get back on my feet and stand, somewhat woozily, among the crush. Other crows' feathers held me upright; other crows' breaths kept me warm.

The girl covered her nose with the blanket and hunched deeper into the box. The walls on the inside were made of shiny tin, and seemed to reflect our breaths, keeping us a little warmer.

She said, "I…have another story." Her eyes looked over at Ibarrazzo, who was still hiding her head in her shoulder. "It is not a true story. And it is all finished up."

Old Loyolo watched her, twisting his head over his shoulder. He had been looking out into the open space in the center of the pit, toward the old truck cab, which was, either fortunately or unfortunately, out of sight. "All right," he said. "You may tell it."

"It's for—"

He shook his head. "It is a story. Never say what a story is for. Or who. Just tell it. Otherwise you take out some of the magic."

"Going to save us from the monster in the truck? From the Crouga?" Facunde snarled. "What crap."

"Sss!" Old Loyolo hissed at her, his tongue protruding out of his beak. But the girl said, "I wasn't thinking of that at all. Just a story."

"Fine," Facunde said. "Just fine. So I have no heart. Tell your story. It doesn't matter."

"All right…"

10. Inappropriate Gifts

I knew what the package for my daughter was before I even opened the box: my grandmother's apron. It was muslin, thick and heavy as an old-fashioned flour sack. For all I know, that's what she'd made it from. She was always giving people inappropriate gifts, crafts she'd made out of things other people threw away. Potholders crocheted over plastic soda-can rings (they melted). Homemade soap bars made out of the stub-ends of Grandpa's Irish Spring bars, with a crocheted yarn holder over it, a redneck soap-on-a-rope. Except Grandma wasn't a redneck, she was a survivor of the Great Depression. One of the things that you never get over, that define you for the rest of your life.

I didn't have to open the box to see it. The apron had roses on it, big, wide-open faded red roses with their petals almost falling off. The paint was the same kind of fabric paint that Grandma used to paint on everything, from dish towels to pillow covers. As a little kid, I'd used the same kinds of paints to paint towels too, carefully brushing the paint onto fabric stretched across a wooden hoop. The lines on the roses weren't as neat as the ones you usually saw on things Grandma made; the black outlining was a little crazed, a little shaky, like she'd been upset when she'd made it. The paint of the rose petals was a little blotchy, too.

She tried to give me the apron the last time I saw her before she died, which was when I was about thirteen. I was young and terrified that boys would never like me. For some reason, I was convinced that my nose was too big and my arms were too thin (they weren't), and thus, I would never find love.

Mom had taken me to the nursing home to see Grandma; she wasn't doing very well, and her mind would wander. One minute she'd be talking about her new house in Springfield; the next, she'd be weepy over being trapped in a nursing home. It was hard to say which was worse.

So there I was, walking on eggshells. I loved her the way you love anyone who's willing to spend time with you when you're little, who has the time to do crafts and bake cookies and listen to your made-up stories and babble. They're nice to you, and that's all you care about at the time. Whether that feeling is too naïve to be love, I really can't say. Since I've become a parent, my ideas of love have changed. You have to do a lot of painful things when you're a parent, but you don't do them out of hate. Ignorance, maybe.

Grandma had scooted herself around in the seat of her recliner, which had a crocheted doily across the back so her head wouldn't rub directly on the fabric, until she had turned toward her side table, where an old, yellowed box was sitting. She picked it up in her hands, which had giant knuckles and twisted fingers—my mother always warned me against cracking my knuckles, or my hands would turn out like Grandma's—and held it hovering over her lap.

"You leish to cookh," she said. On bad days, her Bell's palsy made her words mushy and hard to understand. It embarrassed her, which made her even harder to understand, and less likely to speak. *You like to cook.* "I want shoo to shake gish." *I want you to take this.*

The top of the box was cracked cellophane. It was an old cake box.

I could see the painted cloth through the opening on the top. "What is it?" I leaned forward out of Grandpa's recliner, where I was sitting, and took the box but didn't open it. It wasn't just the gift, with Grandma. It was the story. Often, the story had nothing to do with the gift, like the time she told me about the blizzard that buried the barn—they had to dig air holes for the cows—and gave me a giant candle in a canning jar with a picture of the Virgin Mary cut from a color newspaper ad and taped to the side.

"Ish an aprah," she said. "Opah itch." *It's an apron. Open it.*

I looked at her. Where was the story? I'd come here to do this ritual one last time—with her, back then, everything was done in anticipation of *one last time*—and she was shaking things up. Doing things that weren't the way she was supposed to. I didn't know what to think. It hurt, a little.

I tried to make out what she was thinking. Her hairdo looked a little crushed from where she'd had her head against the back of the chair all day, and her lipstick went off her lips on the left side. Everything on the left side of her face drooped from the palsy; today was a pretty bad day. Maybe she was too embarrassed to tell a long story, afraid that I'd keep interrupting her to get her to say the same word over and over.

But I always understood what she said. It was Mom that had to ask her to repeat herself.

I started to feel self-conscious about staring at her and opened the box. The cellophane broke in pieces, leaving shards of half-sticky yellowed flakes all over my hands and lap.

I pulled out the apron. I was pretty mature for my age, but I was, nonetheless, thirteen and insulted that my grandmother would give me such a thing. I didn't want to be a housewife or a cook. I was the kind of girl who hissed when people tried to open doors for me or called me a young lady. That kind of thing. I liked my grandmother, but I couldn't imagine growing up to *be* her.

Then it started to creep up on me, the sense that someone was shoving a hand into my guts and squeezing.

"Push ish ah," she said.

I shook my head. "I don't feel good." I stood up to hand the apron back to her and run to the toilet down the hall. I refused to use *their* bathroom. Too creepy.

"Push ish ah!" Grandma yelled.

Mom was out with Grandpa—he spent all his time in the wood shop at the home—and there was nobody to hear her yell, but I looked back at the door to their room anyhow, expecting a nurse's aide to come bursting in or something. My hands popped that apron over my head faster than I could think to stop them. I didn't want to get in trouble.

It ripped through me then. Pain so bad I went down on my knees, still trying to turn towards the door. I ended up in a pile at the bottom of Grandpa's tan, threadbare recliner, looking at his footrest, which was so worn it was shiny. I felt like my insides were puking themselves out or like I'd eaten something bad and I was about to soil myself. I wondered whether I already had, at the time, but when I checked later in the public toilet, the only result was a brown spatter of blood in the front of my panties.

"Zeh," Grandma said. "Nah yah zhafe." *There. Now you're safe.*

I put my hands on the linoleum tiles and the green bathrug in front of the TV. The room was so small that my grandparents, with their walkers, had to take turns standing up from their motorized recliners, to go to bed. If they bothered to get up at all.

I breathed hard, grunting every time I breathed out, until the pain stopped. That is, it didn't stop, but the pushing and squeezing stopped, and what was left of the pain was so much less that it wasn't like pain at all, at the time. A reminder.

I pushed the apron back over my head, folded it, and put it back in the box while still on my knees, then hefted myself up to the seat of Grandpa's recliner. Tears were running down my face.

Grandma said, "Keepsh you fwa meh. Zheh hash off you. Zhafe." *Keeps you from men. Their hands off you. Safe.* She leaned between the two chairs and patted me on my shaking hand.

I ran out of the room and locked myself in the public toilet. When it was time to go, Mom had to yell at me through the door to get me to come out. I refused to say goodbye to my grandparents, and my mother yelled at me for that, too.

Aside from that spot of blood, I wouldn't get my first period until I was twenty-three.

By then, my grandparents were dead. Grandma had died within the week, and Grandpa died a few days after her, causing no end of trouble with funeral arrangements. He didn't waste away or anything—there wasn't enough time—he sliced open an artery on a scroll saw while making a pair of angels holding a heart with Grandma's name under it. The aides didn't notice he was bleeding until it was too late. His last words, according to the aide I talked to, years later, were "Don't feel bad, son, it was my own damned fault."

I had left the apron there with my grandmother, but I didn't escape it. I never thought about kissing a boy or touching myself between my legs without a twist of nausea. The harder I thought about it, the worse it got, until I ended up in a twist on the floor and spots of blood in my panties.

But that didn't mean the apron worked. It didn't keep men's hands off me, no. It didn't matter that I wasn't leading them on—I couldn't.

It was after the first time that I'd been attacked, while going to a movie with some girlfriends, that the package showed up in front of my bedroom door. Grandma had been dead for six months by then, and I wasn't talking to anybody. God knows what they thought was wrong with me.

I was coming home after school, half an hour late and a nervous wreck, trying to avoid certain people, and Mom was yelling at me. She broke off when she saw the box. "What's that?"

"Grandma's apron," I said. I hadn't talked to Mom about the apron, either. I couldn't. Every time I tried, the same sick feeling—ugh. I unwrapped the box, opened it, and showed her the apron, trying not to touch it. I had to have been as white as a sheet, with two black holes cut out for eyes.

I knew there was no getting away from it, so I pulled it out of the box and shook it out so it fell straight. It was creased hard from years and years of being folded up like that, and some of the paint flaked off from the creases.

"Be careful with that," Mom said, reaching her hand out for it. I wanted to jerk it away from her. "What on Earth did she send it to you for? She knew I wanted it." Her hand stopped just short of touching the thing.

"Do you want it?" I asked. "I like to cook, but you know I never—wear—aprons." The last words were so hard to say that they hurt my throat coming out, but I pushed them out anyway and closed my mouth before the thing could make me take them back.

"Yes," Mom said. She let her fingers brush the thing; flecks of paint stuck to her fingertips. "She sent me a potholder."

"May I have that instead? To remember her by?"

Mom nodded, and I handed her the apron, holding it like it was as fragile as a baby or the Mona Lisa or something. "Thank you." She sounded surprised that I could be so considerate. Not undeservedly so, considering the way I had acted over the last six months, constantly fighting pain and shame and everything else. But Mom didn't look like she was in the least amount of pain. Whether that was because the thing didn't hurt her or because she was always in that amount of pain and didn't notice it, I don't know. "I never got to touch it, when I was your age. I always thought—" she stopped talking. I think she'd stopped noticing that the words were only in her head. I felt like she didn't need me anymore, so I put the brown paper in the box and stuffed it all in the recycling bin. When I came back, she'd wandered off.

I'm sure Grandma had good intentions. When it came to me, at least.

My daughter's thirteen. My guts clenching and my legs dripping with blood, I took a serving dish out in to the back yard, doused the apron with lighter fluid, and watched it burn away. She'll never know it was here. And if it shows up at my daughter's doorstep again, it won't be me who gives it to her. At least, that's what I hope.

When the girl was done, she looked at Ibarrazzo again. In fact, she had been sneaking the old crow looks throughout the story. And not without cause: Ibarrazzo had moaned and crowed into the girl's shoulder, her feathers shaking as if she were reliving some memory, being haunted by a ghost.

After several moments, the old crow cried out, with her head still buried in the girl's shoulder. "I didn't mean to, all right? I didn't mean to!"

Old Loyolo picked between the claws of one foot, worrying at a patch of dead skin. "Didn't mean to what?"

"To bring it."

"The bead," Facunde said. "*You* brought the bead."

"I picked it up out by the girl's house. In the trash. It was part of a necklace…buried under some old meat…it was on a gold chain and I took it. The chain rotted and turned brown, but the bead was so shiny, I had to keep it. I snapped the chain across a rock and picked the bead up…I spat it out as soon as it started to move, and it stopped. Then I buried it and dragged a rock on top of it…"

"What about the Crouga, then?" I asked, but Old Loyolo raised a claw.

"When?" he said. When she didn't answer, he asked again: "When did you pick up the necklace?"

"A long time ago."

"How long?"

"A long time! Years and years. The babe hadn't been born yet, the girl-child was barely able to talk. A long time ago."

"From the woman's house."

"It was hers, I tell you."

"What about the other beads?"

"There was only this one, dangling on a gold chain that wasn't gold."

Loyolo stopped picking at the dead skin between his claws. "How long was the chain?"

"How long—?"

"How long."

Ibarrazzo shook her head, the feathers fluffing over her neck. "How long? How long? Long enough to snap over a small rock. Long enough that I held one end of the chain in my beak and it did not tangle in my claws. A small chain."

Old Loyolo looked over his shoulder at the girl. There was pity in the slump of his shoulders: when she was a babe, her mother had tried giving her a necklace that would kill her. Oh, we might argue, you and I, about whether the gift was given by someone else, or whether it was meant to harm her. Whether, perhaps, it was a kind of initiation into knowledge: a souvenir from *your* mother, passed down in good faith.

The girl looked down at Old Loyolo. There was grief in her eyes, and I knew, all of us knew, those of us who were paying attention to anything beyond the wingspreads of our own feathers, that she understood what such a revelation must have meant.

I said, "I have another story."

Now, normally, when I come up with a story, what I start with is a seed that I pick up. Or a piece of shit, or a feather, or a straggling length of squirrel-tail, bodiless, abandoned on a wire fence.

What have you. Or I steal the story whole, from someone else. It all depends.

This one, I picked out of the girl's sad eyes. It came to me all of a piece, from beginning to end; I told it just as I am about to tell it to you, like this:

11. Clutter

I could see Mom watching *Days of Our Lives* through the door as I knocked the snow off my boots. I pressed the bell and heard it ring.

Mom twisted around in her recliner but didn't put the feet down. "It's unlocked," she called.

I came in, closed the door behind me, and took off my boots. The smell of dust and rotten cushion batting crept up my nose, and I sneezed. I took another breath and inhaled Icy Hot. Her walker was next to the dining room table, a good ten feet away from the recliner. She wasn't using it.

"Hey, Mom," I said.

"Danny," she said. Normally, she said things like, "It's good to see you" and "It's been so long." I put the box of trash bags on the table beside me, walked over, and gave her an awkward hug.

"Why don't you have a seat?" she said. Testing the waters.

"Nah, too much to do," I said. "I better get started." I picked up the trash bags. "I'm going to start in your bathroom, all right? Did you set aside the medicine like I asked?"

"Not yet," she said, and put down the footrest of her recliner.

I picked up the walker and set it in front of her.

"I don't need that, Danny. Not for just walking around the house." She set the walker aside, took two steps, her hips refusing to unbend enough for her to stand up straight, and nearly fell. I caught her and gave her the walker. She glared at me. "I must have sat still for too long. Just let me sort out that medicine for you."

"Thanks, Mom," I said. "I'll make some coffee while I'm waiting."

I made sure she made it into the bathroom safely. She'd filled up the shower with stacks of blankets and rugs; shirts hung from the shower rod, packed in so tight they bulged around the end of the shower. She left her walker outside the door; there wasn't room. She could barely walk from the door to the sink on her own, but there were half a dozen grab bars in the room, and I'd hear her if she fell.

I went into the kitchen and started a pot of coffee in the cleanest carafe I could find.

Then I started packing trash bags. I'd had the trash company leave us a big take-away container that was going to cost me $250 to have them pick up. I figured I could get most of it in the container and haul the rest in my pickup. I'd have to see how it went.

I started with the garbage under the sink. For some reason, she'd decided to sort everything into compostable and non-compostable trash and leave the compostable stuff to rot. On the way out the back door, I noticed she'd been leaving the non-compostable trash in the laundry room. Fortunately, I was able to toss most of it directly into the container without tracking through the snow; the bags weren't too heavy. I got the compostable trash out from under the sink—the worst of it, anyway—and started on the fridge.

"How's that coffee coming?" she called.

"I was just waiting for you to come out," I said.

"What's that noise?"

"Just taking the trash out from the laundry room. It's pretty slippery outside the back door, and I don't want you to fall."

There was a pause. "I'm not done in here yet. Why don't you bring me a cup of coffee? Make sure you don't throw anything good out."

"Okay, Mom." Damn it, I couldn't find any dish soap, and I hadn't thought to bring any. I'd have to pick some up tonight. I rinsed out a cup with plain water and filled it with coffee. I knew from my earlier peek in the fridge that looking for cream was a lost cause.

When I brought it into the bathroom, she was sitting on the closed toilet seat, panting. The door of the medicine cabinet was open. The entire thing was stuffed with bottles, most of which probably had one or two pills left and had been expired for twenty years. I didn't dare look too closely; she was watching me.

"Here you go."

"Thanks."

I promised myself, yet again, that when it was time for my kids to pack me up and send me to the nursing home, I'd let it go without a fuss. Mom took a sip of coffee and said, "It's too hot."

"Do you want me to put an ice cube in it?"

She shook her head. "I'll just sit a minute and wait for it to cool down."

"Oh, shoot," I said. "I forgot to turn the warmer off. I'll be right back." I went back into the kitchen, turned off the warmer, and started cleaning out the fridge. Later, I'd come back and start scraping off the spilled milk and grime, but for now, all I wanted to do was to get the garbage out of the house. I had to get Mom's collection of possessions down to a couple of cardboard boxes inside of a month—I was driving her over on January second. A new start. The beginning of the end.

Mom came out of the bathroom, using her walker, and said, "Why don't you leave the bathroom for later? I'm feeling a bit tired, and I want to take a nap. You don't mind waiting around until I get this all sorted out, do you?"

"No, Mom," I said. "I like being here. This place has a lot of memories."

She smiled and got settled in her recliner. I put her feet up and helped her get comfortable. After a few minutes, she was snoring softly, like a cat.

I went into the bathroom and took out the trash, my first priority being to throw away anything in the process of actually rotting. In the case of the bathroom, this meant the entire space between the sink cabinet and the shower stall, which had been packed tight with tissue, paper towels, dental flossers, empty toothpaste tubes, and a few pairs of stained underwear. I broke down and retrieved the heavy rubber gloves out of my truck at that point.

For a minute, I thought I had all of the trash trash, but then I remembered she'd always kept a small can in their bedroom, so I went in with another bag. After Dad died, the whole house had started to stink, and their bedroom was the worst. I'd nosed around any number of times through the years. The room had filled up with more and more junk, but I'd never been able to figure out where the smell was coming from. I'd thought it was a dead mouse in a vent somewhere, but the smell never got any better.

I edged sideways into the room past ceiling-high boxes marked "quilting fabric" and "Montgomery-Ward Catalogs 1960–1979," etc. Maybe she'd feel better about getting rid of some of this stuff if I gave it to Goodwill or something. Dad's side of the bed was stacked with more boxes, and the blankets were all rucked up. I sat on the edge of the bed and reached between the bed and dresser for the trash can, which was only about half full. She probably hadn't used it for years—

Something on the bed shifted, and for a second, I thought a stack of boxes was going to topple and kill me. I put up my arms to cover my head, hitting myself in the face with the trash bag. After a second, I realized that something heavy had been under the blankets, and it had rolled into me.

I pulled back the blankets and nearly shit myself.

Under the blankets was a dead woman that looked a hell of a lot like my mother. Recently dead. The room suddenly smelled like pee, and I felt a wet spot on my pants. It was on the leg of my pants where it had rested on the bed, though, and damned cold: not mine.

"Holy shit," I said. "Holy shit." My mother had woken up from her nap, come past the bathroom and into the bedroom without me hearing her, and died. Holeeee shit.

I stumbled out of the bedroom and into the kitchen, poured myself a cup of tepid coffee, and sucked it down.

I went into the living room to use the phone, and there she was. My mother. In her recliner. Asleep. Alive and asleep, still making those faint snoring sounds. Fast asleep. Holy shit.

I went back into the bedroom. Dead Mom. Living room. Living Mom. A couple more times of this, and I was going to make myself dizzy.

If it wasn't my Mom, then who was it?

I checked the body again. I wish I could say that I knew where my Mom's birthmarks were, but I didn't. I mean, who wants to see your mother naked? But as far as I could tell, two things were true: one, I couldn't find any difference between the corpse and my Mom. They were even wearing the same clothes with the same stains on them. Two, one of them was dead, and the other one wasn't.

Beyond that, questions of whether I'd lost it or my mother had a twin sister, I couldn't tell you.

I can tell you this, though: I rolled up the body in a couple of blankets from the shower stall (the ones on the bed were wedged tight under the boxes, and I didn't have room to move them off) and put it in the back of the truck, under a tarp. I was pretty sure that the trash company would have found the body, even as surrounded by garbage as it would have been, had I put it in the container.

I went back in the house and watched Mom snore for a while. Then I got back to work. I finally had all the trash out; I started bagging up extra dishes from the kitchen, throwing away used paper plates and plastic forks as I went. At first I told myself I was going to take the dishes to Goodwill, but when I took them out to the truck and saw the tarp with Mom's body in it, I threw them in the trash container instead.

That night, I drove out to the reservoir and hid the body in a drainage tunnel. I figured the body would freeze until spring, then get either washed away or disfigured so badly there was no way they'd track her back to my mother.

Unless the dental records matched.

But that was just stupid; they'd know my mother was alive when they saw her.

When I came back the next afternoon (with dish soap), the big trash container was empty. Mostly empty. The trash was still there; the bags and bags of extra dishes and pans were gone. I knocked on the door. The same ritual followed: Mom was watching the soaps; I egged her on until she went into the bathroom to sort out her meds; I made a pot of coffee. The dishes (still dirty) were all back in their cupboards; the garbage bags were folded up under the sink.

Fine. I washed the dishes and repacked them in clean garbage bags. Then I carried them carefully out to the truck and put them under the tarp. She didn't want her stuff thrown away. Fine. Fine. I filled up the back of the truck and looked around the kitchen. The cupboards were covered in grease; the ceiling tiles were stained over the oven; the wallpaper was peeling; the gold-and-orange carpet had a black streak down the center from decades of footprints and wear.

I wanted to pull everything apart and make it habitable again. Do something nice for Mom. Peel off the paper and paint the walls sky blue, pull up the carpet and refinish the floor with some tile. You shouldn't have carpet in your kitchen. I don't know why they hadn't let me do it years ago, instead of now, a month before I had to kiss the house goodbye.

I walked into the bathroom. Mom was asleep on the toilet. I should have checked her hours ago, but I'd lost track of time. It was ten o'clock, and she hadn't eaten a thing since I'd come in.

I shook her shoulder. "Mom."

She twitched but didn't wake. I'd just have to get her to bed and make sure I brought food tomorrow. I should have packed her up a year ago. Two years ago. Nobody should live like this. I'd let her put me off for too long. I couldn't stand the thought of what she'd been doing to herself, here alone. What the hell was wrong with me, that I let her—

I sighed and went into the bedroom to push back the covers, so I could put her in bed and cover her up without jostling her too much. She'd carried me to bed many times when I was a boy; I could still remember the warmth of her arms.

There was already an old woman in the bed.

I leaned back against the closet door and almost tipped a box of photos onto my head. After shoving the box back and wiping my eyes to clear out the dust, I had almost talked myself out of it, thinking that it was just a lump in the covers. Then I pulled the blanket back.

My mother's dead twin lay in the bed again. The sheets were even dirtier than they had been yesterday, covered with wet leaves and slime. It was as if my mother had followed me out to the reservoir, picked up her body, and brought it back with her. Tucked it into bed. Not that she had a driver's license anymore. And surely Dad's old junkers wouldn't start.

I put the footrest up on the recliner and laid my mom there instead. No wonder old people slept in their recliners, I thought, if this is what was hogging their beds.

I'm not one to keep doing the same thing over and over, expecting different results, so I didn't wrap the corpse up in a blanket and shove it in the back of the truck again. This time, I took it out to Dad's old shop. I looked around; the old shed he'd been using was falling down. I should have started out here; it needed to be done anyway, and it would have meant less time trying to deal with Mom in the house. Maybe I'd start out here tomorrow.

There was no power in the shed, and I didn't feel like trying to start the generator, so I got a flashlight out of the truck and hunted around until I found a hacksaw. It was dull as shit, so I went into the house and got a kitchen knife, which was even worse.

I ended up pulling the body apart like a raw chicken with a utility knife from the truck. It wasn't messy; the blood was more like dish soap than ink, and the longer I was outside with it, the colder and thicker it got. It was midnight before I was done, so I stuffed everything in a bag and shoved it underneath some bags of trash in the big container. The truck was full up, and I'd be back tomorrow anyway.

I dropped off the kitchen stuff at Goodwill, picked up some fried chicken, and drove out to Mom's.

"Hi, Mom. Brought you some chicken," I said. But she already had a plate in front of her. "What's that?"

"Roast," she said.

"Someone brought you roast beef? From the church? Nice. I'll just put this in the fridge for tomorrow, then." I carried the chicken into the kitchen, half-expecting the dishes to be back again. I checked a few cupboards, but they were empty. The one skillet that I'd left mom was in the sink, soaking in cold, brown water. I reached in and pulled out the drain plug.

Mom muttered from the living room, the way she did when she was about to lay into you. "*Someone* shouldn't throw perfectly good things away."

My stomach went as cold as the water in that sink. I dropped the stopper, shook my hand off, and ran back into the bedroom.

The body was there again, laid out in pieces under the covers. A chunk had been cut out of one thigh; the old skin sagged around the hole.

I went back into the living room. Mom was still eating.

She stared at me, daring me so say something.

Hell. What's one more month of living in squalor?

"I'm going out to the shop while you finish sorting out your medicine cabinet," I said. "It's not too cold today."

Mom nodded. "Your father never would get rid of anything. I'm sure there's a lot of crap out there, pardon my French."

I nodded and left.

With a little gasoline, the generator started just fine.

God help me, I don't think it's going to take me a month to clean up Dad's shop. And I don't know how much longer I can wait.

When I had finished, I ruffled my feathers. I will not lie to you, I felt naked under the stares of the other crows. If there was ever a time that I might have been pecked down for a bad story—although it *wasn't*— it was then, I was so nervous afterwards.

But I swallowed my fear, and the others settled.

The girl said, "I don't need to keep the bead, do I? It's mine, but I don't need to keep it."

I bowed in front of her. When we crows tell stories, we always tell them to entertain—it would be blood and dead storytellers if we did not—but often we tell them to sway the course of some event, some mood. Instead of making laws or casting spells, we tell stories. It is a subtle magic—not even magic at all, it is so subtle.

I had been the first to talk to the girl, your daughter. She was swinging on the swingset in the front yard. It was just after the dog had accidentally—or so you claimed—eaten poison, the first time her heart had been broken. Two years ago, before the babe was even a thought in your mind.

She was telling herself a story about the dog, about how it had eaten poison and lived, for a short while longer at least, and had attacked the rats who hid in the barn, because they were the ones who had put the poison in his food. Her dog killed the rats, killed them until they lead him to their king, crying, "Save us! Save us!"

The dog killed the rat king, then dragged himself back to the house, where he lay on the ground by the door and panted, dying. A crow, curious, landed next to the dog, and asked it what was wrong. "I am about to die," the dog said. "And while I have killed the rats who murdered me, and I will leave the farm free of rats for a time, there will always be more rats." And then he begged the crow to watch the farm, to protect it from the rats, to guard his humans.

I had been listening this whole time, perched on the branch above her head as she was swinging. It was a bad perch, smooth and wide and prone to lurch back and forth under my feet, but I did not wish to interrupt her.

Until then.

I flew down and landed in the dirt under the swing next to her.

I said:

"No," the crow told the dog. "I will not guard against the rats, who are not evil and only wish to live their lives, and who suffer enough already. Nor will I guard the humans, who put out the poison that murders you, and whom you would never blame for what has happened to you, although it is undeniably their fault."

"But they didn't mean to," the dog whimpered.

"They meant something," *the crow said. "They meant to kill. And they will be saddened that that they have killed you—but it will not stop them from doing it again. Not in the slightest. They will say that now that the dog is gone, they will have to set out even more poison and traps, and bring in the cats. And I can never countenance anyone who supposes that the correct answer is to increase the number of cats sauntering about."*

And then I waited for the girl's response.

She stared at me consideringly, not seeing me as a crow as much as she saw the story, and happened to be staring in my direction. "Papa wants me to think it was poison because that is what he thinks. But it was *not* poison, it was a spell. Mama says that Mr. Dog was old, and needed to rest, but that was another lie, too. Grandmother on the phone said that Mr. Dog was in Heaven, but I'm not sure how she would know, so that must be a lie, too."

"A spell," I said. "How do you know that?"

"Mama does cooking magic. Sometimes it smells like pumpkin pie, and those are the good spells. Sometimes it smells like chemicals, and those are the bad ones. The whole house smelled bad yesterday. And now Mr. Dog is dead, and his breath smells just like the bad spell."

"Hm," I said. "That *is* suspicious."

"What should I do, Mr. Crow?"

I did not know what I know now, but that does not excuse what I said then: "Wait and see. Your mother may have cast the spell on purpose, or there may have been an accident. We all tell stories about the world, the way we wish it to be seen. Perhaps that's all it is."

"We lie, you mean."

"No," I said. "We tell stories. They are not true, yes, but they are not true for a reason that is not just not wanting to be punished. Spanked. They make us special, they tell us that some things are good and others are bad. They give us hope and ease from pain. They tell us that we are brave and noble. And those things benefit everybody, when they are believed. A lie is very selfish, and it makes everyone worse, whether it is found out or not. A story is generous, and keeps us from despair."

She looked into the distance toward the barn where the cows were, where her dog had died. "I think Grandma is telling a story about Heaven. And Mama is lying about Mr. Dog needing to rest."

I cleared my throat. Despite my noble words, I had my doubts about you, even then. "I think I agree with you."

"You are a crow." The chains creaked incessantly. She often came there to think, and she was thinking then, traveling nowhere yet thinking so hard that she was leaving her childhood behind as she kicked up the dry dust.

"I am."

"Can all crows talk?" Her eyes were following me now.

I bowed. "No. But all crows speak the language of stories."

"Is that true? Or just a story?"

"You shall have to come and visit us and find out, someday."

"Someday I will run away from home," she said. "And then I will come visit you before I follow my destiny." She frowned. "Destiny is a story, isn't it?"

I bowed again, and flew up over her head, and out of view. She had many things to think about, as did I; I had great many things to discuss with Old Loyolo and the other elders. Perhaps it was because Facunde loved another and I never took a mate; at any rate, I suddenly thought to myself then, *if I had chicks, I would like them to be as cynical and as wise as that girl, as full of stories, as perceptive of lies.*

In the cold snow, then, I questioned her as though I were her sire: "If you aren't going to keep it, what are you going to do with it?"

The girl twisted her lips. It was deep night by then, the deepest kind of night, where the storms cover the sky and the snow stalks through the air, looking for prey. Between the cast of the light and the cold, her lips were turning a greenish-orangish blue. We needed to find her better shelter, now that the terror of fleeing the Crouga had passed. The trunk of a junked-out car, an inside-out tractor tire covered with plywood and held down with rope.

"I want—" the girl said, but then Facunde interrupted her, pinching on her ear until it turned pink.

"I want to tell you a story first," Facunde said. "Before you make up your mind."

"Is it a long story?" the girl asked.

"No," Facunde said. "It is short. Very short."

"All right," said the girl.

12. Lord of Pigs

It was the pigs that told me that Uncle Chuck was dead.

I was just a kid, no more than seven or eight. Maybe ten. We were staying overnight and Grandma and Grandpa's house for some reason. Mostly we drove there in the morning and drove back at night on the roller-coaster hills, Dad always driving too fast, the snake of dust from the gravel roads shouting out that we were coming, we were coming from miles away. By the time we'd go home, it was dark and I'd sleep.

But like I said, we were staying overnight, Uncle Chuck in his room, Mom and Dad in the guest room, and my brother and I in the baby's old room, which I guess would have made it Uncle Chuck's, when he was little, anyway the one that was full from top to bottom with craft stuff, mostly paint-on dish towels, which you could smell all night long, the smell of those little tubes of paint with pen balls at the tip, so the paint would come out in a thin line, following a pattern that you ironed onto the towel in black ink. I wasn't too good at following the lines.

So, surrounded by all those stacks of you-can't-do-it-right ghosts, with my brother sleeping up on the tiny, creaky bed and me on a stack of blankets on the floor, with the darkness under the bed staring me in the face all night long, I didn't sleep too well. Smell of paint, smell of dust, smell of dusty paint, smell of pigs.

You could smell pigs everywhere on Grandma and Grandpa's farm, because Uncle Chuck raised them.

When I was growing up, I was proud of being able to smell shit without pulling my shirt up over my nose: that was for town kids. So was being afraid of seeing animals being butchered, turned into meat. We knew where food came from. The garden, filling jar after jar of canned corn, applesauce, strawberry jam. Tomato sauce, ground up in a tin food grinder that you turned one way to make the sauce, the other way to scrape the screen clean.

And the axe.

The pigs talked all the time, in grunts. At night they were quieter, but they still talked.

Grandma and Grandpa had the loudest damned clock, that chuffed when it ticked, and it chimed all night long. It was past two in the morning, and I was staring into the darkness under the bed. My brother was sleeping.

I heard a clack from someone's door, and I thought somebody must be getting up to go pee. This was after Grandma and Grandpa put in an indoor bathroom—I can remember having to bathe in a tin bathtub—but sometimes the boys went outside to pee anyway, so I wasn't too surprised when the floor creaked all the way through the house, and the front door opened, and the screen door opened, then clattered shut.

The geese honked, one at first, then all six of them. Those geese were better than guard dogs, but they knew Uncle Chuck, so it was just because they were annoyed to be bothered so early in the morning.

I counted to five hundred, and he didn't come back.

I kept counting, but I lost track when I realized that the pigs had gone quiet.

They'd been quiet a while by the time I figured out that they were the sound I was missing, and I suddenly got it in my head that they had eaten him.

No lie. That's the kind of mind I have. Once the thought got into my head, I couldn't stop it from going around and around. I was always having horrible nightmares; when I was six I used to wet the bed, which was one of the reasons that I was on the floor on blankets (one of which was pink and wooly and scratched even through the old blue-flowered sheet on top), because they could be washed. And the thought was in my head that Uncle Chuck had gone out to go feed his pigs and had slipped into the pen, and the pigs had eaten him, and that idea wasn't going to come out.

I didn't want to get up, but I did. I rolled the blankets off me, one inch at a time, and snaked my foot onto the bare, painted floor. The floor was white, chipped, and cold, and felt tacky under my bare feet. Every time I picked up a foot, it sounded like ripping off a bandaid, no matter how slowly I did it.

The great secret of my childhood was that I knew how to open doors quietly. It doesn't seem like a big deal now, but it was then: I knew that I'd mastered something special. I leaned on the door in the frame, then turned the handle, which was just as thickly covered in paint as everything else in that room. Noplace else in the house had been painted that much; noplace else had paint directly on the floor. But that room did.

The handle turned with just the barest, secretest scrape, which I was sure was covered up by the sound of that damned clock. I pulled the door open a crack. I had intended to just listen for a few seconds, but the clock was so loud I was scared of it waking up my brother, so I opened the door just enough to go out, and slid around the corner so fast that my nightgown got caught on the latch plate, and I had to let go of the handle in a hurry, and it clacked anyway.

I froze, and the phrase is, "My heart was in my mouth," but I didn't know it then, and that's not how it felt. It felt like my heart was going to explode in my chest. When you're afraid as an adult, there's a flash of coldness that goes starts on the backs of your hands, that squeezes and freezes you all at the same time, but as a kid, it's your heart. It feels like you're going to die, when you're that scared. We never feel that scared again, but we never forget what it's like. I think we're convinced that that's what death is like, like being as scared as you were as a kid, convinced over the stupidest little things that you are, no shit, going to die.

The clock kept chuffing, and, from inside Grandma and Grandpa's room, their little white fat dog, Radar, wheezed loudly twice, then went back to sleep. Or it could have been that he died of a heart attack, which is what I thought for just a moment, then dismissed: I could only be afraid of so many things at a time, and my heart just wouldn't take any more dread then. I had to know about Uncle Chuck; therefore, I couldn't know about Radar. In my heart, I wanted to believe that everyone was dead, everyone in the whole house, or even in the whole world. How was I supposed to know? Where were these people? Maybe it was all a dream: I was asleep, having a nightmare about wondering whether Uncle Chuck had been eaten by the pigs. Or else I was having a nightmare that I was somebody else entirely, and I had never been myself; my whole life was a nightmare leading up to that point; or else I was in a horror movie, just some stupid extra little kid, a horror movie about the pigs eating people, bursting out of their cages and slaughtering our whole family, one after the other, in revenge for having their families eaten every year. It would have been justice.

I could have tried to go back to bed. I could have tried to talk myself out of it. In horror movies, the characters look, they always look where they shouldn't look, they know it, but they have to look anyway. They do it because that's what we're really like. Stupid.

That was me, turning the handle all the way, pulling the door tight, then slowly releasing the handle so it didn't clack. That was me, shifting my weight carefully from foot to foot on the barenubbins carpet that was all colors of the rainbow but mostly black, onto the linoleum tiles, into the rag-rug entryway past the bathroom.

The light was bright enough to see everything, because there was moonlight everywhere. Not just coming through the windows. I remember it as being everywhere, bright, without shadows. That's probably just my imagination, but that's how it was: light so bright and thick that it bounced off the white, gold-flecked kitchen table and filled up the room. That was it. It wasn't bright in the living room, but it was, in the kitchen. It must have been the white tile, the white walls, the white table. Just a bunch of moonlight bouncing around.

The entryway was bright, too, because the door was open. The screen door, being on springs, was shut, but the winter door was wide open.

I shivered. There wasn't a breeze that I can remember, but the air had leaked in through the door, thick like the moonlight, and it was chilly out there. If anybody else had been awake, they would have yelled at Uncle Chuck for leaving the door open, letting out the heat. They wouldn't start up the furnace until the end of October, no matter what weather came before them—at least, that's what Grandma would say, and Grandpa would just grunt with a smile on his face. If it got cold enough, she would complain that he wasn't listening to her, when she'd told him to light the furnace early this year, and he'd light it when she wasn't looking.

I slipped into somebody's boots, probably Grandpa's. They were too big for me but too small for him. The leather had been stretched tight. You could see every bulge of his foot in the shape of the boot. There were patches where flakes of mud had fallen off: cleaner in the middle of each patch, lines to show where the edge of the mud had dried. The mud on Grandpa's farm was dark, but weak. When you stirred that mud into water, it didn't look like coffee, and it didn't look like chocolate. It looked like a blackboard that hadn't been washed in a while.

Not the best land for farming, but it was what they had. I think Uncle Chuck did better with the pigs than Grandpa ever did with the farm.

I also put on a coat, my coat, which was pink and stuffed in squares, and dirty, and had worn places just under my wrists from me leaning on things, and never felt warm enough, but I had to wear it, damn it, because it was the one I'd wanted, begged for, and Mom wouldn't let me get a different one. It didn't matter that the one I'd wanted had been purple with paisley on it, and that she'd told me we couldn't get it (it was probably too expensive). What was important was that it was the story that would make her feel like I deserved to be cold and miserable, and that it wasn't her fault, for marrying a farmer and living her dream to be a farm wife. We all change the story to fit what we think what should have been, but it was the way she did it, and the way it hurt me, that I noticed first. Grandma's shifting stories, I didn't notice until later, and they never really hit home the same way, so I never resented her for what I saw as Mom's pure, self-serving lies.

Now I know better. Now I know that Mom couldn't have faced the idea that she'd failed everyone, that it was her dream that was holding us all in place, that it was her insistence that Dad stayed farming when he didn't really love it as much as anything else that kept him there. I doubt she'll ever drink from that cup, and I doubt that she ever should. Me, I'm not like that. That cup full of fear and self-loathing and horror, I go looking for that cup. I feel baptized by it. I crave being able to tear myself apart, from time to time, like some people like to go to the chiropractor, just to hear their bones snap.

I thought about putting on a hat, but I didn't see one, except for Grandpa's greasy cap, so greasy I couldn't tell you whether it was a sports team or a tractor brand on it. I remember my dad running around with John Deere caps all summer long, riding tractors. But Grandpa, I'm not so sure. I can still smell it, though: the sourness of bearing grease, that came in long tubes like caulk (so you had to check to make sure that you handed Dad the right tube), sweat, and the sweetness of engine oil, like grape jelly mixed with cough syrup. It's a smell that I knew and loved, but I also knew that I didn't want to put that hat on, because it would stick to my hair. Disgusting.

I opened the screen door as narrowly as I could and slipped out sideways onto the concrete front step. The moonlight was even brighter outside, of course, but at the time it shocked me. It was impossible that I wasn't dreaming.

I went past the iron boot scraper, down the four stairs, past the long, bare planks of the cellar door, and towards the pig barn.

The geese were waiting for me, wide awake. They were moon-geese. I was terrified of those geese. They didn't honk then, thank God. They hissed at me, and two big, fat tears rolled down my cheeks. I wanted to run away. All the advice that people had given me about those geese welled up in my mouth. I wanted to spit from fear and anger at all that stupid advice that didn't work. Don't run. Don't act like you're afraid, or they'll bite you.

I had no bravery for that kind of thing, to calmly walk through a bunch of shining white geese that were after my blood, to attack anyone who tried to get onto their parts of the farm. You could go out in the shelterbelt of trees, out into the mazes of long, rustling, sword-sharp grass across the road, but the hell if you tried to go close to the pig barns. You had to run past them as fast as you could and climb up onto the hay bales and swing a stick at the geese until someone yelled at them to knock it off, and even then they would stand back and hiss at you when they thought nobody else was looking.

I was some other kind of kid, not the brave kind, so I said, "Please let me go. I have to see what happened to Uncle Chuck." Like they were moon-geese for real, and all I had to do was ask.

Here was the first miracle: they did.

I walked straight toward the pig barns with three on one side and three on the other, and they hissed at me. I was shaking, with my fingers curled up around the sleeves of my coat and my nightgown swishing around my legs, my legs swishing as the dry skin on my knees scraped against each other. I regretted putting on those boots. I wouldn't ever be able to run, not in those boots. They thumped every time I took a step on the bare, dry ground, because they would start to fall off every time. The air was cold in my mouth, and my breath steamed.

I walked across the yard, following the dirt path that led from the house to the fence that marked the edge of the pig pens. I didn't look back, but I felt like the geese were following me, step by step, ready to bite me the second I hesitated. I could hear them behind me, getting further and further away, but I didn't actually believe it. I got to the gate, which was red-painted wood, and climbed over it. I had trouble at the top, trying to sort out my nightgown and the loose boots, but I eventually got down the other side. The geese were all in a group again, right where I'd left them.

The pigs were talking again, but it sounded different.

Normally, at night, they were all outside, and on a moonlit night, you could see them sigh in their sleep: a big inhale, a sudden exhale. They would snort and mumble and shift around, like little kids who didn't want to go to sleep. Some of them would stand at their food trough all night, as far as I could tell, just so they could be first when Uncle Chuck came to feed them in the morning.

That night, they weren't. I could hear them, mostly making soft, repeating snorts, like the chuffing of the clock, except sometimes I could hear a long sigh, too.

I walked on the packed dirt between the metal wire of the smaller pens to the door of the first barn. The door was shut, but not latched.

I grabbed onto the handle with both hands, which was not as cold as I'd expected, and jerked on it, but it was too heavy for me. The door was one of those big sliding affairs, and the bottom dragged in the dirt, and I was seven or eight or ten or whatever.

I took a deep breath, held it, and jerked on the handle with all my strength. My breath came out of me in a grunt. The door barely twitched; it shifted a little in its track, maybe half an inch, then rolled back into the wall of the barn with a clonk.

The pigs went silent again.

I heard footsteps coming closer to the door, dragging through straw.

"Uncle Chuck? Is that you? Are you okay?" I leaned my head on the door, which, too, wasn't as cold as I'd been expecting it to be. "You haven't been eaten, have you?"

Something heavy thumped into the door, and the bottom of it slid out a couple of inches. I jumped back. From the bottom crack of the door, a pig's nose stuck out, pale pink. That side of the barn was in shadow, but I remember the nose being touched by moonlight anyway, the hairs of it sparkling. That was probably another memory, from another night. But that's how I remember it.

The nose sniffed, the edges of it curling and twitching.

The pig grunted, it sounded like a question.

"Uncle Chuck?" I said. "Are you in there?"

The pig kept sniffing around. I started to cry.

Back then, I would cry over everything. I would cry over anything. People would make fun of me for being a crybaby. To this day, I can't cry without feeling like I've made a fool of myself. Even at funerals, with cold eyes looking at me, as if to say that if I believed in heaven more, I'd cry less, and tears made me a sinner. I do still cry, though, no matter how much I wish that I didn't have to, that people and sadness couldn't make me.

The pig grunted again and slammed into the door, which bounced outward, caught on a rock, and stuck open at the bottom. Not much, but maybe just enough for a little kid like me to get through.

That was the second miracle.

The pig's nose reappeared for a second, and grunted a question at me.

I took step by shivering step toward the door.

The closer I got, the worse it smelled.

I had never wanted to cover up my nose like some stupid town kid before, but I wanted to then. I didn't. I didn't want to be rude.

And then I was on my hands and knees in the dirt, crawling through the hole of the pushed-out door. The dirt went from dry and cracked into sharp pieces on the outside, to a line of wet mud that I knew was full of pig shit, to clean straw. Clean-ish. Cleaner than I expected. Pieces of it were still gold-colored. I don't know why I didn't notice it before, but the lights were on. I should have seen the glow through the windows, which were only green, corrugated plastic that matched the silver corrugated walls of the pig barns, that let in a glow of light but nothing to look at, that were so dirty anyway that you probably wouldn't have noticed whether it was day or night, if you were a pig. But I never really noticed anything, back then. I still have this idea that I can't. Notice things, that is. But what it is, is that I don't notice the same things as other people. The things I notice used to get a circle drawn in the air around somebody's head: cuckoo. And the things I didn't notice used to get a circle drawn in the air, too. But now I know, nobody notices everything.

I'm the only one who noticed when the pigs stopped talking. And that wasn't cuckoo at all.

I finished scooting through the crack, with my nightgown getting drug all through the dirt and the mud and the straw and doing nothing but getting caught under my knees as I tried to crawl forward, and got to my feet like a little kid, both hands on the floor until I had my feet under me. Then I brushed off the front of my nightgown like a fool. It wasn't coming clean; imagine that. I think I smeared more on from my hands than I scraped off.

My guts were in knots. Luckily, my nose was already numb by that point. The smell was so bad that it was fading and leaving tingling behind. I didn't want to look up, so I brushed the front of my nightgown again, pointlessly. I knew I had to stop, I knew I had to look up. I knew I couldn't.

I heard a soft grunt in front of me, and then the squealing of a younger pig, maybe even a piglet. Not in pain, but just yelling. Like it was saying, "No, no, no!" Like a little kid throwing a temper tantrum.

To this day, I blame the parents when I hear a temper tantrum. Wherever I go, I hear kids pitching a fit, I blame the parents.

You.

I blame you.

Did you forget what it was like to be a kid?

That constant, raw pain?

It's you throwing the fit, but you're throwing that fit by picking on your kid until they lose it.

Really, what you want to have happen: your kids look at you one day, they could be six years old, they could be six days and still shitting themselves, and they say, "Wow, being a parent is hard, and I should be the one to make the compromise here."

Fuck that. Fuck that for a stinking pile of pig shit.

I can't tell you how many times I've heard a kid try to get their parents' attention, get ignored, try a little harder, get ignored, try a little harder, get ignored…right up to the point where they break down and cry. And get yelled at, because they don't understand why your fucking coffee selection is more important than they are.

When you're a kid and that happens, you think, this means they don't love me anymore.

Your heart breaks. You're a kid. You don't understand.

That was the sound coming from that piglet.

I looked up. I couldn't help it.

I closed my eyes before I could see, I could really see what was there, but it was too late. It was on the inside of my eyelids, burned in. It was spinning around in my head. It was there, and I couldn't get it out, I knew I wouldn't be able to get it out, and it would be better to see it than to hope it would go away. Just like looking into the darkness under my brother's little bed. It's better to see what's there than what you imagine.

Uncle Chuck was on the floor of the pig barn. The pigs should have all been outside, or locked up in their pens, but they weren't. Some of the gates were just standing open; others were twisted up and pushed out. Some of the latches had torn out of the wood; some of the big squares of wire had just been pulled up and out of the way.

The pigs were surrounding him, mostly.

Big ones, little ones. Their hair sparkled in the wire-cage lights overhead. Black hair on pink pigs, white hair on black pigs, all mixed up. I didn't know them all—we weren't allowed to hang around the pig barn too long—but I recognized the one who had let them in. He was standing next to me still. Pink, all over pink, with just a little bit of mud around his feet, and some in one long streak along his side, where he'd pushed open the door for me.

My legs shook, and he leaned against them. I stumbled sideways for a second, then clomped back close to him, leaning into him as much as he leaned into me.

The grunting started up again, I think from a big female who was laying on her side, toward the wall. Her side heaved, making her rows of nipples jiggle. It sounded just like she was crying.

Uncle Chuck was in the middle of them, in the middle of the floor. He was this big blue blur, from his overalls. One of the larger pigs was shoving a smaller one toward Uncle Chuck, and the little one didn't want to go.

Uncle Chuck's skin was the color of a fresh-scrubbed pink pig; he wasn't wearing a shirt or a jacket with his overalls. In the middle of the smears of blue and of pinkness were streaks of red.

I took the backs of my hands and wiped them across my eyes. I was having trouble breathing. My body wasn't remembering to breathe, so I had to do it, but I couldn't seem to remember how to do it, either, so mostly my breath just jiggled back and forth in my lungs. Tears of snot started to run out the end of my nose. My face was wet, but I could only tell because tears were running off my chin and into the neck of my jacket, cold streaks going down my chest.

I lowered my hands and sniffed hard about a thousand times, and the snot went down my throat.

The older pig pushed the little one up to Uncle Chuck's body, the little pig shaking its head the whole time, squealing louder and louder, so loud I thought it would wake up everybody in the house. But the older pig pushed it right up to Uncle Chuck's body, to his shoulder, where there was a long smear of blood that was already starting to turn flaky and fall off around the edges, like mud off a boot.

The pig beside me nudged me on the back of the knee, and I knew what it wanted.

I…I walked forward, shuffling in those too-big boots.

Uncle Chuck's feet were bare; he'd walked out here in bare feet. Muddy.

My eyes felt heavy, like I was going to fall asleep before I got there. I kept forgetting to breathe, then I'd gasp, and the smell would feel like a taste, a shitty taste. My mouth wouldn't shut, but the sides of my jaw ached and ached and ached. I stumbled forward until I was next to the piglet, and I dropped to my knees, and I picked him up and hugged him to my chest.

He went all the way across my chest, from one side to the other, and stuck out over the sides. His split hooves where sharp. He tried to run away, but I wouldn't let go, and he scratched up the tops of my legs trying to escape. I leaned back so his feet would scrape mostly on the bottom of my coat instead of on my nightgown.

After a while he settled down and buried his snout in the armpit of my coat, and I scratched his back. The hair got up under my chewed-off fingernails and hurt, but it felt good, too. I was crying, and he was grunting with me. He took his snout out from my armpit and put it up by my ear, sniffing me, and the edges of his snout curled around and under my ear. I pet him a few more times, then let him down.

He stood next to me, shivering.

I looked at Uncle Chuck, I guess really looked at him for the first time.

His eyes were open. I know it couldn't have been true, but the way I remember it, his eyes were black like beads, all the way across, with long black lashes over them, that curled just at the ends. His beard covered most of his face. Underneath it, though, his cheeks were white, just plain white, not pink or red like usual. White like a doll's. I reached one hand past the little piglet and touched his cheek. It was warm, but it didn't move right. You touched Uncle Chuck on the cheek, and he smiled. He looked at you and smiled.

If you were sad, he picked you up and sat you on his knee and made fun of you and laughed with you and told you stupid jokes that weren't even funny. If you were sad, he heard you. If you were mad, he heard you, he might tease you, he might roll his eyes at you, but he heard you.

I brushed my hand across his beard. I didn't want to say it, in case my little brother heard, but I knew that he was Santa, too. He'd put on a Santa outfit and put powered sugar in his beard and his hair and show up at the back door with a black plastic trash bag full of presents, and if you'd say, "But who's bringing Uncle Chuck's presents?" the rest of the adults would shush you, in the middle of the smells of spiced apple cider and chili and oyster stew, in the middle of eating too many piped cookies covered in sugar, in the middle of fighting with everyone over the olives stuck on the outside of the cheese logs.

The pig that had been pushing the little one over to Uncle Chuck's body sighed a long sigh, shook herself all over, and lay on the floor with her feet sticking out. I petted the little one again.

Uncle Chuck was covered all over with bites, mostly on his arms, but one big one on his foot that left his little toe hanging sideways.

I leaned over to Uncle Chuck's face, with one hand on either side of his head, and kissed him on the cheek. His skin felt like someone had put wax all over it, like a candle. Or—cold grease. Cold lard.

He smelled like pigs.

Not like pig shit. Like pigs, like the warm skin of them, but going cold.

I couldn't bite him, not like the pigs had. I didn't have the right teeth. I didn't have the right kind of heart.

The little pig next to me, still shivering, took two shaky steps closer to Uncle Chuck and nipped him on the arm, not a wholehearted bite, just a little nip. And then he ran, squealing, back into one of the pens that had the wire all bent out of shape.

My eyes were flooded over again; I couldn't see. But I knew that…I knew, I didn't want to know. I stood up. Uncle Chuck didn't.

The pig who had let me in grunted a question at me, and I answered it like he could understand exactly what I was saying.

"They're going to kill you. You gotta get out of here."

I went over to the door and grabbed onto the inside handle, hoping that it would work better from the inside, but it didn't. I jerked and shoved on that door, my feet slipping in the straw, the door rocking but not moving anywhere. I just wasn't strong enough. And there wasn't anybody I could trust to help me, either.

And then I remembered the side door.

The side doors were where the people were supposed to go in and out of the pig barns. Pigs through the big doors, people through the sliding doors. But Uncle Chuck never used them, so I never thought about it, except in the sense of whether or not I could sneak through them, like a spy.

I found the door. You went through a gap between the pens to a cement ramp that led down from the human area to the pig area, or maybe up from the pig area to the human area, which was maybe only a couple of feet higher, but there it was, and there was the door, and up in the human area were big white-plastic tubs of pointy oats with their hulls still on, and some ground-up pellets that I think had vitamins and things in them, that smelled like chalk or maybe Vitamin C tablets, although that last bit could have just been my imagination.

The door was only latched with a wire latch with a pin that went through the door so you could open it from the other side if you had to, and when I unhooked it, the door swung open.

"Come on," I said. "You have to run away. As fast as you can. So they can't catch you. They'll kill you for biting him, they'll think you're crazy pigs or something."

At first, none of the pigs came to me, but then a few did. The other pigs looked at them nasty, but I ignored them. When the first pigs reached me, I walked with them out of the pig barn and into the yards. We walked all the way across the yards to the edge of the field.

It was very dark and cold now, and I was shivering hard. It seemed like the moonlight had gone all weak and lost its thickness; it was bright but far, far away.

The gate to the field was chained shut, and covered with barbed wire so the pigs wouldn't get out and wreck up the fields. I climbed over the fence okay but forgot to check before I jumped off the other side, and my nightgown ripped one long, unforgiveable rip that seemed to go on forever. One whole side had come off, up to my waist.

I didn't have time to mess with it, so I gave it a big jerk, which left me with a couple of loose flapping parts over my legs.

The last link of the chain was on a nail; I lifted it off and unwrapped the chain, trying to make sure my coat sleeves didn't get caught on anymore barbed wire. That chain got heavier and heavier the more of it I unwrapped, too. But finally it was done, and I dropped the whole heavy thing, which fell down along the black tarred log of the fencepost with a too-loud rattle. I froze.

One of the lights came up in the house.

Quickly, I grabbed onto the gate and pulled. The gate was a rigid, long piece of metal all welded together, but different types of wire had been added to it, from chicken wire to square metal fencing to barbed wire. I tried to keep my fingers between the barbs, but it didn't always work out.

"Chuck?" someone called.

I jerked harder, but it wasn't moving much. It hadn't been opened for a long time; there was mud built up all around it.

"Help me," I whispered. "Push!"

That was the third miracle.

The pigs dug their snouts into it, pushed their sides into it, and pushed, grunting from the barbs poking into them, but doing it anyway.

As soon as the gate was wide enough, I dropped it and whispered, "Good enough! Please go, please hurry!"

And the pigs started running out of the gate. A couple of them tried to push ahead in line, but they got bitten, and the pigs started pouring out of the pig yard and into the field, like they were marching.

The front door opened, and my Grandma yelled, "Chuck! You out there? I think something's got into the pigs. Chuck!"

But that wasn't the worst part; Grandpa's shadow was coming up behind her, and I could see that he had something long in his arms. A shotgun, probably.

It seemed like a lot of pigs went running through the gate, but also not enough.

The geese woke up and started honking to beat all hell, and Grandpa shouted at them, but they didn't stop. I hoped they were getting in his way, but I didn't dare look.

As soon as the last of the pigs went through, I went back inside and clomped toward the barn. I hoped that Grandpa wouldn't shoot me. He was already walking across the grass to the barns.

He saw me.

"Deanna? What are you doing out here? Did you let all those pigs out? Chuck is going to skin your hide if you're messing around out here."

I ran.

I almost tripped on the two cement steps up to the people-door on the pig barn, but I made it in and ran down the ramp to the pig area. The smell hit me again, about at the same time that remembering hit me, and I couldn't see for a second, just blurs. I blinked it all back. I couldn't cry then. Most of the pigs were gone. The little one was gone, even though I hadn't seen him go by. Good. But the one who had let me in, the big mamma, and a few more were still there.

"He's coming with a gun. You have to go, you have to go…"

But they didn't seem to see me anymore. I wasn't a person, I was just a human. Their eyes were flat beads, dead. Stupid.

Exactly the kind of crazy animals that would chew up a dead guy.

I backed up slowly.

I wasn't exactly afraid that they would hurt me.

I knew they would, but only if I pushed my luck. I wasn't a part of it anymore. What was happening, I didn't know what it meant, I didn't know why they were doing it. I only knew that they would do it, no matter what I did.

Grandpa appeared in the people doorway. "Deanna! Get back out of—"

He gasped.

I would have, too.

The big, fat sow got to her feet, her flesh shaking like a fat lady's. She walked over to Uncle Chuck, bit into him, gripped down, and pulled backward against him, shaking her head back and forth. The skin on his arm bulged out like a tent. The place where one of the other pigs had bitten before started to tear, and then…a big hunk of his skin ripped off, leaving…stuff behind.

Grandpa lowered the shotgun at her, and I pressed back against the wall.

The pig who had let me in squealed a crazy squeal, jumped in the air, and ran around in circles around the body, thumping into the cages, running over the top of Uncle Chuck's body, digging gouges into his skin. The big fat-lady pig dropped Uncle Chuck's skin onto his arm, then started stalking toward us.

"Come here, Deanna."

I edged along the wall. Grandpa stepped forward, expecting me to go out the door behind him, but I grabbed his arm, making the front of the shotgun go up and down.

"Stop it," he said.

"Don't shoot Uncle Chuck!" I cried.

"He's—" He shook my arm off, but I grabbed it again.

"Don't shoot them! They're just pigs! They don't know you're not supposed to eat people!"

Grandpa lowered his shotgun again. The big fat-lady pig was coming up the ramp toward us, one heavy leg after another. I could hear her breath wheezing. The more she walked, the harder it was for her to keep walking.

"Please run," I begged. "Please run away."

She shook her head just like she understood me, her ears flapping back and forth on her neck. She stopped, tried to turn around a little and grunted.

The other pig stopped running across Uncle Chuck and watched her.

She grunted again. She had blood on her snout and all the way across one cheek. On her teeth. I wanted to tell her, so she could wipe it off.

She grunted again.

Grandpa fired the shotgun at her, and she screamed.

Somewhere in there, I closed my eyes and prayed that I wouldn't have to look. Grandpa fired again. Instead of screaming, she made this sucking noise that was probably worse than anything I could have seen, but then I couldn't open my eyes anymore. I couldn't look. I was kneeling on the cement, and it was cold on my knees, and it hurt, because it wasn't smooth. Something was digging into my knees, but that was all right, I always had at least a scab on one or the other of them. I was dizzy, so I put my hands on the cement, too. I felt tiny rocks that had been mixed up in the cement, that felt like Braille, like I was blind and trying to read a book made of gravel. You know. But I could feel mud and shit, too, both dry and wet. Mostly dry, flaky. The shit was flakier than the mud, that's how you knew what it was, when you couldn't see. I was crying. I might have been crying out loud. I was shut up inside my own head, and I wasn't coming out. My lips were sealed together, I could feel them stuck together. If anyone was going to open them, it wasn't going to be me.

That was the fourth miracle. And if it wasn't much of a miracle, it was what I needed for those few seconds, until I smelled the blood.

I smelled it, and then I had to look.

The fat-lady pig wasn't dead yet. She had…she had a hole in her throat, the edges were moving as she breathed, blood was squishing out of her like a hose that was almost turned off and your mom was about to yell at you, and when she breathed out, the blood sprayed out and splattered the concrete and it splattered my nightgown.

I was already on my hands and knees, so it wasn't hard to crawl towards her.

I think Grandpa said, "Stay back," but I didn't understand what he'd said until later, after it was too late.

Those rows and rows of nipples were shaking. The bottom ones were covered with blood, that made a miniature swimming pool all along one side before streaming out from under her bottom leg and running the rest of the way down the ramp.

The other pig was still there, frozen.

"Run," I said. "Go away. Shoo pig, shoo." I flapped one hand at it, then finished crawling toward the fat-lady pig.

Her side was hot. Her blood was hot on my knees. She flinched when I accidentally rubbed one of the places that the shotgun pellets had punched into her. I found a good place and laid my hand on it. She went up to my chest, she was so big. Her legs were bent out of the way. I laid my head on her shoulder, on a good place, as gently as I could.

She couldn't make grunting noises anymore, but her side was quivering, up and down, like she was crying.

I think she was in love with Uncle Chuck. I don't mean—well. As a kid, I didn't think about things like that, and I think less of myself for it even crossing my mind. I think—she was willing to die for him. It was either that, or she was willing to die so the rest of the pigs could get away, or at least try to get away. It was love, either way.

I heard the click of metal on metal, and then Grandpa tried to lift me away, but I wouldn't let go, and I cried "no, no, no," and maybe he had a change of heart, but anyway, he left me there.

The fat-lady pig's feet tried to run, but they were only twitching. I felt her head move and looked: her mouth was opening and closing.

The sucking noise stopped.

Her eye looked at me.

And then it didn't move at all, and it wasn't looking at me at all. It wasn't until after that that, that her feet and mouth stopped moving. By then her eye was drier, and it didn't sparkle.

I looked up.

The other pig was gone, and Grandpa had gotten down on the ground next to Uncle Chuck somehow, and was talking to him, but not out loud, just under his breath, like he was cussing him out or something.

I heard the geese honking outside, and Grandma yelling, and then my dad showed up in the door, and then I really did get picked up and carried back to the house, the big boots dropping off my feet into the grass as I hugged my dad. They made me take a bath in cold water for some reason.

And it still wasn't morning after all that, so they told me to go lie down on my bed of blankets again, dressed in a shirt and underwear was all. My brother was awake, but there was nobody saying he should go back to sleep; it was pointless. So they put me alone, in that room, in the dark.

I could have lay on the bed, but I didn't.

I lay on the floor tucked between two sheets and sandwiched between piles of blankets. It was cold again; I'd been gone long enough for the blankets to get as cold as though I'd never been in them.

An ambulance came.

I heard someone shouting at the pigs, and one gunshot, but I didn't think they got anybody.

I heard a tractor start up, and the water run through the pipes, and the sound of coffee bubbling in the pot, sounding wheezy and sucky, like the fat-lady pig.

I heard footsteps everywhere, and the voices of strangers.

The light got brighter and brighter, until finally I could see under the bed, where my arm was getting cold from being out from under the blankets for so long, reaching out for something.

I closed my eyes. There was nothing under there. I was finally ready to go to sleep.

I felt a touch on my hand, a sniffing, the edges of a snout curling against my palm, and then it was gone.

I hope that Uncle Chuck went to pig heaven. "Hog heaven." For years, every time I heard that phrase, I thought of him. Even as my need for the story of it faded, I still held the idea of it close.

They caught some of the pigs, but not the one who had let me in. I think. That's another story that I want to believe: that there will always be wild pigs running around in that country, getting into crops, chasing off dogs and coyotes, making mischief.

"That was not a short story, not at all," the girl said. "Why did you tell it to me?"

Facunde shrugged, ruffling the feathers on her shoulders as though it were as warm as a summer's day instead of nearly a blizzard. "To pass the time, that was all."

"You never tell stories *just* to pass the time. None of you. Except that young crow guy. He might just want someone to listen to him. The rest of *you* are all telling stories to get me to do something."

Facunde stretched her neck and riffled through her feathers. "How *vain*," she said. "To think that every story has to do with *you*." But she wasn't fooling anybody, least of all the girl.

Enough time had passed that the sky had begun to think about turning into morning, and our bellies had begun to think about turning into begging chicks fresh from the egg. "Well, no matter what you say, I'm going to take the bead to Mother's house," the girl said. "I'm going to take it there and let it eat her up."

"It's *you* that'll be eaten up," Facunde said. "And you shouldn't be murdering your mother."

"Oh?" the girl asked. "Then who should be? She's killing my baby brother and used a spell on Papa that ran him off the road and killed him, too, and she's killed my dog, and she'd kill all of you in a heartbeat if she weren't busy with my brother."

I felt the sky calling to me. The girl's house—your house—wasn't far away. I danced from foot to foot, I hopped up, fluttered once, and landed.

Almost too late, almost too late, whispered a voice in my head. *Go now. Now!*

I cawed and leapt up into the blowing snow. I flapped desperately to get my bearings in the ground storm, rose above the worst of the wind, and flew quickly toward your house, tall and white in the darkness, a kind of fortress against the snow.

Quickly, quickly!

By the time I had reached the house, dawn was breaking. I hopped to the place on the roof where the air from the kitchen sometimes pours out, to see if I could smell anything foul, but there was nothing. Not then. I peered through the windows at you, and you were sleeping with almost the stillness of the dead.

The babe's crib was filled with shadows.

At first I called myself a foolish chick, to have panicked: simply because a girl issues vague warnings does not mean that all crowdom was about to be attacked!

But I found myself affixed to the window outside the babe's room, staring within, unable to look away: the room had been painted pale orange, and there was a quilt on the wall, which was made of blocks with pictures of angels on it, childlike angels with fat, baby faces. The crib was under the quilt and against the wall; a changing table stood nearby, stacked with cloths on its shelves. The floor was wood, the lights were darkened. Within the crib was only shadow, a small dangling toy hanging over the pit, as though waiting to be looked at, played with. Perhaps, I thought, the girl was wrong, and the babe was untouched. But I had watched you a great deal through your dusty windows, and I knew that it was a lie that I was telling to myself.

And yet I could not fly away.

Instead, I found myself telling a tale under my breath…

13. The Edge of the World

There's not much difference between the real world and the land of fairies. Just take the number of assholes times ten. Bang! You're in fairyland.

When I said "no," Felix bound and gagged me, tied me onto the back of a prairie dragon, and flew me back to the Edge of the World anyway.

I watched the Edge coming up to meet me, the cottonwoods rustling louder than the dragon's feathers in the heavy wind. The dragon landed right on the Edge, about a thousand feet above the prairie below.

About a thousand fairies had come to see Roberto burnt to ashes. Some were dressed in feathers and quills, as if it were a powwow; others wore Air Force uniforms or business suits with bare feet. The only ways to tell that they weren't human were their ice-blue eyes, and they didn't scream in terror at the dragon. Only mortals scream in terror. It's a selfless act, a way of warning people to stay away or get their guns or whatever. Fairies are too self-involved for that.

I was still wearing my football jersey from practice. Felix cut the rope, and I rolled down the dragon's side and the ground knocked the wind out of me. Felix jumped down and cut my ropes; I had to tear the gag off myself. I couldn't believe they'd sent Felix. Then again, he'd been able to trick me long enough to cast the knockout spell on me when nobody else could have.

They'd laid Roberto's body on a platform made of rough, green pine branches they'd dragged in from Hermit Mountain, rising above the last hills of the Edge. Rick Chamberlain held a bough burning with blue fire, which he tossed onto the base of the platform. Yeah, they'd just been waiting for my feet to touch the ground before they torched him, to make it official.

As soon as I could stand up, I ran over to the man who had abducted me, eighteen human years ago, and spit on his face. I screamed obscenities at him, and, "Why did you do it? Why couldn't you leave me alone?" The man who had abducted me as a baby and held me prisoner in a razor-grass cage when I disobeyed him was dead, and the rest of them wanted me to take over his job.

Stealing kids.

The fire spread quick and hot, until the whole bier was black with smoke and sent sparks over the Edge. My last sight of Roberto was my spit running down his face, like a tear. And turning to steam.

Fucker.

"I won't do it," I said. "I'm a human now. I'm done playing fairy games. I'm done being a changeling. Done."

But they didn't understand, of course. Fairies don't have souls. It was like trying to talk to someone at the DMV.

Chamberlain stood with me beside the fire. Roberto's body collapsed, tipping and sliding between the larger branches, which fell onto the red-hot bones. Bodies burned quick once the heart was cut out, and they'd cast spells to keep the fire twice as hot as a glass-blowing oven, so it'd only taken a few hours, and spells to keep the fire from spreading. I couldn't leave; I wasn't about to walk back to Oregon, and I didn't have money or an ID with me.

Chamberlain was a big, dark-skinned guy who passed for as much as of a king out here as the fairies ever had. "A changeling picked you; you pick the next changeling. More than one, if you want. Pick one and we'll let you go."

"I won't," I said. We both had our arms crossed over our chests. Me, because I was cold, and Chamberlain because he was copying me, trying to make me feel more at ease. I'd heard he was working for a company's HR department, which, come on. Or maybe he was perfect for the job, I don't know.

"I know that you had difficulties with Roberto," Chamberlain said. "But that does not invalidate the tradition."

"Difficulties?!" I shouted. "Difficulties? The man raped me when I was eleven. As a birthday present. He deserved what he got."

Chamberlain rolled his long black hair into a knot to keep it out of his face. "He said it was a human custom."

"I'm not doing shit for you fuckers. You swore you'd leave me alone. Or doesn't it mean anything to the fairies if they don't keep their words anymore?"

"You should have died first," Chamberlain said. "You would have died a mortal death by the time Robert passed out of fairyland, but the girl killed him. I told you, 'I swear that as long as Roberto lives, you will never return to fairyland.' Roberto is dead. He picked no more changelings."

I shoved him. "Fuck Roberto! Let me go!"

Chamberlain stumbled backward toward the Edge of the World. I took another step forward and shoved him again, until he slid off. He stepped into the air, his suit jacket flapping in the breeze and exposing his naked chest.

I shook my fist at him. "Keep away from me!"

From behind me, Felix said, "You shouldn't get into fights at funerals."

I nearly jumped out of my skin, but I wasn't about to let him see that. "Fuck off, Felix," I said.

"Hey, boss?" Felix asked. He was wearing jeans and the t-shirt of a band that had never existed, chewing on a lollypop stick and peeling off the paper with his teeth. "You know that thing you said I should do if he said no again? I did it."

"Did what?" I said.

"Killed your parents," Felix said.

There I was, standing in fairy, where the sound of semis rushing by was replaced by the wails of ground lizards that burst out of the prairie to mate in the long grass. The prairie dragon was digging around, trying to find them. Its head lurched into the dirt, and it pulled a squirming lizard out of its tunnel tail-first.

Maybe it should have hit harder than it did, but I'd never known them. The only parent I'd known was Roberto, and he'd been one of *them*.

"I'm sorry," Chamberlain said. His hair came unbound and blew into his eyes again. "We didn't want you to come back, either. He died trying to collect another baby, so we'd never have to see you again."

"How did he even die?" I asked.

"The girl's family had one of the knives, as a keepsake from the East. She cut him down."

"And then what?" I said. "Did you have Felix kill her, too?"

Felix squatted down at the Edge and watched his dragon crunch up the last of its meal. "Against the rules," he said.

I snorted. "What do you even need babies for?"

Felix paced back and forth, flattening the dry grass that stretched between worlds. "To keep the link with the human world open."

"So, if I don't do this, you'll lose contact with the human world, and I'll never see you again?"

"Nah. There are lots of people like you. Dozens. All over the world. We'd just get someone else to do it." Felix started kicking the hot ashes over the Edge. He stuck a boot under one of the logs, lifted it, and pitched it over the edge. It scattered sparks on the way down.

I took a running kick at the skull and punted it over the Edge, which was probably the best thing that had happened to me all day. "Then get someone else to do it."

"It would be embarrassing," Chamberlain said. Then, to Felix: "Do the next one."

"Who's that?" I asked.

"Somebody who's destined to be your lover in the future," Felix said. "It's not hard to find out."

"So? I'll find another lover."

Felix ignored me. "I'm tired of waiting, Chamberlain. You promised."

"Very well," Chamberlain said.

Felix whistled, and the prairie dragon jumped up the cliff, spreading its dirty yellow wings for balance.

"Do I have to tie you on again?" Felix asked.

I shrugged. "If I let you kill him in front of me, will you let me go?"

"Sure," Felix said, too easily. He leaped and landed gracefully. I climbed up the dragon's ankle and knee and pulled myself up into the saddle behind him. The dragon's skin was covered with what felt like horsehair, and I couldn't help petting it a few times after I strapped myself in. It snorted and took off.

"What's it like?" I asked Felix. "Being such an asshole? You're either going to kill somebody, or you're going to bully me into stealing a kid. And then it's going to die anyway, as far as its parents are concerned. It's going to dry up and die after a week or two. Do you know what it's like being here? As a human?"

He shrugged. "At least it'll be warm."

I ignored him. "You promised me. When I was a kid, you promised me that if there was ever a chance for me to get out, you'd help me."

"I did," he said.

"And then you brought me back!" I screamed into his ear. We kept flying.

We didn't have to go too far, only a couple of hours into the prairie. It was full dark by the time we landed, in the middle of nowhere, under a streetlight that didn't have a street. As we slid off, the dragon nickered and trotted into the dark, folding its wings close to its body so it could creep up quietly on whatever it was hunting. The Wild Women howled on a nearby hill, their silhouettes against the moon, coyote muzzles and naked breasts.

We let ourselves in the old wooden gate as quietly as we could and approached the house. The place looked pretty nice, with vinyl siding and a sidewalk and cut grass inside the gate. As a fairy, I'd crept up on a hundred places like this, pulling pranks on them more out of boredom than anything else. Usually with Felix to help me.

"We been here before?" I asked. "Playing lost boys?"

"Nah." Felix pointed over the door, where a horseshoe hung, points up, and then to a bottle of beer just outside the doorway. "They keep to the old ways, mostly, so Chamberlain had us leave them alone. They didn't do the window, though, so we can still get in."

I bent down to pick up the beer, and Felix stopped me. "One way or another, it's going to hurt them," he said. "You can't come here with me and drink their beer. That's not how it works."

"I'm not going to hurt anybody," I said.

"Then take it on our way out," he said.

I put the beer down. We circled the house; as we went around the corner, a collie-mix dog ran out of a doghouse and barked at us, sounding tougher than she felt.

Felix squatted in the grass and whistled her over, beckoning with his fingers.

"Leave her alone," I said.

"I don't like dogs," he said.

"You know I always wanted a dog." An old argument.

Felix stroked the dog's head, then grabbed her under the chin. He crushed a piece of dried leaf in the dog's eyes, and she sighed and sank onto her belly. "She's asleep." He pointed to a window on the upper floor with a dim glow from behind some thin curtains. He rose halfway, then looked at me. "Aren't you coming?"

I hissed, "I can't fly anymore, you dumbass."

Felix swooped behind me and grabbed me under the arms, which wasn't fun. He lifted me up to the window ledge and waved the tips of his fingers. The curtain slid sideways, and I looked inside.

It was a kid, of course. A little kid in a crib. I couldn't tell whether it was a boy or a girl; the room looked kind of yellow and had elephants all over. "Put me down."

Felix lowered me back on the ground, and I swung my arms around to get the kinks out. "It's just a baby," I said.

"Take it, or I'll kill it," Felix said.

"I thought we were friends."

He shook his head. "If we don't steal another one soon, we'll lose the connection. And we'll all die if we're cut off from the mortals. No mortals, no spirit. You know that."

"Don't I get time to decide?"

"If you were one of us, yeah, you could have time to decide. But we don't have a living changeling anymore, so no. It has to be done by dawn. If you're not going to do it, then I gotta fly to the Summerlands and find a changeling who will before then."

Felix reached under his fake-band t-shirt and pulled, hard. There was a tearing and sucking sound, and then he pulled a knife from under his shirt, a knife made out of his own breastbone. Those things are almost impossible to keep from striking true, as long as your heart's in it. Felix turned the knife back and forth; it glistened clear fairy blood, which he wiped on his pants.

"I thought you were my friend," I repeated.

"You gotta do what you gotta do." Felix floated back up to the window, slashed through the screen, and pried at the window with the tip of the knife.

I ran. I ran to the door and tried the handle: we were out in the middle of nowhere, so it wasn't locked, and I was mortal, so I could pass under the iron. I ran through the house, yelling, "The baby! He's coming for the baby!" A couple of scared faces looked at me as I spotted the stairs.

I slammed into the railing and pulled myself up four stairs at a time. There were a bunch of doors, but then the baby cried, and I knew which one I wanted.

I threw open the door. Felix had the baby by the scruff of its neck and the breastbone knife at its stomach.

"Put it down," I said.

He pushed in the knife tip, and blood stained the baby's white one-piece and ran down its leg. The baby screamed.

"I'll do it," I said, offering my hands face-out. "Put it down."

Felix lowered the knife. The baby screamed. Felix wrinkled his nose and handed it to me. Its diaper felt ice-cold and stank like shit.

I felt the change coming on. It wasn't much of a change, and I'd felt it before. The baby hadn't though. It screamed as its heart stopped beating and its blood turned to living ice.

"Who?" Felix said. "You have to name someone to take its place."

I shook my head. "Nobody. Let's just go."

The parents had shaken off their shock and were running up the stairs.

Felix grabbed my arm that wasn't wrapped around the baby and put my hand on his chest. "Me," he said.

"You?" I asked, but the magic must have taken it for an answer, and Felix started to shrink. His face wrinkled up like a dried apple skin and he collapsed on the floor as his bones shrank. His band t-shirt and jeans turned into rags and a wet, shit-packed diaper.

I ducked out the window and closed it behind me as the parents ran into the room. They pulled back the covers in the crib and shrieked at the empty sheets, but Felix wailed at them from the floor. The mother picked him up and held him tight, then held him away from her chest. She said, "It's your turn, Jack." The father made a face and carried the baby to a changing table, where he pulled out a couple of wipes and a diaper.

I knew my hands were cold, but I couldn't feel them.

The parents would make sure Felix stayed warm, for the little time he had left. It was the food; a fairy could never live on mortal food.

All I had to do was hand the baby over to Chamberlain and be done with it, be human again. I'd get on the dragon, cross the Edge, and fly back to football practice and business calculus and getting ready for my real life.

Then it hit me that I didn't know anything about the baby, its name, its gender, who its parents were, nothing. I slipped inside the window over the kitchen sink while the parents were fussing around upstairs and found out.

I wrote down their names and the address on the back of an envelope. "But," I said, "While you're with me, your name is Felix."

I finished the story, watching the darkness in the crib. Nothing moved…nothing breathed. And yet I could *feel* the presence of whatever was in that small, dark place, with its embroidered cushions lining the sides. The angels' faces on the blanket seemed wicked now, as though they were fallen angels, now whispering evil into the hearts of the one who laid in the crib.

That was the moment I finally believed that the girl's baby brother had been traded for something else. Why did you do it? A longer life, youthful beauty? The perfect slave? The girl's heart?

Protection from the monster you had summoned below?

I flew back to the place I had left the girl and what was left of my flock, but they were gone.

I circled the dumping ground, looking for the others. As my gyres widened, I saw movement: the girl, dragging her blanket over the snow, sweeping the thin white dusting off the ground behind her, leaving darker earth behind. She was surrounded by metal and machines, the antithesis of the kind of magic that you do. *You can't find her here*, I thought. *That's what's protected her. Until now.*

But I had gone straight from the girl, to the house, and back again; there was no telling. My guts squirmed like worms in a corpse, and I couldn't resist looking back over my shoulder, even when it seemed that I would dash myself into the ground.

The daylight was thin, thinner than milk, as thin as a pale sheet of wind-whipped ice over a bottomless pond. The wind seemed to have settled, although it would dash itself at small drifts of snow here and there, disbursing them with small devils that tossed the snow into corners and crannies, then chased it off over the higher tops of the gullies and onto the endless fields.

The girl was walking toward the truck, wending through the narrow bottoms of the trash-filled gullies, still clutching the white-streaked pink blanket around her.

Her face was as pale as the sky.

On one shoulder was Facunde; on the other was Ibarrazzo. Old Loyolo was nowhere to be seen. I circled overhead, then landed between the girl and the truck. She didn't stop. She saw me; the skin between her eyebrows pinched together, her lips turned down, and she kept walking.

Her feet stepped higher, though, as if she intended to step on me, if necessary, in order to pass. I waited until the last moment—then flew up in front of her, beating my wings in her face.

She pushed me aside, bent forward, and yanked on the handle of the door.

It groaned and lurched, its bottom edge burying itself in the dirt: the entire truck had tilted a little. The glass had been broken, and it was scattered on the ground around and under the girl's feet.

The inside of the truck smelled of harshness that burned in the back of my throat, even from my perch on a sagging cardboard box on the ground opposite the truck. A slow, black rain of dust was sifting from the wires at the top of the cab where the seat had been and piling on the ground in shimmering black mounds. A waver like that of the sun on a hot piece of metal rose above the truck. The snow had melted from between the axles.

A long, low moan echoed from the darkness above the wires, and more dust fell, hissing on the roof of the truck.

"Machado…Machado," the voice called. It was Old Loyolo's. Almost. "Is the monster coming?"

"Could be," I said. "The babe's been traded away for something dark. I know that."

"So there is nothing good left in that house." Its voice came from a story, it came from nightmares. It was rough and hollow, as though it had come disembodied from his throat and had gone wandering around the underside of the truck, touching wires, scraping off rust.

"No," I said. "Nothing good is left in that house but for a jar of jam or two, and we don't have hands to open it with anyway."

"Good," Old Loyolo said, or something not very like Loyolo anymore. "Good."

Something dark and crow-shaped dropped out of the wires onto the shit-layered roof of the truck cab, kicking up black dust as it landed. Its claws were as black as its feathers, and no light reflected from its wings or its eyes. It was not a thing. It was a kind of shadow cast by something else.

"Loyolo," I cawed, with grief. Ibarrazzo echoed me, a moan that was almost madness.

The shadow chuckled, a sound like a distant rumble of spoiled summer thunder. "No," it said. "Guess again."

"The Crouga, then."

"Close enough."

I hopped to the ground and squinted, trying to get a better look at it in the darkness of the truck cab. The clouds had thinned, seeming to make the shadows even darker, but not so dark that I could not see that its form seemed to flatten as I turned one eye at it, then another. A shadow indeed. "You're wearing his skin?"

"The memory of it. The taste."

The girl was reaching her hand out for it, her fingers clenched, her wrist bent.

"Stop!"

She hesitated, then stretched out her hand. The Crouga hopped onto it, digging its claws into her skin.

"Ouch!" She bit her lips.

"Just a little cut, so that I can find my way," the Crouga said, that deep voice still rumbling.

"You're lying," the girl said.

"Yes, of course." The Crouga rustled its black wings. "I am, at the very least, not telling you the entire truth. Why should I? Now let's go, my little flock, and see what mischief we can get up to, that the old one traded his life for." It twisted its head a little, and seemed to peer up at the girl's eyes. "And what do you think about all this? We'll be killing your mother, you know."

"I know. She killed my Papa and my baby brother."

"That's still not a good reason to kill someone, you know. Revenge. Half the world's tragedies come out of that one idea, revenge. More than half. You're sure?"

She nodded.

"It's good to be sure. Back soon, little love."

As one, the Crouga and we three crows took flight. I felt as though my wings had been jerked out of their sockets, as though I were a puppet.

The wind—or some other power—carried us across the garbage, to the fields; and from the fields, to the yard of your big white house. The four of us—that is, the three of us and the Crouga—landed on a tree that looked at the front door. In the house, the lights inside were out, the chimney cold. It was in the fat part of the morning, when the air was still, and if I held myself perfectly still on my branch, I could almost pretend for a moment or two that I was warm.

The Crouga sniffed at the air. "It smells of fairies."

Facunde snorted. "Fairies."

The Crouga flicked its beak at Facunde. "You know so much about fairies, then? Do you have all their stories memorized? Know the Seven Houses, do you, all the way to the House of Aeons? You're a brave one, that's for sure. Even I'm not stupid enough to tangle with the Houses. It's bad enough that they have a darkling huddled upstairs, let alone that witch. The only reason I'm doing this is that she threw me out, you know. Tried to pass me off to a *baby*. After all I'd done for her. No, I'm only here to collect what's mine. *You'll* have to deal with the darkling. And good luck with that, o scoffer-at-fairies."

The Crouga crouched, then sprang off the branch, flying straight for the house like a swarm of leaves. It cast no shadow, and the glint of sunlight off the windows seemed to twist around it, reflecting indirectly onto the powered snow below. I tried to follow it, but I couldn't move my feet; they felt as though they were tied with black, sticky string.

In a moment, the Crouga had swept around the house and returned to the branch.

"They are within," it said. "The witch is exhausted from the summoning and in her bed, fast asleep with the door shut. The darkling is prowling the hallway, trying to find a way to get through the door, but she was too clever for that and put up wards. As soon as she wakes, she'll send it out for your flock and to do whatever with the girl."

"Whatever?"

It flipped a wing. "Kill her, drink her blood and bring it back, squeeze her up into a bead. Might bind her as an apprentice, might cut open her skull and put in a bunch of honey to make her sweeter, brew her up for a couple of years with mushrooms in her lungs, that kind of various horrible thing. You only need a darkling if you need something that doesn't care what you do around it."

I looked at the house.

Facunde cleared her throat. She was on the other side of the Crouga, so that I had to lean forward to see her. "So...you will kill the mother. How do we kill the darkling?"

"You don't," the Crouga said. "You just keep it entertained until I'm done with the witch. And then it ought to disperse, contract over."

"Ought to."

It clicked its beak again. "It's a fairy. Who knows? It could decide you have a pretty throat and decide to look at it from the inside out. Just keep it from going in the room, that's all. If the witch wakes up and get her hands on it, we're all done for."

The Crouga flew us like puppets down to the front door, the rug made of thin strips of old tires woven together with long, thick wires. The cracks were packed with mud and cow shit and flecks of frost. The Crouga flew toward the door, a flicker across the green-painted panels, and then it was inside.

The door creaked open, and the three of us hopped inside.

The walls were mint-green. The floor was covered with mud prints on the rubber-backed rug, and streaks of blood had run from inside the sink over the edge, and puddled and dried on the floor. The ceiling belonged to a slaughterhouse, as though the pipes had backed up with blood so fiercely that they had nearly burst. The air was cold, but it was warmer than it was outside.

The Crouga was nowhere in sight.

With hops and short flights, we passed a door leading downward along steep steps into shadow. It looked as though something large and muddy and bleeding and furred had been dragged downward, and not come back up. The fur was white and rust-red and had come off in patches. As I learned later, it had been the milk cows.

The passages were filled with more mud, more blood tracked along the floors, bits of fur and what looked like curls of skin covered with fine, black hair, as though a bat had been ravaged to shreds several days ago.

I had an idea about telling the darkling stories to distract it: we would stall, that's all. But Facunde and Ibarrazzo had other ideas.

The house had seemed to groan quietly to itself, as though it were caught in a powerful wind that made it lean back and forth a little, its bones shifting and complaining. There were ticks and pops from upstairs, as though something with claws had taken a step, then halted. A smell of dead flowers filled the air, not dried blossoms but dead ones, piles and piles of them, turned into an oversweet, sticky perfume. The closer we came to the stairs up, which led from a room with a large table that had been split the long way down the center, as if by lightning, the stronger the smell became.

We hopped and fluttered up the stairs as quietly as possible, with Facunde in the lead and me at the back, constantly looking over my shoulder. I felt a prickle between my shoulder-blades, as though I were being watched. The thickening darkness that followed us up the stairs confirmed it slyly, as though it were pleased with itself. As though it were some sort of cat.

At the top of the stairs was a twisted mass of darkness.

Part of it was liquid, flowing.

Part of it was dissolving, like old paper that has been yellowed by the sun, and was being eaten through by a hailstorm. It was full of holes. It steamed, although I could not have said what it smelled like—the smell of dead flowers was too thick, thick enough to choke on.

Help me, the Crouga said, as black slime twisted through it, dissolving it.

Facunde and Ibarrazzo flew at the darkling, pecking and kicking and screaming. It twisted on them and tried to pin them down, but they had been harrowing cats for years, and they kept it always attacking the places where they had just been.

So much for my plan to tell it *stories*.

The last of the paperish darkness collapsed, leaving behind a bead.

I snatched it up and glided down the stairway.

The cellar, it said.

I flew through the passage, careful not to beat my wings against the narrow walls, careful not to swallow. At the top of the stairs I opened my beak to fling the bead into the darkness.

No…further down…you must take me further down.

It was then, I must admit, that I thought to myself, *This is all a plot to kill Machado the valiant storytelling crow*. A moment of vanity, or rather of fear: what would happen to me, in that darkness?

I shuddered all over, then spread my wings and jumped.

What is down in your cellar, you would rather not know. If your curiosity begs to differ, then I won't stop you from opening up your door, going downstairs, and having a look.

I crawled out of the cellar a different crow than when I went down. The horror of the thing, if you will permit me to dwell on it but a moment, is not that it is *horrible*, although of course it is. The horror of the thing is that you brought it here, what must have been long before I was born, long before my sire's sire was born. You brought that thing here for some reason, and, before I bleed to death on your windowsill, I would dearly like to know why.

14. The Strongest Thing about Me Is Hate

Brian,
~~This is Lisa~~
~~I gotta tell you something. I'm~~
~~Mom & Dad and Martin and Dave &~~
~~I want to tell you that I'm sorry~~

You remember us hiding out in the scrub trees across the highway? We'd crawl through the big runoff drain, the metal ridges hurting our knees, getting all muddy and me tearing my skirts. The whole thing would shake and roar when the semis drove over top of us. In the winter the bottom was full of ice and in the summer it was stinky puddles and whining mosquitoes. We'd crawl and crawl and it felt like it took forever. And then we were on the other side, running over the muddy ground and losing our shoes in the mud half the time.

You and me, we'd sneak away from chores on the farm and make stuff up. We'd leave Middle of Nowhere Reservation, South Dakota, and we could go anywhere. We hid all day out there, eating government cheese on mushy white bread with mustard and pickles.

You remember how we used to pretended there were monsters out in the scrub trees and cattails next to the river? We pretended there were caves under the muddy grass banks where they lived, and we either hunted them or ran away from them or pretended we were them.

I want to tell you something, but I don't want you to know what I'm telling you yet. I want you to save this letter for later, when you're older. You can read it now. But I want you to save it for later, too.

The night before I left I found you downstairs in your hiding-out closet and hugged you through the sleeping bag you had wrapped around you. You had a bandaid on your head but you said you were okay. You wouldn't tell me what happened to you. I told you never to go back there. You asked me why and I told you nevermind just do what I told you, but now…I've been gone long enough that I can tell you. Kind of. In a story.

There's a lot of things I haven't told you.

I was tired of wearing K-mart shoes with cracks across the bottom and my toes sticking out while the stuckup rich white kids wear $200 jeans and complain about their allowance.

I was tired of getting called a half-breed. Now I tell people I'm half Hungarian, and they think that's cool.

I was tired of not being in sports because we have to ride the bus every day. I felt like I could run faster than any of them, even the ones in high school. I was as good as anybody. But when they chased me, they backed me into a corner with no way out. Nowhere to run.

When I came home I always changed clothes right away because they were ripped up, spat on, covered in boogers and piss and shit. My knuckles were always swollen because I hit stuff when nobody was looking. I had this dream. Sorry if it's too mushy for you. Someday I'd have a man, and he would hold up my hands and say, "Hey baby. How did you get those scars all over your hands?" And I'd snuggled into his arm, 'cause he's my protector, and I'd say, "I don't remember, baby. I got in a lot of fights at school when I was a kid." I'll say that. I'll say "kid" like being sixteen was the same as being ten. Only now you're eleven.

Anyway he'd say—he'd kiss my scars and say, "They make you look strong, baby. Tough as hell. I like that."

And then we'd get all kissy kissy. He'd never, never find out how weak I am. Because when people find out you're weak you can't trust them anymore.

That was my dream, anyway.

You don't have to tell me what happened for you, but I am going to tell you what happened to me, so you can understand what I did. I don't want you to forgive me. I'm not sorry for what I did, except for what you had to see, the next morning.

I told you I wouldn't sit with you because I was too old to sit with a little kid. But that's not true. It's because it was too dangerous to sit with me. I used to think it was because I would sit in the back of the bus, where I wasn't supposed to. You know, "only middle-school and high school boys are allowed in the back of the bus," or so they said. But that wasn't it, because when I quit sitting back there, it didn't stop.

Do you remember when one of the high school girls sat back there two years ago? She used to bring a knife with her on the bus every day. The day of the big fight after Christmas break the high school boys got it away from her. That's why she was screaming. That guy, X, fucked her. He raped her. The bus driver saw it, too. He looked at her and just kept driving. Why should he care? He was an old white guy.

That's why she left. She didn't graduate early. She got pregnant and killed herself. I used to want to kill myself. I didn't want to end up like her, and it was starting to look like I was going to.

I will *not* write down his name. You know who I'm talking about.

Anyway I'm riding along in the middle of the bus by myself and trying to do my algebra. I secretly do all my homework twice, once at school and once on the bus, in case it gets ripped up.

(You can't skip homework, not even a little bit. That's what happened to Martin and David. They skipped a little homework because Dad told them they had to help out around the farm, and every week they had to do a little bit more, and a little bit more, until Dad told them they better quit school because they were flunking out anyway, even though it was his fault. ~~That's when they started to go~~)

So I'm doing my algebra and my socks are wet from the holes in my shoes and my feet itch from walking in wet socks. It's supposed to be spring but there's still a ton of snow on the ground and ice on the road, but when I breathe on the window, the fog disappears right away. Barbed-wire fences and weeds flick by. I stick my pencil in my algebra book and hold it closed. The notebook paper is already falling apart on one corner where a drop of spit hit it. Stupid cheap paper.

The reason nobody sits with me isn't because I'm a snob. It's because X told them not to.

After a few minutes someone sits next to me. I don't look. I already know it's him. He says, "You keeping it wet for me, eh?" He's talking about sex stuff.

"Fuck off," I say.

I used to feel bad for him. In the morning he gets off the bus and he's a nobody at school, just like me. But by that point I hate him.

He leans closer and breathes on my face. I don't move. I'm shaking. I feel him shift and my algebra book starts to move. He's trying to shove his hand in my crotch again.

I think, "This is it. I'm going to go home and kill myself tonight."

Something goes *pop* in my chest. I have tears exploding down my face but I don't feel afraid anymore. The bus bounces up and down like we just ran over something, and I bounce off my seat for a second. I feel sad, because I'm already thinking about myself like I'm dead, but I don't feel afraid.

I reach into the book where I have it closed over the pencil and start rolling the pencil back out towards me. I say, "I will fuck you up, X. If you don't knock that shit off I will fuck you up."

He laughs at me and shoves the book out of his way.

That's when the bus starts swerving, like the bus driver's going around a dead animal in the road or something. I don't know if you saw what it was later or not. It was a tire. A tire blew. That's when we started to swerve. It was ripped up so bad that a loose circle of rubber was just hanging down across the side of the upside-down bus.

Everybody around us stops talking. I feel more breath on me, the stink of chaw. The other high school and middle school boys are gathering around us. I can hear them breathing. The other nobodies are pushed back in their corners and praying to God that they aren't next.

X shoves his hand into my crossed-over legs and I decide to stab him with the pencil. It doesn't matter what I do because I have nothing left to lose. Do you understand? I wasn't even a virgin anymore.

Then the bus swerves again, harder, and everyone's heads jerk forward. My body slides forward on the green fake leather seat stuck together with green tape. My algebra book falls on the floor and I step on it before I can even think about it. I knew I could not lose that book. Better to turn in a book with a footprint on it than no book at all.

"Ungh," X says. "What'd you do that for, bitch?"

I didn't do anything but I know better than to argue with him. The bus jerks again and he takes his hand off my legs and puts it on the seat in front of us. The bus bucks up and down. We're sliding off the road. The brakes are squealing, people start screaming.

We tip forward. That's when we start to go down into the ditch. He's staring out the far window. For just a second, while he's not really paying attention, he's weak, and I'm strong.

I pass the pencil over to my left hand, turn the point around so it's facing his hand, and stab as hard as I can.

I don't know if he sees me, but his hand slides to the side as we go over an especially big bump. I don't stab through the middle of his hand but I don't miss, either. The pencil rips a red line along the side of his hand, digs into the bone by his pinky finger, and jumps over it, leaving a gray line. Before his hand even starts bleeding bad the pencil hits the fake leather and snaps in half. The back half of it stabs through the back of the seat and falls inside the hole.

Then we start tipping sideways and I get thrown right into him. He hits me and blood from his hand goes into my face but we're all falling and the slap turns into a grab, and I'm shoved up against him with my face against the side of his head. He bounces off the other seat and his head slams up against mine. I see an explosion of white pain. I don't know how else to explain it.

"Bitch!" he shouted. "I'll fucking kill you!"

Right in front of me is his ear.

I hated him, Brian. I hated him so much. I knew I was going to die. One way or another, either I would die in a bus wreck or I would kill myself. I didn't matter what I did, so I opened my mouth and grabbed the bottom of his ear between my teeth and bit down.

Let me say something about hate. You shouldn't hate the people below you. If you have to hate, you should hate the people above you. That's what makes you strong. If you hate weakness, it makes you weak. But hating the strong gives you strength. Not much. But a little.

I feel the slick of meat between my teeth as the ear starts to slide out of my mouth. I bite down harder, and he screams. Everybody's screaming by then but me, I think. We're falling in all directions. I pull back with my head. His ear stretches. I feel something tearing. We slam into seats and other kids and the roof and the floor and the windows. Hot blood fills my mouth, mine or his, I don't know. Sometimes he's on top of me, sometimes I'm on top of him. It fucking hurts.

Someone kicks me in the head and I pass out.

By the time I wake up, you're gone. Everybody's gone, except for the person on top of me, although I don't find that out until later. I must have ended up on the bottom somehow. Except the bus was upside down, so I was really on the roof.

The metal is sticky and cold under me. The inside of the bus is supposed to be mint green but it's brown now, from muddy footprints. There's streaks of blood, too, but all of it except for a puddle next to my head has turned brown already too. I can't move so I don't see much at first.

I spit bright red blood and move my shoulders from side to side, trying to get the body off me. Whoever it is, he's heavier than I am. It must have been one of the teenage boys, maybe X, maybe not.

Suddenly he starts moving off me.

Not like…not like he's getting up. He slides off me like someone dragging a pile of blankets. His head knocks on mine and I see bright white lights and bite my tongue, which means more blood in my mouth. His fingers get stuck in my hair for a second, not grabbing, just tangled in it. My scalp hurts and my head starts to pull back, which makes me feel like puking. I jerk my head forward and it hits the metal. Great. But his fingers come loose. The boy is still sliding off me, and I hear a thud as his head hits the metal of the upside-down roof. He doesn't say "ouch."

I try to say your name a couple of times but I can barely speak. It's like someone took my voice away. The more I lift my head, the more it hurts, until I'm so dizzy I just lay it back down again.

I spit again and figure out one of my front teeth is gone. I'm never getting that back. My skin feels torn up all over. A cold breeze comes in through the broken windows and my skin feels like it's burning with cold. Sometimes when there's too much pain your body gets all confused. Gas rumbles in my gut, it feels like it's knives stabbing into me. I fart and it feels a little better.

It turns out I had a tear in my large intestine and I was lucky not to get it infected. I'm okay now.

I hear a grunt from outside, and then a crunching noise. A horn honks. Honk honk honk. It doesn't stop for a long time. Then there's a woman shouting from outside but I don't know what she's saying. The grunting and crunching stops, and then someone's walking through crunchy dead grass. I turn my head and that's when I know for sure that everyone else is gone. I also know I'm going to throw up for sure by then, it's just a matter of figuring out when and where. A gun goes off, a rifle. Don't ask me what gauge, I don't know guns as good as Martin and David. There are more shots and more shouting. Glass sprays over me and I turn my head the other way but it doesn't hit me. The bus rocks with a jerk, and there's a squishy thud outside, like someone jumped off the top of the bus into mud. The puke is coming up now. I spit again but it's too late.

I puke.

I close my eyes because I don't want the puke to splash back into them.

I think the stupidest things. While I puke I worry about that algebra book and what I'm going to tell Mom. I think about what she's going to say. "We don't have that kind of money, that you rip up your books like that all the time." I want to tell her that I never do it but you know. She never listens. She's just upset about the money.

I'm to the point where I'm still puking but nothing's coming out, when someone touches me on my back. "Kid—kid—what happened? Where is everyone? Where's the bus driver? Did you see—?"

It's a woman's voice, hoarse from shouting. She sniffs. I guess she's crying.

I open my eyes.

In front of me, mostly buried in my flattening mountain of puke, is a ripped-off piece of ear. It's like a piece of corn, you can see it when you throw it back up again. There's the red-brown of X's skin and the bloody pink of fat from inside it.

"Kid? Hey, kid?"

"I don't know," I say. Barely any sound comes out. I'm staring at that piece of ear and hoping that it doesn't look too much like a piece of an ear. There's a long hangy piece of skin from where it ripped upwards. "I don't know what happened. I just woke up."

The hand stops touching my back.

"Let me help you up."

I shake my head. "I'm going to puke some more."

It's not that much of a lie. As soon as I say it, I start heaving again. Nothing comes out.

"Okay, okay."

While I'm puking I have this fantasy about a handsome guy coming into the bus and picking me up, and carrying me to his home. He'll love me forever. He'll tell me I'm beautiful.

I'll only have one secret from him, I promise.

"What's that?" the woman asks. Her hand brushes my hair as she tries to pick up the piece of ear.

My feet are tingling, they're numb, they're burning, all at the same time, and this shooting fear runs up my skin and I desperately shove my face into the pile of puke. My teeth close on a mouthful of ear and puke and…I suck the whole thing into my mouth like it's spaghetti. It tastes like the powdered cheese you put on top of spaghetti. I am never going to eat that kind of cheese again.

But anyway I swallow it.

I mean, I try.

I swallow it, and then I puke it back into my mouth again.

And then I have to swallow it again.

This time it stays down.

The woman's hand is stroking my hair. "Shh," she says, even though I'm not making any sound.

The bus shifts a little. I know I should say something but I'm still gulping back the last strings of skin from the ear. I hear a grunt, and then the woman says, "What?"

The bus shakes and there's a thump and then the woman falls on top of me and knocks the air out of me. My head hits the floor again. I don't actually pass out, but it's close. I see blackness closing around the sides of my vision. I feel puke falling off my face in clumps. Every time I puke I swear I'll do a better job of chewing my food but I never do. I'm never eating spaghetti again. Never.

The bus shifts a little, and this time I hear footsteps. The woman slides off me, just like the other person did. Her head hits the ceiling of the bus with a thump, just like his did.

I put my hand on top of the puke and lay the side of my face on my hand. I know I have to get out of there, but I have to rest for a second.

I try to puke up the ear again but it won't come.

I get up on my hands and knees. I'm facing the wrong way and there's glass everywhere. I turn around and start crawling across the mud and the blood toward the door. I pull the sleeves of my coat over my hands, and I push the biggest pieces of glass out of the way as I go.

I crawl to the door and that's when I see them. The monsters.

They're just like we thought they were. They have white skin and rough bristles all over their bodies, like pigs. ~~They don't smell bad, though.~~ Some are red, some are black, and some are white, but most of them are different colors mixed together ~~like pigs. They grunt.~~ They grunt, but it sounds more like they're talking than pigs do. Their legs are up to the knees with mud, from walking through the icy water by the old cattails.

There's only two, plus the woman on the ground. She's on her back with her head flopped over funny.

And X.

He's on the ground, too. Most of his face is gone. For a second I think I did it, but I think I would have known it if I puked it all back up again.

The monsters are by the front of the bus, and they're grunting at each other, pushing each other back and forth. One of them is bigger than the other.

They both know I'm there.

The ~~younger~~ littler one wants to kill me. ~~I think that's what he's saying.~~ He keeps running toward me, and the big one keeps pulling him down. The big one is bleeding from a cut on his side.

I crawl away from the bus.

In the grass by the bus is a rifle. I think the woman was shooting at the monsters with it, and thought she killed them before she came to save me. I pick up the rifle. It has a wood stock, ~~just like~~

The barrel is kind of warm, warmer than the ground anyway. It smells like someone's been hunting with it. I use the bolt to load a .22 short shell. The two monsters are still fighting, the big one knocking the little one down again, only this time, the little one finds a rock and smashes it into the big one's face, then comes running toward me.

I'm sitting on the ground with my skirt in muddy water and my boots in front of me. I aim. I take that little bit of extra time to aim, because I know I'm not going to scare him off. If I don't hit him the first time I'm dead. His head keeps moving up and down as he runs toward me but that's okay, I know how to shoot.

I breathe out and relax, then squeeze.

It's a pretty good shot, it goes a little high. I hit the monster right below the collarbone. It goes in. I work the bolt again and fire. I don't have time to aim so I don't. I just fire again and again, until the monster falls and I'm out of shells.

I roll to the side or he would have fallen on top of me. Instead he falls face down in the mud and the dead grass. I get splattered with blood and mud. I wait for him to get up and try to kill me.

He doesn't move. He doesn't breathe. His skin gets paler and paler, and the cold breeze makes his hair bristles twitch.

I stare at his back for a long time, until I hear someone walking through the mud and dead grass toward me.

It's Martin. He's walking toward me with a rifle in his hands, pointed off ~~to the side~~ toward the other monster, but he's not shooting it.

"Hey, little sis," he says. He squats down next to me, puts the gun down, and picks me up. I grab his neck and start crying. "Shhh…you had to do it. He was going to kill you."

He starts to lift me, then says, "Pick that up for me, will you?"

I rub my face on his shoulder and try to grab the rifle, but it keeps sliding out of my hands. He grunts and turns around on his boots, grabs the gun while he braces me on his knees. He keeps looking at the dead monster.

Martin pinches me tight and stands, up the gun braced in his hand under my knees.

He walks backwards for a while, almost falling into the mud.

Finally he turns around and starts walking faster. He jogs up the hill toward the road. I'm bouncing around in his arms. But that doesn't stop me from looking past his shoulder at the dead monster on the ground.

"Don't look," Martin says.

But I do look. I don't stop looking until he starts threatens to hurt me.

I'm not afraid of going to Hell. Hell is a joke. Hell is getting detention after you've been raped. Hell is…hell is sending a letter without a return address to tell your little brother how, later that night, you crawled and crawled back through the tunnel, found another one of the monsters, a girl monster this time, and made her come back with you into the house, so she could kill Mom & Dad and Martin.

Hell is taking a shower, going through Mom's purse for money, and walking back out to the highway to hitchhike the fuck away from the middle of nowhere, and leaving your little brother behind, because you know that he'll get taken in by foster parents, somewhere far away from nowhere.

Hell is leaving your little brother behind so he won't end up like you.

Hell's not that bad. I'm not afraid of Hell anymore.

I hope you get this and you're safe.

I'm sorry it turned out that I couldn't tell you the truth. I meant to. I swear I meant to. I tried to, but I couldn't. ~~I hope someday you'll understand.~~ Just know that I love you, and I promise I'll never see you again.

Don't go back to the farm. Don't look. I went back there a couple of days ago, I hitchhiked on a semi. Already the paint's peeling off the sheds and everything's full of weeds. There's yellow tape that was supposed to be all around our yard, but a lot of it came off. The letters are all faded and they flap around in the wind. I saw some of the pigs back up in the shelterbelt past the house. They're wild now.

The bus is still upside down out there. The water is a lot higher this year, everything's flooded out there. It's so deep that it's covering a lot of the trees that were there. It's all flooded. The monsters…they're all drowned out. They're gone.

It wasn't in the news. I mean it was, but they lied about it. So I'm not the only one. They just said the bus crashed into Mom and Dad's car and ran off the road and killed everybody, and they decided to have closed caskets.

~~I know I'm a monster but~~

I don't want to kill myself anymore. I'm okay. I found my strength. Maybe someday I'll find peace.

Love you, your big sister,
Lisa

Ah. Thank you. That explains—not everything, but a great deal.

When I had reached the top of the basement stairs, it seemed as though an eternity had passed—and yet I knew that there was another flight of stairs ahead of me. I dragged myself through the passageway, leaving behind a trail of blood, shit, and feathers. I told myself that I would never fly again. Better to die quietly, I thought, if the desire to find out what had happened to Facunde and Ibarrazzo had not tortured me so.

The rumbling from below had already begun to echo up the stairs in what would have been an alarming fashion, if I had been able to sustain that particular emotion at the time. The noise from below drowned out the possibility of hearing what was going on upstairs. I thought I heard a bed creak, but I might have been mistaken. It is not as though we crows spend a great deal of time around beds.

I reached the stairs upward and hopped up to the first step.

Rather, I leaped, scrabbled my claws on the wood, hooked my beak on the edge, and dragged myself upward more by accident than anything else. Afterwards I lay on the step and panted, waiting for death.

It did not come; it was busy elsewhere.

I heard two things then: a knock at the door, and, in the sudden silence from below, the sound of car tires on gravel.

"Hello?" the girl shouted. Did you hear her? She was here, briefly.

No? You didn't even hear her. How sad. I would have liked you to have seen her, one last time.

"Go away," I croaked. As though that would do any good. I heard the door open, and footsteps come inside. "Mother? Mr. Crow? Mr. Crouga?"

Outside, a car door slammed.

I rolled off the step and onto the floor, and struggled until I was able to stand. I walked, one claw in front of the other, into the passageway, and saw the light from the window outside shining over that long, filthy floor in front of me, and thought, *I'll never live to reach the end of this passageway.* The noises from downstairs hadn't yet resumed. The thing that was below might have been behind any doorway, waiting to pounce.

A shadow fell over me, along the length of the hallway.

I walked toward it, dragging my claws in the mud. It reached down for me, and it was gentler than I had thought it would be.

It was the girl, although at that point, I wouldn't have cared if it were the monster.

She carried me outside and put me down in the grass. The pink blanket lay beside the door, and she had scuffed mud into the doormat. Her feet were bare, the socks and shoes lost. Are human children always this way?

She could not go back into the house; she could not stay outside.

The front gate creaked, and a man stepped inside onto the pitted cement sidewalk leading to the front door. The priest. I knew him, as well as any crow knows a human—he had told me his story. It was an odd one, but the strength of stories is not in the believing of them, but in knowing who would tell such a thing, and so he felt very familiar, the tall man in the dark clothing, wearing thick glasses and keeping a silver medal around his neck.

After a few steps he stopped and sniffed deeply, then frowned.

"Is your mother home?" he asked the girl. "I thought you had run away. There are still searchers out looking for you."

"I didn't run, I was carried," said the girl. Her tangled hair dragged across her face as she straightened up. "The crows took me."

She said it as though daring him to disbelieve her. But he only looked at me and said, "I see."

"Mr. Crow is hurt. You have to take him while I go fight my mother."

The noises had resumed within the basement by then, groaning and creaking, and just then a terrible crash echoed across the yard. The thing in the basement had, I knew, come out. It snuffled around the bottom of the stairs. Wood burst and fragile things shattered; there was the sound of distorted music for a moment, the twanging of a hundred strings as it destroyed the piano in the room beside the entrance, a piano that only the girl had ever played.

The priest knelt down next to me and said, "Are you the one I spoke to before?"

"Machado," I said. "My name is Machado. And if you would do me a favor…" I twitched my beak toward the girl.

He pressed his lips together. The girl was watching him.

"You want him to take me away," she said.

"I do."

"I don't need to be rescued."

"You don't need to see what happens to your mother, either."

"I want to."

The priest cleared his throat and pushed up his glasses with a torn, scabbed fingernail. "What we want and what we need are very different things. Imagine what your mother might have been like, if she wasn't getting what she wanted all the time."

"Don't talk down to me."

"All right, then: *stay here and you'll turn into a murderer and an evil magician like your mother.* You can choose to watch her die. I won't stop you. But the first time you call up dark magic, I will start hunting you."

"You're not so scary."

He sighed.

"If you're worried about me scaring you, then you're worried about the wrong things. I warned your mother, once, about the time you were born. She bided her time. I thought she was done with all that, she was a woman who was struggling with a heavy past who had chosen to walk in the light."

"I don't want to walk in the light."

He put a finger to her lips, and she quieted. "She didn't, either. She kept her life in the darkness, and let hate twist her, over and over again. Do you know why I am here?"

The girl shook her head.

"Because your mother called me. She said she had done something so terrible that she wished to die. She said she knew she would never be able to go to

Heaven. She only wanted me to come and kill her, to make sure she was dead and wouldn't be a slave to some demon walking around in her skin."

"The Crouga," the girl whispered. And then she began to shiver.

"No, child. The Crouga is a little boogeyman. There are things much, much worse that are waiting to eat your mother, coming up out of the darkness to climb into her skin and pretend to be her. She was so terrified of them that she killed your Papa, and your baby brother, and now she is trying to kill you, in order to escape them. And that is why she called me. Not because she wanted me to save you. Only because she wanted the pain to end."

He stood. The crashing and groaning and thorough breaking of things inside the house was continuing, loud yet methodical and measured. Unhurried.

"Is that who you wish to become?" he asked, sweeping a hand toward the house. "A creature of hate?"

"I want to see her suffer."

But her voice wasn't as sure as it had been, a moment ago.

"I will watch for you," I said. "If the priest will raise me up on a stick and set me at her window. I will watch and tell you all about it later. If that's what you still want."

The girl's lower lip trembled.

"Mama," she said.

No tears filled her eyes, but she broke then: her limbs came undone, and she fell on the ground, with the cold cement under her cheek, and her eyes sightless.

The priest carried her into his car, which was still running, and closed her inside. Then he returned, broke a long stick off the elm tree closest to the house, and lifted me on it to the high window on the second floor that I showed him. He murmured to himself in a language that I don't know—it might have been prayers in Latin. I clutched the stick and nearly fell…it seemed as though my entire journey through the air was one of falling, although I was doing the opposite.

The sweet smell of dead flowers oozed from the cracks in the window. I looked inside, and there you were, awake then, with wide eyes, staring at the door, looking at your hands. The large, flesh-colored telephone on the small table next to the bed had been, by then, taken off its hook.

As the priest carried the girl, he had been telling her the beginning of a story, one that I had heard before. If you had heard it earlier—well. Let me tell it to you now.

15. The Rock that Takes Off Your Skin

The wind stung Omanu's eyes as she floated in the bay and she wondered if her whole body would sting, when she took her skin off and became a human.

The waves rocked her up and down but she had found the place among the currents where part of it wanted to pull her in and part of it wanted to push her out and part of it wanted to pull her down, but with that many currents all at once, she didn't have to be pulled by any of them. All she had to do was balance on the tips of her flippers and she could stay there forever, or until the tide started to go out.

Seagulls cried at her but she had never learned the language of seagulls. She blew the water out her nose and breathed in sea foam, then sneezed. Her throat ached. She sneezed again and tasted sweetness. The water in front of her splattered with mucus, hissed as she burst the foam. Now she smelled blood. She would lay on the beach in the sun and wait to feel better. She wouldn't go to the rock now.

The tide started to go out. So much for her skill at finding the one place where no change need be made. She slid backward. No. Not now. The rock that would take her skin off turned into a shadow, then a shell, then a pebble, then gone. She hid in the cave that no one else could reach, because she had brushed the rock with her flipper before, and now she could change that flipper into a—a hand.

She could climb.

But only her sister Ma'a knew of it.

Their beach was a shifting pile of pebbles that could be hollowed into the shape of a seal's belly and warmed with sunlight or with one another's flesh. Omanu flopped to where her sister was sleeping and shoved her with her shoulder to wake her up and to push her out of her spot. Ma'a grunted and slapped her, but allowed herself to be moved a little to share her spot.

Where have you been?

To the cave.

Ma'a quivered and twisted her head to bite her own shoulder where it touched Omanu's side. Hide your hand. I don't want to see it.

I changed it back.

You can do that now? You couldn't do it before. Maybe you should stop going to the cave. Who knows what would happen to you.

I could scratch your back, Omanu grunted mischievously.

Not here. I don't know why you want to do this.

I'll come right back.

No you won't. You'll go up on shore and a man will take your skin and you'll—

People go all the time and nothing happens.

Something will happen to you. You will walk around with no skin on until something happens. I see the water flowing out to sea as plain as you.

I won't go anywhere. Not the first time.

Her sister stopped biting her itch and shoved her out of the hollow of warm pebbles she had made, putting her heavy head under Omanu's shoulder and shoving until Omanu rolled over on her back.

Ma'a flopped down the pebbles that clattered over themselves and said, You will have no sisters and no family! Man will take your skin and you will have no fish but what he gives you! You will learn nothing but—her head splashed into water and took the rest of her words.

Ma'a was always afraid. Omanu was not brave. But Ma'a was always afraid.

Her chest ached.

With Ma'a gone she couldn't stop herself from coughing.

More blood ran through the yellow spatter. Before she could stop herself she flopped down the beach.

The water was so still she could hear the stones chatter as the small lapping waves flipped them over. Ma'a used to say that the stones would tell her other seals' dreams when the sea was quiet enough to for her to hear them. They told Ma'a the character of the tides and the weather and all the gossip from up and down the coast for a hundred days' swim, and it was true that Ma'a knew Omanu's heart before Omanu did. Today even Omanu could almost hear what they said, so she hurried off the beach as fast as she could. Under the water she was free, except from the tides and the things left behind when man came and went, and herself.

Ma'a shouted, her voice echoed off rocks. It really was a calm day, to hear her from so far away.

Just go. Every day it's the same, just go.

What if I go and nothing is different?

But Ma'a did not answer.

The seagulls cried and she snapped her teeth at them. She did not need to understand the language of seagulls to know they laughed at her. Well enough. She was laughable.

The place where she could balance in stillness among the currents had shifted, she searched for it with her nose. She could feel the edge of it, where the long river that fell swiftly from the echoing rocks, passed under the bridge over which the men flashed in their quick and reflecting boats, and met the sea with the flavors of earth and green tangle, but she could not find the down current, without which she would spin slowly. As a calf-child she had spun and spun in such waters but she was sick and today it would make her vomit.

The tide poured toward the river, so she let the current take her closer to the rock. She could feel the rock before she could see it. The ocean had gone silent, the clacking rocks at the beach popping and sucking instead.

Omanu put her head under and swam, but her breath hurt in her. She surfaced and coughed again. Her breath came back foul in her own mouth, like death, and coated her teeth with sweetness mixed with blood. She kicked and floated, and even though the tides should have pushed her forward up the river, they pulled her fur, turning it sleek.

She swam forward as fast as she could, under the bridge, the water falling back to the ocean and sucking at her. The rock split the sky in front of her, but now she didn't want to touch it and she swerved away.

Suddenly a seal hit her from the side, knocking her toward the rock that would take off her skin.

Ma'a!

A wave was coming, filling the sky as she twisted and Ma'a hit her again from the other side. She turned her flipper into a hand and tried to hold onto Ma'a but the wave took them. End over end, the rock sliced her from throat to tail, and then the water lifted her up into the tangle above the river. To a place where her hand could hold.

The seagulls cried in her ears so loud she thrashed and grunted to get them off her head. Oah my god. Take her hand deyeh. Get it oahf her. The stoahm must have thrown it all the way up heyah on toppah her. I cannoaht believe it. Heyah, help me lift this, it's crushing her.

Her eyes could see only light and dark. The shadows of the seagulls were all over her, pecking her, ripping her apart. Anoahdda one. Landing on her and pulling, screaming at her.

She sobbed and flailed and grunted and twisted but they had her. Don't do it don't make me do it I changed my mind don't do it.

The air around her bit the back of her throat and she sneezed and the last of the ocean dripped from her mouth. Oah my god Bobby she's bleeding out her mouth. She won't die befoah we get her to the hoaspital. Shouldn't you check her now? I already checked her as much as I need to. We should take her offa dis rock is what we should do, now help me lift her.

She was a tangle of white under the gray sky in the tangle on top of the rocks. Her skin stung, but not from the air, from the tangle that reached for her, the tangle that cut red lines onto her. She screamed. Put me back, put me back inside.

The men pushed her inside a boat that stung her skin and pinned her arms to her sides and pulled her hair to keep her from moving. Why you gotta…Bobby, what is that? It's disgusting.

She shouted my skin where is my skin you have to put me back!

Weyall, I cannoat rightly say what it is. You don't know what it is and you put it in the trunk. Why noaht? Just throw it away.

The smell of seagull shit stung in her mouth and nose and the world was the white of winter sunlight on the water, pale. The men had wrapped her in tangle and the seagulls shrieked but they didn't talk anymore, just barked a high squeal over and over. She lay on a high shelf of seaweed or moss surrounded by metal.

Next to her a man's dark-furred head, with a tangle of white—clothing. Clothing covering his shoulders and arms and hands, hiding his hands entirely with his arms over his torso.

She reached her arms across her own self and shuddered, it was like being tangled in seaweed. She untangled one arm from herself and it was as heavy to lift as though she had tried to lift her whole body out of the water to stand on her tail. Her hand fell on his shoulder.

His head wobbled and his eyes opened. His arms reached in front of him for a second, then folded over his chest again. Holding something tangled. Oah! My deah, you're finally awake.

With her breath taken in, the coughing came out. Don't talk, my deah, you have pneumonia. Youah very sick. But you didn't have any identification on you, we need to noah who you ah.

She said her name but it was a grunt.

Sorry my deah, I should noat have asked you to say anything.

My skin, where is my skin?

Heah, drink this. Water to her mouth that tasted of poison from man, coating the inside of her mouth and all of her teeth. She coughed it out. Noah, you need to drink it. The water shimmered next to her mouth, and she butted the glass with her head.

My skin.

Maga? Margaret? Your name is Margaret?

My skin.

He must not have her skin, or she would have to mate with him and bear his pups. Her skin was gone. What happened when your skin was gone? Ma'a would have told her if she knew. Ma'a had argued all horrible things to keep her from taking off her skin. And now Ma'a was gone. Omanu pushed the metal on the side of the shelf with her shoulder and it creaked. She grunted, hunched her back, and unleashed into the metal again.

Doan't do that, you'll hurt yourself. The man moved the metal out of her way, and she rolled onto the floor, without thinking, slapping her hands on it to break the surface. The floor was a beach made out of a single rock. She flopped forward, dragging the tangle with her. The seagulls shrieked louder.

Whoah, my deah, don't do that.

She turned from side to side. She was inside a cave full of thin winter sunlight. Before her were a dark cave that smelled more of seagull shit than the cave they had put her in and a bright cave that echoed of seagulls and pebbles rattling on the beach. She turned toward the bright cave on her belly. That was not how the men walked, but she didn't have time to learn how to walk.

The man pulled on her arm. She butted his legs with her shoulder and he let go of her. She flopped into the bright cave, her human skin sticking to the floor and stinging when she moved. She had no fur. She coughed from the smell of death in the bright cave but did not taste blood.

Wait! He pulled harder on her arm, and she whipped her head around and bit his hand, crushing down with her teeth, and tossing her head to break his bones. It twisted, his hand could twist about, as she should have remembered from her hours of curling around to see her own human hand, in her private cave. His hand grabbed her again. His fingernails scratched in her mouth, blood again, she bit and his hand left her with a yell.

What had she wanted? Her skin cut open on a rock and a woman to come out. She had imagined herself shining in the sunlight like a seagull laughing, her hair blowing in the wind. She would walk and turn around in circles with her arms out like a pup spinning in the current.

But she could not even stand.

Other men in white clothing lifted her up. My skin, my skin! Her arms were not strong but they could twist around, the men could not hold Omanu with their hands if she had hands to twist back with! And then her feet were under her, three slaps of her feet on the ground and she was falling on the floor, no water to hold her up. She had not walked but she had run.

She keeps saying something. Maga? Maska?

I think her name is Margaret.

Back on the shelf again, the walls around her. She shoved them, she thrashed, they tangled her up so even twisting could not get her hands free.

She cried, my skin, my skin!

The others left, the first man remained.

My skin!

When she could no longer move, one of the man's eyes opened and closed without the other. Yoah looking for yoah skin, ahn't you? This is yoah skin now.

She tried to twist away again, but they had tangled her like a fish. She kicked the metal on the sides of the shelf and beat the back of her head against the cave wall. The man laughed.

The side of the boat opened and the wind from the sea came in like a sister, making her tangle of dried-out hair billow around her face like seaweed in a current.

Come out, come out. He showed her his hand. He would pull her out of the boat like a seagull pulling a clam out of its shell. We're all the way on top of the ridge, which is lucky. A house lowah down on the hill didn't make it. Too bad foah Curruthahs. Now come out, theyah's someone I want you to meet.

They had tangled her in more clothes, so it didn't sting when she slid out of the boat. The car. Her feet weren't sure of the ground, but he grabbed her arm, and rather than twist free, she grabbed his arm back and walked on top of her shoes more like a turtle walking on sand than a long-legged bird picking its way through the shallows.

Remembah, you must do what I say, or I will throw your skin away.

I remember, she said.

The seagulls laughed at her. Look at you, look at you!

She grunted. Through the tangle of trees the gray sky turned into the line of the sea, her beloved waves running and leaping and jumping white on shores that she couldn't recognize, looking out instead of in.

Oah no. This way, to the house.

She looked toward the cave. The house, the house. Gray like a fish, gills running from end to end, gasping on the beach. A red door like washed fish flesh to be torn and eaten. Dark, gaping holes flat like dead eyes, the last glint of sunset on them. He lived in a dead fish. With the smell of the car still around her, the house smelled foul, too foul to eat.

The red door opened, and out of the flesh of the house came a man with long black hair and white skin and an open mouth that opened and closed as though near death. The man had teats under her clothes, a female.

Say hello, deah.

Hello.

Omanu hobbled toward the female, taking the last few steps on her own. The female leaned on the wall, and Omanu leaned with her, smelling sharpness from the wall as her clothes scraped on it. She bumped up against the female, and the female bumped her back. She tried to remember the smell but could not.

The man laughed and laughed.

She grunted and the female grunted the stones told me he would bring you to me today.

Ma'a!

It's all your fault I'm here. He has my skin, Omanu.

Ma'a! She tangled her arms around the female. The smell was not the same, instead of the sea and the seaweed and the smell of even the pebbles they lay upon, which she had not known was a smell until she had not smelled it on her sister's skin, her sister smelled of flowers and poison and seagull shit, the same smells bleeding into the air from the red door.

She grunted in the language of seals we will kill him, Ma'a.

He has my skin. Ma'a shivered under her clothes. I have to lay with him and bear his pups until I have my skin.

Then *I* will kill him, Omanu grunted.

What a nice little reunion, Bobby said. Now come in the house before you get cold. I just got your lungs healed up.

Beside the door was a sharp, black stone that looked as though it had been broken off the rock that would take off her skin. She would not have thought anything much about it before but now she had hands.

Later that night, Omanu pushed her ear onto the wall. Ma'a barked with pain but without speaking either in the human language or the seal language. The wood door was nothing but hollow sticks, rotten on the inside, but it would have made a sound if she slammed her shoulder into it to break it.

The gaping black eyes of the windows, however, could be opened more quietly, the glass moved like so. She clawed open the clothing that covered the hole, opened the glass, and dropped down onto the rocks below the window. They clattered under her flat shoes made out of skin but told her nothing.

She watched the moonlight through the tangle of trees, the sea and the moonlight, then turned to the red door and found the sharp rock. With both hands she carried it to the window, squatting low to keep from tipping over. One foot. Another foot. She lifted it and it hit the wall. She froze, reaching out with every hair on her skin to feel the current. The wind blew from the land, carrying scents of tangle and flower and the long trees that pointed shadows onto the beach at sunset. Rotten leaves and other things, from the ground.

She rolled the rock up the ridges of the gray wall, over the white stick at the edge of the window, and over. Then no more time for silence, she put her hands inside the sticks around the window and pulled and pulled and her feet left the ground but slid down again. She had no wave to lift her. She pulled again and went nowhere. Ma'a shouted. Omanu jumped and her shoes kicked on the gray fish wall and she climbed through the black fish eye, scraping her torso from one end to the other as she flopped through.

She fell on the floor and grabbed the sharp rock and shouldered into her door, which sould not open unless the man opened it.

Her shoulder broke though part of the sticks but not all the way through. She shook her shoulder away from the broken sticks, lifted the rock to her chest, which was losing its clothes, and charged the door again, with her head and her chest.

Ma'a shrieked.

What ah you doing, woman? I told you not to look in theyah.

Omanu stumbled over the broken door and the rock pulled her down and over.

What's that?

Omanu!

Omanu grunted. Then she lifted hard on the rock. It hit her shins and scraped through the cloth, but she got it back up to her belly with both hands. She could not run.

Omanu!

She carried the rock to the door where Bobby kept Ma'a at night. She lifted the sharp rock to her chest.

Before she hit the door Bobby said Good gahdamn, woman, would you let goah?

Two rocks cracked together and Ma'a grunted.

Omanu ran at the door with the rock, and it kicked her chest so she couldn't breathe, but the hollow door popped open and crashed away from her. Bobby was behind the bed looking at the floor. He looked up at her with a long face and a mouth like a fish. She settled the rock on her chest and leaped at him, over the bed, into his chest, and the two rocks cracked again.

The ceiling of the cave rippled and stretched and fell away from her face.

She barked in pain. She had thought it was only a rock but he had punched her with a harpoon somehow. Salt filled her mouth.

Ma'a! Where are you, Ma'a?

Shit and death and the smell of Ma'a, Ma'a skin.

Omanu tried to find the hole in her side but she could not raise her head enough.

The man grunted, his head on the wall and his arms in front of him. He had blood on his mouth and the rock under his far hand. It had not removed his skin, not at all.

He lifted his hand from the rock and coughed, more blood from his mouth, then leaned forward with his hand in front of him. On the bed was something dark and shimmering and heavy.

The moon loved it, the way it loved the sea, and it was Ma'a's skin, her fur shining in the light.

He pulled it onto his legs, then onto his belly, and onto his chest.

Omanu rolled onto her knees with one hand on the spongy floor but she was too slow.

He lowered his face under the fur and coughed and fell onto his side, slapping the floor with his flippers. He coughed more blood onto the white floor, then charged at her.

He crushed into her chest and tried to snap her backward, the way the males do to each other in mating season.

She threw her shoulder back, and his weight tossed her aside, against the wall.

Part of it broke from her weight and part of it was a piece of sharpness across her back. She rolled to the floor and lay with her mouth breathing grit and salt.

Further and further away she could hear him thumping and crashing and barking.

Ma'a's hand touched hers, under the bed, and Omanu grabbed it. Ma'a coughed.

He has more skins in the secret cave.

Ma'a!

He has my skin.

I will kill him for you.

Look behind the door. Ma'a's hand relaxed.

Ma'a!

Her voice flowed to sea. If you let my skin get away I will never forgive you.

Omanu crawled backward until the bed was out of her way. Ma'a's smooth white legs lay straight and spread open, like a flipper ripped apart.

On her chest was the place the harpoon had been ripped out of her, but Omanu could not see the harpoon anywhere. A black pool of blood rippled as the tides went out to sea, across her breast, over her teat, down the fold of her shoulder, and into the white, white floor.

She coughed and the blood crashed against a rocky shore, splashing high, throwing spray.

Ma'a!

Behind the door. Your skin is behind the door. Her words pushed blood faster. Omanu looked at her sister and knew that her sister would be dead before the sun rose again. To stay by her side, to bellow and wail while Ma'a demanded her skin, then begged for her skin, then fell still with her mouth open and sagging and monstrously white, still longing for her skin, Omanu could not do it.

She crawled away from Ma'a, not trusting her feet.

The blood coming from Omanu's side was a thin stream that neither whispered gossip nor tossed seals on the rocks, a stream without tide or any other urge than to flow.

Behind the door.

She pushed the door aside with her nose.

There was another door inside the small room, stronger, and secret. A crack in the secret door breathed out the scent of seals, of home, of warm pebbles hollowed out on the shore.

She nosed it further open.

She did not know what she herself smelled like but skin upon skin upon skin upon skin she found.

She grabbed one with her teeth and backed away from the door.

The skin followed her and thumped on the floor.

The moon did not love it as it had loved her sister's skin, but it smelled fresh, a bull's skin sharp with strength.

She crawled next to it, lay down on her stomach, and slid under one edge. It curled around her back, it rolled over her legs, it pressed her arms to her sides until only her fingers could move. It gave her strength.

She bellowed as the face sealed over her own.

Ma'a!

She flopped onto the door, toppling it closed then knocking the trash into flinders.

Bobby stood naked at the red door to the outside with Ma'a's skin in his fist. She would reach him, he was moving so slowly.

One leg outside, his head gone, his shoulders, the skin dragged behind him.

The door bounced open, then slammed shut and caught her whiskers.

She bellowed and slammed into the door. The metal of it bent but not burst. She bellowed again.

Her hands slipped out of her flippers and clawed at the inside of the bull's skin.

She screamed her seagull scream and shook the skin away from her face. She shrugged and tossed and thrashed until the skin slid forward off her shoulders and slumped on the floor.

She could hear his feet slapping on the flat rocks, then go silent after the end of them.

She squeezed the latch of the door and pulled it with the whip of her arms like she was trying to break the neck of a fish.

Then she tangled the skin in her arms and ran with her bare feet past the flat rocks.

They both knew the way of it now and neither would use the skins until the water.

The arms and the fingers and the hair of the trees tangled her arms and her fingers and her hair and scratched her and tried to take the skin from her and make her fall. They were his trees.

The crash of Ma'a's skin filled her ears and her teeth and she shrieked at the man who had filled her sister's skin.

Yaaaaaah!

The seagulls shrieked overhead, not laughing now, because she spoke of their language.

Turn toward us, toward us, go this way to the sea, we will lead you to the sea!

Yaaaaaah!

She threw the skin at a branch and the branch broke under the weight. She climbed the skin then ripped it free, the tree subdued and bleeding.

No, no, not that way, the seagulls cried, even though she could see the moonlight on water. She followed the seagulls instead of her sense.

The man wearing her sister's skin, he ran between two boulders down a line of tangle and dirt toward the beach.

He slipped and landed on a boulder, and over the side of the boulder sliding on top of Ma'a skin like her skin was a boat on the ocean of rock.

She climbed the rock and leaped, the skin flapping like crow wings on her back.

Yaaaaaah!

Her feet landed next to his head and she kicked at him.

He slipped and she missed.

And her weight took her off the rock to the place he had been, but not on her feet.

Her head bounced against the skin, the folds between her head and a rock. She grunted and vomited, then slapped the rock to push herself away.

The beach was close. He was already on it and running toward the water, one leg not as fast as the other, his white legs churning like long fish.

The wave is coming. Shh.

She screamed at the beach in the language of gulls, don't tell me your secrets! Tell them to my sister!

He fell into the water on top of the skin. The pebbles scattered under his weight, chattering with anger.

The traitor skin wrapped around him.
His dark sleek head turned into a ripple, then less than a ripple.
She reached the water, threw down the skin, and left it there.
The water sank under her, the pebbles popped and spat and sucked as the water lowered.
A bull called from the land, the bull of the men.
She did not believe in the language of the pebbles or that they could gossip to her, she did not know the language of the seagulls. But they guided her to where the sea had left the man on the beach, flopping to reach the water but not as quickly as she could run on her feet, the pebbles chanting justice and revenge with every step.
The tangle had found him. It could not hold him long, but it found him and kept him from the sea.
The wave was coming.
She grabbed her sister's skin and tangled it tight.
She did not believe in these things but she would let herself be used, for Ma'a's sake.
The man bucked in her arms but she was no woman. Under her woman's skin was something else, and her arms held him.
He tried to open the skin and come out but she trapped his human arms at his sides.
Even her hair tangled into his mouth to choke him.
The wave shook the ground, it was coming.
The pebbles shook in fear and said their goodbyes.
Ma'a!
Woman, let me goah! We have to get out of heah! Itsa sunami! Ma'aaaaaaa!
She could not hear anything but death.
The pebbles hushed, the seagulls fled.
Water washed her skin and Ma'a's skin together. The man inside froze.
The fat of Ma'a's skin lifted them with the wave together, up, then over, tumbling down the side of the wave, over and over,

rising as they fell. Omanu saw the moonlight, the depths of the sea, the moonlight again.

And then they hit the rocks.

The man in Ma'a's skin hit first, arced his back, and flung his arms free of her and the skin.

The water carried her further, took her by the feet and turned her the long way around, then pressed her against another rock. Her arm slid against the rock until another rock joined it and the water drove her arm into their vise.

Her body flopped with the water until her feet felt as though they would go where the waves willed, even if it meant her arm ripped off.

She could not see except for greenness. She could not breathe, but only taste the salty water as it drove into her mouth.

Unknown tangles hit her body, clung to her.

A white monster flashed by her and tore her foot. She kicked and kicked, and it was ripped away.

With the last of her breath she screamed. Yaaaaah!

She coughed and spat out her hair but no blood came. The seagulls shrieked and the waves flipped the pebbles at the tideline, end over end, a clatter that said nothing to her anymore. Dull gray light coated the pebbles, and she was a man.

She curled her fingers in the pebbles with one hand, but the other hand shrieked in pain when she tried to move her fingers. She screamed and the seagulls laughed at her. That she could still understand.

She barked into the pebbles.

Ma'a!

Ma'a!

A wave lifted her up and pushed her toward the shore

I'm going, I'm going.

She pulled her legs under her chest, rolled back and stood. Her toes felt the rocks more widely. The tangle fell away from her, fishing line and sticks and seaweed and other trash.

She did not recognize the beach, and the corpse of the dead fish on the hill above her might have been the man's dead fish house, or it might have been some other house.

In the rocks above her a white monster from the deep, deep ocean lay broken, speckled with leaves. The man's white leg jutted from its teeth. Ma'a's skin was nowhere to be seen.

She felt the tug as if from a downward current below her. One current toward the ocean, one current toward the land, and one current that would pull her down into the cold and the blackness. She could balance here forever, or at least until the tide went out again.

She use the tangle to wrap her arm to her side and found a place where she might, by pulling herself upward, climb to the top of the hill, to see what was left inside the dead fish house that had been broken by the wave.

The wind still stung her eyes, but not her skin.

She was used to all kinds of skins now.

In a sense, I pity you. I am grateful that you chose not to answer the knocking at your door, not to let the darkling in. And I am, of course, happy that you listened to my stories, and that you told me your own. I will remember it, for as long as I have a memory, and I will tell it to others, although I will never say that what you have done is justified.

It is your fault that the best of my flock is dead, leaving behind little more than chicks who have hardly heard our stories once or twice, at best. I suspect that even Zubalo is dead. Much will be lost; many stories will never be told. At least there is the girl. She has an ear for it. Someday she might write down what stories remain, and help us remember.

It is dark now, and the wind has come up, pulling snow off the ground and out of the sky. It will be a long, cold night, and I think that neither one of us will see the other end of it. It has been a long battle between the thing from the cellar and the darkling. The Crouga was right—a fairy is nothing to sneer at, and if that was one of the weaker ones, I shudder to think of what the others might be like.

The darkling screams in pain now, unendurable agony, and then stops. You might tell yourself that it is the other thing. You might beat your hands on the wall, you might think of throwing yourself out the window.

If you do, it will pursue you. Better, I think, to get it over with quickly, than to run and make it catch you again. If it is angry now…

Now the door creaks, the knob clacks as it fails to turn.

While we wait for the door to break and you decide whether you can bear to end it here, and let your daughter live instead, let me tell you what might have been, if you had turned away from your hate, and especially from your fear. The heat from your hand and cheek against the glass are faint, but they still warm me enough for me to finish this one last tale. Your skin is pale, you know. As if all the blood had run out of your veins long ago.

That doesn't have to mean you have lost your heart.

Close your eyes. Don't look. Just listen.

It will all be over soon.

16. Things You Don't Want But Have to Take

When it's time, you know.

I opened my front door. The deliveryman, a guy of about twenty with sun-streaked hair and the musculature of a young god, had his fist up in the air; either he was going to hit me, or he was just about to knock.

"Hey, Joe," I said. I plucked the signature pad out of his other hand before he could say boo and signed for the package. "Do you want some chocolate chip cookies?" I asked. "I made them last night." In fact, I'd had such a bad nightmare last night (about the box) that I hadn't been able to go back to sleep. I know, cookies, right? But cookies are wholesome. And they smell good. I'd eaten about a dozen already.

Joe gaped at me and retrieved the signature pad. "How do you know my name?"

I pointed at his nametag and walked into the kitchen. The cookies were still a little bit warm. "Want some milk?" I yelled into the hallway.

"No thanks," Joe called back. "Uh—"

I put the cookies on a paper plate and wrapped it with plastic wrap. "You sure?"

No answer. I brought them back out. Joe had picked up the package and was staring at it. He looked like he was about to vomit. Probably from the smell emanating from the box.

You know, Joe reminded me of an old boyfriend I had, who was always trying to keep me out of trouble. Hadn't worked. Joe looked up at me, and I knew he was going to try to run off with that box.

I hate it when people try to be noble.

"Trade you," I said.

Joe hesitated. "I—"

Damn it.

"I know," I said. "It smells. It's some really stinky cheese."

"It isn't cheese, ma'am. Let me get rid of it. Nobody needs to know."

I hate it when people call me ma'am. But I'm married to a company man and stay home all day. I wear color-coordinated pants and sandals and get matching manicures. So I guess I can't complain. It's what I've made myself look like, after all. Protective coloration.

Something heavy in the box shifted across the bottom, rattling the packing peanuts.

Joe jerked the box away from me and started walking back towards his idling truck.

"Joe!" I trotted after him, my sandals clacking along the sidewalk. "You give that back, or—"

The box slammed him in the gut like a strong man's fist, doubling him over, then knocking itself out of his hands. The box rolled—flopped—a few turns toward me before it stopped against a step.

Joe and I both bent down to pick up the box. He got there first, but as soon as he touched the box, it twitched out of his hands and started growling. Joe jumped back, breathing hard. The smell must have hit him again, because he gagged. Well, if he thought it smelled bad then, he should hang around until I had to open the damned thing.

I smiled and brushed his hair back, an automatic reaction to the guy who looked like a boy I hadn't seen for twenty years. I couldn't help feeling fond of him.

"Ma'am," he said, breaking the spell. "I'm sorry. You're going to have to take it." His teeth were chattering.

"It's okay," I sighed. "I had it coming."

After a few seconds, Joe stood up, walked back to his truck, ground gears, and sped away. Without his cookies.

So. The box. It was still growling.

I cooed at it as I picked it up. "It's all right, darling. I'll have you out in a jiff." I brought the box inside, set it on the hall table, and locked the door. The box was heavily sealed with brown packing tape. I rubbed my fingernails along the tape, trying to find the edge. I found one, but the tape split off to the side, and I had to start all over again. I wouldn't have minded—I like to pick at things—but the phone rang. Doreen from church was calling to let me know that one of the parishioners at the nursing home had died last night, and would I please help serve refreshments after the service, since Annie was next on the list of helpers but her six kids all had the flu at the same time, can you imagine?

Gotta love Doreen.

"And please bring some of your wonderful cookies. Oh, Madeline, it's so kind of you always to be giving your time to those in need."

"It's nothing," I told her. "I don't have any children to take care of."

"That's true," Doreen said. I could hear the pity in her voice. What did a woman have to live for, after all, with no kids? Her husband? That's a laugh. Men didn't need to be taken care of;

trying to take care of a man was like dressing up a cat for a tea party. "But thank you anyway."

I hung up.

I brought the box into the living room and set the thing on the coffee table. I started running my fingers along the tape again, cooing. "Shh, darling. It'll be all right in a minute."

The phone rang again, and I cussed. Some telemarketer wanted to ask me a few questions about my lifestyle. I almost laughed in the girl's face. What kind of hair-care products did I use? Did I use any non-prescription medications, and if so, what brands?

Telemarketers are damned souls, busted out of hell for eight hours a day to do Satan's bidding. Do they even know?

I answered as politely as I could, turning down any and all offers for free products, trial offers, and coupons. Then I jerked the phone cord from the wall jack.

The thing in the box had run out of patience, and the box was wobbling on the coffee table, winding itself up with a good howl, like a cat with its tail lashing. I cooed to it for a few seconds, got it settled down, and ran down to the furnace room to find the black knife. For a few seconds, I was sure I had lost it, but I found it in a box of cooking magazines, still wrapped in its black cloth. The knife was the only thing that could hold the thing off, if it decided to attack. And it was good for opening boxes.

The blade was damasked with oily black and gray streaks and eight inches long, about as long as a chef's knife, but double-bladed. I took care for my fingers as I brushed the knife against the box seams. The knife was so sharp the cardboard didn't make a sound as I sliced into it, here and there. I put the knife to the side—within easy reach—opened the flaps, and scraped back the packing peanuts, sticky and wet.

There it was. Something I didn't want but had to take.

It reached out a cornstarch-white hand, pasty and sluggish. The smell hit me, and I almost stabbed the thing out of some kind of primal reflex. Instead I lifted it out—it was heavy and slippery—and held it to my chest. The thing was cold and smelled like something that had been left lying dead and wet under the leaves, until some asshole had come along and stirred it up with a stick.

I'd tried to wash it once, after I'd first made it. Bad idea. Where the soap had touched it, its skin had peeled back, revealing a black mess like a rotten tomato. My fingers had sunk into it, splitting the flesh and sliding through it. I don't think it had any bones, just that rotten, fruity mush that had oozed back together and crept up my arms. Finally its skin, humping along with a wet slurp, wriggled back over the flesh until only the eyes were showing. Never again.

I tucked the flaps around each other one-handed and tucked a stray peanut back inside. Then I cleaned the knife, wiped it with some light oil, and wrapped it back in its black cloth.

"I won't fight you this time," I told the thing. "But you have to stay hidden. My husband can't find out." I intended to make a nest for it in the furnace room and clean up the stains—oh, there were already stains on the coffee table, not to mention my blouse—as best I could. "He'd leave me."

The thing purred against my chest, apparently content with my plan.

I threw the box in the trash, wiped up the mess on the coffee table, and filled a plastic crate in the furnace room with old t-shirts, the soft ones that smelled most like me. The thing was as cold as a piece of refrigerated meat, despite the fact that I'd been holding it for—I looked at the clock by the TV. Jesus. And hour had passed in the blink of an eye. All I could think about was how tired I was, especially after all the nightmares and insomnia last night. I laid the thing downstairs in its crate even though it scrabbled at me with its claws, trying to stay close to my chest and the sound of my heart. I peeled off my blouse, stuffed it in the box in the trash, showered, and lay down on the couch for a nap.

—

I jerked awake as David pulled into the driveway, around six.

The thing was back on my chest. David was coming into the kitchen through the garage, slamming the door behind him and throwing his keys on the table, so I grabbed a blanket off the arm of the couch and wrapped the thing up in it. My lungs hurt, they were so cold, and I felt a wet cough bubbling up. The hell with my lungs. The bones in my chest hurt, like they were being crushed from the inside out. The thing reached an arm out of the blanket and trailed the icy, nubby things at the end of its arm across my cheek. Oh, sure, they looked soft, but they were sharper than my knife and left cuts on my face that stung with black slime. I shoved the arm back in.

David walked into the living room and kissed me on the forehead. "What's that?" He nodded toward the bundle of blanket and monster.

I tried to tell him, but my throat seized up, and I started coughing so hard I started to worry that I couldn't stop. Of course, once you start to worry about not being able to stop coughing, you make it worse.

Regardless, it was too late to hide the thing. Finally, I croaked, "You'll never guess what came in the mail today."

He grinned. "Is it bigger than a bread box?" Sniffed. "Smells awful, whatever it is." He pulled back the blanket.

The thing was clinging to my chest. Its skin stretched where the blanket had stuck to it, and I prayed the skin wouldn't tear. The thing shifted until it could glare at David through its black, fleshy eyes.

David stepped back. "Oh God, Madeline. What is that?"

"A mistake," I said.

"Get it off," he said. "Get rid of it."

"I can't," I said. "I made a deal—"

Without warning, David grabbed the bundle away from me. The thing tried to hang on to me, but its claws slipped.

"David, don't. It'll hurt you. Put it down slowly—"

But the thing had done something to me. It had hurt or drained me so bad I couldn't get off the couch to try to get it away from David.

I heard David from the kitchen. "Ugh." A shriek louder than a fire alarm made me flinch. It cut out with a crunch. I heard the rustle of plastic—it sounded like he scraped everything into a garbage bag. He went out through the garage door and drove away.

By the time David was driving back into the garage, I was feeling better.

Then the thing was mewling at the front door, getting louder every second. I opened the door. The thing had left a black trail on the sidewalk and front step and was reaching up to me with both arms. Its knees were scraped down to black jelly. I scooped the thing up and closed the door.

I didn't think I was going to be able to help at that funeral tomorrow. I laughed with hysterical relief. No more cookies for Doreen! I picked the thing up and held it. Small blessings and all that.

David came back through the garage to the kitchen. He opened the cupboard above the sink—the booze—sighed, and closed it again. Then he opened the fridge and poured himself a glass of something. Probably milk.

The thing hissed and dropped to the floor, creeping on its skinless legs to the kitchen door.

"David!" I screamed. "Stay back. It's trying to come through the door."

The thing nudged the kitchen door with its head, which caved in like a gelatin mold. The door had latched; the thing beat the door with its head so hard—despite the way it stretched the thing's skull like a balloon—it cracked the wood around the hinges.

David jerked the door open and kicked the thing across the room. As it hit the wall, the thing curled its legs under it and sprang at David, sharp nubs streaking toward his throat.

But I'd been fighting that damned thing a long time. Losing. But fighting. I caught the thing, swung it around in a circle, and wrapped my arms around it until it clung to me, shuddering with rage.

"Well?" David walked toward me, standing so close I could feel the heat from his body.

I held on tight and closed my eyes. The thing jerked in my arms as David tried to pull it away from me, but he wasn't fast enough this time. The thing's claws dug into my throat as David pulled harder. I felt the claws slipping: the blood running down my shoulders.

"Please don't," I begged.

"Don't make me do this," David said. "Let it go."

"You don't know how bad you're making this," I said. "Let me—"

"I'm still going to try." He pulled on the thing, but it only coiled its arms around me tighter. I screamed. David wouldn't let go. I couldn't let go. I felt blood on my breasts now. The harder David pulled, the more it choked me, but David wouldn't let go.

I passed out.

When I woke up, I was covered with black slime, crusted blood, and bruises, but the thing was gone. My bones hurt, but not as bad. I put my hand inside my blouse and tried to feel if my heart was still beating. It was. I was in the bedroom, lying on the bed—David must have put me there. We'd made love only a few days ago, and I hadn't changed the sheets.

David didn't understand. The thing would only come back. I'd made it. I'd made a deal with it. I got to live a few more years without being sick, and it would poison everything I loved. It had come. It would always come.

I wasn't going to be able to hide the cuts on my throat—they were fine, like red hairs, but they'd swollen up. The slime was probably full of something nasty. I dabbed around with rubbing alcohol, but I didn't think it was going to do much good. The cuts went all the way up to my ears and across my chin. My blouse was shredded almost to the waist. I took another shower.

Poor David.

No. It was going to be fine.

Until I realized the thing was clinging to the wall above the bathroom door, waiting for David.

I started screaming again. I backed into the corner of the bathroom between the shower and the toilet, knowing I was only going to bring David running. I was naked but for the towel around my head, screaming nonsense and howling. My throat was already raw; the screaming quickly died into a painful croak.

Something touched my shoulder.

"Aaahh—"

"Don't try to talk," David said.

"Where is it?" I whispered. It was all I could get out.

David clenched his jaw and said nothing.

"It was above the door, it's back already—"

The thing slammed into the back of David's head and sliced him across the face with both claws. David bucked, turned—but the thing had its arms around his neck already.

I beat at the thing on David's head with my hands. Useless. I tried to scream, but it was useless.

David snarled. His face was already turning red, he was running out of—

"I told you not to try to help me," I hissed. I shoved him out of the way and ran downstairs. By the time I'd come back upstairs with the knife, David was lying still on the floor, unconscious or dead. The monster still had its arms around David's throat and was dragging its teeth across his cheek.

I couldn't stab it; the knife was too long.

I held the knife behind my back and stroked the thing's soft head. "Come on, dear," I murmured. "Don't be afraid. It's over now. You know I'll do anything for you. I haven't forgotten what I promised. I told you to hide from my husband, didn't I? He's not reasonable. But you and I, we'll find a way to work it out. Why don't you come here?"

Its head swiveled toward me, and one arm reached out. I grabbed it by the arm—it swung toward me like a monkey to cling to me, sobbing. I patted it a few times, rubbed my face against the top of its head, soft as silk, and used the knife to slice across the thing's back. It screamed. I pushed my hand inside until I found the one solid thing inside: a tiny heart. The scream stopped as I pulled it out. I knelt down to the tile floor and traced a pentacle on the ground with the tip of the knife. The tile split like butter under a blow torch. I dropped the heart awkwardly in the center, then set it on fire with a black word.

The thing writhed and smoked in my arms until it fell into ash.

I cried. It was gone. I cried with relief, I cried with longing, I cried out of betrayal, I cried because my chest was burnt and my bones were falling apart, I cried because I couldn't stop.

I sat on the bathroom floor next to David until I couldn't sit up anymore, staring at my hands and trying to make the fingers move. Eventually I slid down until I was lying next to David, watching him breathe.

When David woke, I had to laugh out loud: it looked like we'd been strangling each other.

"It's gone," I said. "For now. I'm so sorry, David."

"What was that?" he asked.

"A mistake," I said.

He stared at me. "A mistake? What's going on?"

I couldn't tell him. He was going to stare at me and decide I wasn't worth it, and he was going to leave. "May I have a glass of water?"

"The sink's right there," he said.

"Please?" I asked.

While he was downstairs getting a glass, I struggled to sit up. It wasn't as bad as it had been right after I'd killed the thing, and I started to hope that I wasn't going to collapse into a pile of dust and dried bones, like in a movie. The burn on my chest wasn't too bad, so I pulled on a silk blouse and a pair of panties while David dawdled downstairs.

I caught myself jumping at nothing, looking for the thing out of the corner of my eye. It would be faster when it came back, stronger. And I would be weaker.

I thought I heard something move inside one of the drawers, so I jerked it open and pawed through the socks, apologizing. The thing wasn't inside. Another rustle of cloth. Now I was looking through the closet, scraping the metal hangers back and forth. I thought I saw something moving in the back, so I tossed the clothes out, chanting, "I'm sorry, I'm sorry." I shoved the mattress off the springs, and the springs off the frame.

I ripped open the pillows and shook my makeup out into the trash. "I'll never do it again. I swear. If only you leave David alone—"

I looked up. David was standing in the doorway, holding a glass of water and a couple of aspirins, watching me.

"Here," he said. "Take these."

I took the glass and flung it across the room. "I told you not to do it! It's going to kill you. You think it's gone because it's not here?"

The heavy glass left a dent in the drywall but didn't smash.

"Leave. Get it over with." I tried to yell but I couldn't, I had to speak in a reasonable tone to get the words out.

"Whatever you want," David said. He handed me the aspirins and went downstairs.

"Fine!" I screamed unintelligibly. "Then leave! I don't want you. I don't want to hide in this house and wait for the phone to ring so I can bake cookies for another funeral. I don't want to wait for you to come home, wondering if the thing killed you on the road. I don't want to wait for another box full of a monster."

Eventually, I was so embarrassed by my ridiculous, phlegmy babble that I stopped. I gargled some cough syrup, put on some pants, and slunk downstairs. David was slumped over the kitchen table, half asleep on one elbow.

"I've been hiding from this monster almost half my life," I told him. I don't know how he understood me, but he did. "Please tell me I don't have to do this anymore."

"You don't have to do this anymore," he said. "But you probably will."

I opened my front door. Joe had his fist up in the air, about to knock.

"Hey, Joe," I said.

"Hi," he said. "Uh, I guess I'm back again. I'm sorry."

I shrugged. "It's time."

"I had a weird dream about you last night," he said. He stared at my scars. "Do you have cancer? Is that it?"

I laughed. "Cancer doesn't come in a box, Joe. No, I've had six good months, and what comes to me I've brought upon myself." I scratched my neck; the wounds had turned into puffy wrinkles. I was tired, but only from being awake all night. If anything, I was stronger than I had been before I'd made the deal in the first place. Which goes to show you shouldn't make deals with monsters built like a rotten tomato; they lie.

"You don't have to take it," he said.

"All right," I said. "How about I mark it 'Return to Sender'?"

He looked at the box as it rattled in protest. "That won't work. It's your name on the return address, too. Some people do that, so you don't know who it came from."

"Sorry," I said. "Bad joke. Here—" I pulled out a pen and printed my name on a bare spot of brown paper next to the return address.

The handwriting matched.

"Good God, ma'am," Joe said. "Are you sending these things to yourself?"

Then I scratched through the return address and wrote in a made-up address for someplace in Siberia. I wrote "Return to sender" over the front of the box. "How's that?"

He frowned at it. "It might work. It'll probably end up in the undeliverable mail bin."

The box twitched, and Joe gripped down on the box hard. The box wasn't going to get away from him again. I could tell.

I sighed. I didn't want a postal rampage on my conscience, on top of everything else. "Forget it." I signed for the box.

David walked down the hallway in a ragged bathrobe, carrying a mug of coffee; he'd taken the day off work when I'd told him about the nightmare. "Morning," he told Joe.

"Don't let her do this," Joe said.

"We're ready for it," David said. "I hope so, anyway."

Joe stared at David for a few seconds, then shoved the box into my arms. I handed the box to David so I could wave goodbye as Joe drove away. David laid the box on the coffee table, where the black knife was sharp and ready, and everything was laid out.

We opened the box together.

The End

In the end, you chose death.

The priest returned near dawn and went into the barn, and returned with a ladder, and took me down from the windowsill. If I was not dead then, I was very close to it. He held me to his chest and paused for a moment, and we both looked inside the window.

The door had been shattered, bent and twisted inward, and the room splattered with something old and green, like the algae off the surface of a pond. It was still wet. The faint light of dawn glistened from it.

The bed had been crushed, the plaster on the walls broken off the drywall and fallen in chunks. The glass vanity mirror had been driven into the wall in shards, and covered with more of the greenish fluid.

There was no blood, no bones, no flesh. In the middle of the crushed, stinking bed, a small, shimmering spot. A bead.

The priest brought me down the ladder, once again praying to himself, and laid me in the car on an old towel. He folded the towel over my body, then laid a piece of embroidered cloth over the towel. The inside of the car was warm but smelled strongly of gasoline. My skin seemed to burn, but not unpleasantly so.

When he returned, he smelled slightly of smoke.

It has been a long winter, a long wait until spring.

The Crouga's bead is nowhere to be seen; the house is a shell falling in on itself. The priest holds the girl firmly by her wrist, even though she is standing perfectly still. Her hair is in ponytails. She is taller.

I flutter through the ruins, looking for my dead, but they are gone, gone like everything else is gone, which, all things considered, is a mercy. In a few moments, I will fly back to my flock's old haunts, to see who is left alive and hear the gossip.

Your daughter looks like you, a little. Her eyes are dark and hard and they stare at me as though they will stab into me. Then they shift and catch the sky. She looks up, and watches the sparrows swooping irrepressibly through the air. They are pretending to hunt, but really they are only flying, happy to escape their chicks for a moment. They will catch insects—almost by accident—and return back to the nest to feed their young, who will grow, and fly, and leave the nest, and feed themselves, and repeat the cycle.

And she smiles.

Not all cycles will be repeated; not all stories will carry themselves out in our young. Your daughter learns subtler magics, plays with dolls and friends, heals.

And, by all that is holy, forgets.

Copyrights

All material copyright by the author.
"Be Good," copyright © 2011
"The Vengeance Quilt," copyright © 2010.
"Abominable," copyright © 2010
"Winter Fruit," copyright © 2010.
"Family Gods," copyright © 2010.
"A Ghost Unseen," copyright © 2010.
"The Haunted Room," copyright © 2011.
"Inside Out," copyright © 2010, first published in *Big Pulp*, Winter 2012.
"Treif," copyright © 2011.
"Inappropriate Gifts," copyright © 2011, first published in *Penumbra Magazine*, 2012.
"Clutter," copyright © 2010.
"Lord of Pigs," copyright © 2012, first published in *Horror Without Victims*, 2013.
"The Edge of the World," copyright © 2010, first published in *Three-Lobed Burning Eye*, 2010.
"The Strongest Thing About Me is Hate," copyright © 2013, first published in *Black Static*, Nov-Dec 2013.
"The Rock that Takes Off Your Skin," copyright © 2012, first published in *New Realm*, 2013.
"Things You Don't Want But You Have to Take," copyright © 2009.
All other material copyright © 2014 by the author.

About the Author

DeAnna Knippling is a freelance writer, editor, and designer living in Colorado Springs, Colorado, USA. She grew up on a farm in the middle of South Dakota and attended a country school with two outhouses and no running water. She and her brother ran loose on the prairie, often spending entire days in the back of a pickup truck playing with prairie dog holes and waiting for the adults to come back. She is the author or numerous SF, Fantasy, and Horror short stories, and has been published in *Crossed Genres, Penumbra Magazine, Black Static, Big Pulp* and more. Her short story "The Third Portal" took first place in the 2012 Parsec Ink. Short Story contest. She received an honorary mention in Ellen Datlow's *Best Horror of the Year, Volume 2* for "The Edge of the World." She is a member of the Pikes Peak Writers and blogs for them regularly. She runs her own small press, Wonderland Press (www.WonderlandPress.com).

Printed in Great Britain
by Amazon